Up to this Pointe

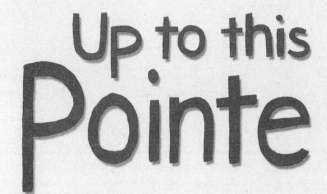

Also by Jennifer Longo

Six Feet Over It

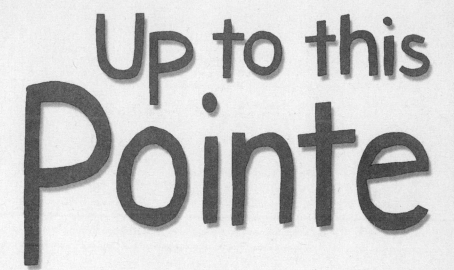

Up to this Pointe

JENNIFER LONGO

Random House ⌂ New York

Text copyright © 2016 by Jennifer Longo
Jacket art copyright © 2016 by Noelle Stevenson

All rights reserved. Published in the United States by Random House Children's Books, a division of Penguin Random House LLC, New York.

Random House and the colophon are registered trademarks of Penguin Random House LLC.

"The Age of Anxiety," copyright © 1947 by W. H. Auden and renewed 1975 by the Estate of W. H. Auden, from COLLECTED POEMS OF W. H. AUDEN. Used by permission of Random House, an imprint and division of Penguin Random House LLC.

Visit us on the Web! randomhouseteens.com

Educators and librarians, for a variety of teaching tools, visit us at RHTeachersLibrarians.com

Library of Congress Cataloging-in-Publication Data
Longo, Jennifer.
Up to this pointe / Jennifer Longo. — First edition.
pages cm
Summary: Devastated when her dream of becoming a professional ballerina falls through, seventeen-year-old Harper Scott takes a job as a research assistant, wintering over at McMurdo, a U.S. science station at the tip of Antarctica where, for the first time, she considers other possible futures.
ISBN 978-0-553-53767-3 (trade) — ISBN 978-0-553-53768-0 (lib. bdg.) — ISBN 978-0-553-53769-7 (ebook)
[1. Ballet dancing—Fiction. 2. Research—Fiction. 3. Scientists—Fiction. 4. McMurdo Station (Antarctica)—Fiction. 5. Antarctica—Fiction.] I. Title.
PZ7.L8634Up 2016 [Fic]—dc23 2015000808

Printed in the United States of America
10 9 8 7 6 5 4 3 2 1
First Edition

For Melissa and Chelsea,
North Stars in a southern sky

- - -

- 1 -

Antarctica

THE THING ABOUT ANTARCTICA THAT SURPRISES ME MOST? The condoms. They're absolutely *everywhere.*

I've been in Antarctica a total of eighty-three minutes, so I'm positive more exciting surprises will probably (hopefully) reveal themselves, but for now, the most intriguing thing about McMurdo, the American science station, is all the condoms.

They're on all the tables, shelves, and bathroom sinks. Their abundance, combined with McMurdo's abandoned mining-town/ski-lodge ambience, is giving the place a real frat-house-during-spring-break kind of feel instead of the for-the-betterment-of-the-world vibe the scientists might be aiming for.

I have come here to understand how I got here. Retrace my steps. Sort of metaphorically but, then again, no—actual steps. Every step I've taken since I was three years old and first walked onto a dance floor. Since the day I tied my first pair of pointe shoes on my soon-to-be-thrashed feet.

Apparently I've been walking all my life on shifting ice, falling snow covering any trace of the path I've made, so now I look back and I'm panicked because I've left no trail. I'm frozen, paralyzed, no clue behind me to find the way back. How did I get so horribly lost? How, when I was never alone? All this time, people have been beside me, helping me walk straight into this blizzard.

How did I get here?

I told a lie and got on a plane. Four planes. Ninety minutes from San Francisco to LAX. Fifteen hours from Los Angeles to Sydney, Australia. The National Science Foundation sprang for Virgin Atlantic, so I had *Seinfeld* episodes on the tiny seat-back screen the whole way. Then three more hours to Christchurch, New Zealand. *No ... sleep ... till Christchurch.* Overnight in a nice hotel, and the next morning, they handed out sack lunches of cheese sticks and granola bars for the five-hour cargo plane flight to The Ice.

We landed inland, far from the water, on the solid polar ice cap. (Less solid every day. Thanks, Global Warming.) Five hours of roaring engines whined to a stop, and our ears rang. We breathed a future-familiar jet-fuel smell and stepped out onto The Ice. And it was quiet.

Deep, heavy, *loud* silence in a world of white and blue and black and red. White-blue sky, white snow and ice, black mountains, and our huge shocking-red National Science Foundation parkas.

We slipped and slid all over the ice. Treacherous grooves carved into the ice as texture for the landing strip were so wide I tripped in one and nearly broke my ankle. Weeks ago that would have been a tragedy, but now it wouldn't matter at all. Now I can sprain all the joints and break all the bones I want. Bring it, Ice.

An hour-long ride in a giant red Terra Bus to McMurdo and we stepped onto The Ice once more, and a precise spot of pain, otherworldly cold, flared in my forehead. Oh my God, it's like being stabbed with an icicle. Yes, I know—*Antarctica,* so what did I expect?—but I'm telling you, this is not regular cold. This is . . . it is unreal.

McMurdo is a town. Buildings, muddy roads, tractors, snowplows, trucks, and metal sheds. A winter population of two hundred. The scientists (*Beakers,* they're called here) go their way, and I am ushered into bright royal-blue Building 155 with the other support staff. We are janitors, line cooks, research assistants, and flight schedulers. We support the important people. We are mostly Americans and New Zealanders. Kiwis? All this slang I'm picking up already from eavesdropping, and I am the lowest of us all. I am a fingy. (*Fucking New Guy.* Charming.)

We're here together for six months. Soon we will watch the sun disappear into the gray cold of the Ross Sea. No planes in or out. No way on or off The Ice until winter ends in September. Which is why we have all undergone stringent medical and dental exams before arriving, and explains all the condoms; conditions like this surely encourage certain warmth-inducing indoor activities, and getting knocked up here in winter would be a dicey, life-threatening thing to do.

Two hundred people at the frozen, dark bottom of Earth: scientists, researchers, support staff.

Me.

I am one of three pioneers: high school students, seventeen and barely allowed on The Ice but for a coveted National Science Foundation grant for high school seniors looking to enrich our scientific education. (The aforementioned airplane lie.) We are Wintering Over. We are the Winter Overers. On purpose. We have willingly given our two hundred lives to The Ice and the dark for two hundred reasons. *Ninety-nine problems, what?!*

See, I'm already delirious.

The huge mittens encasing my hands make it a chore to pull out my earbuds blasting hits from the London Symphony Orchestra, the music of My People, but I do when a McMurdo staff member walks forward to shake our hands. Everyone but me seems to know each other, and no one else looks seventeen. They're hugging and laughing and talking, and I suddenly really want to lie down.

"Scott!" the guy in charge calls through a humongous beard. "Harper Scott. *Scott.*" The party is quiet as I raise my huge down-encased arm.

"Scott?"

I nod.

"*Scott* Scott?" someone calls from the assembled mass. All dudes. Bunch of dudes and me. The three women we flew in with must be scientists, already off to their science dorm building. Beard nods, and I think he smiles, but I can't tell, because *giant beard.*

Now everyone turns and looks at me.

So much for not being known.

"All righty then, *Scott.* Let's find your room. . . ." He flips through the stack of papers on his clipboard and hands me a key stamped 1123. "Right here, main building, second floor. All yours. Bathrooms near the stairs in each hallway. They'll bring your stuff up later. Welcome Dinner's at six, so you've got a couple of hours. You'll meet your supervisor then. You're with . . ." He searches the pages again.

"Charlotte," I say. She is a marine biology grad student who was once Mom's research assistant, a favor called in to get me here. Bunch of lying liars who lie. For me.

"Charlotte, right. So I'm Ben, Building One Fifty-Five gatekeeper, personal point person, security. Check in with me when you're in or out. Here if you need anything whenever. Whatever. Want me to take you up?"

All the dudes are just standing here, listening.

I shake my head. "Thank you."

I walk to the door marked STAIRS, and some of the guys

take no care to whisper, "Amundsen's straight-up grandkids were here last year" and "Never heard of her."

Yes, being a Scott helped the lie along; I applied late. Not the strongest science résumé. Okay, no science résumé. But I'm here now, so screw off!

Delirious *and* cranky.

I follow Beard's directions to the concrete stairwell lit with fluorescent bulbs to another long, dingy hall to the door marked 1123. Home. For six months. Tiny dorm room with a three-drawer dresser and a small desk with a CD player on it that someone probably left behind, because who even has CDs? There is a rack to hang my giant, wet parka on and two single beds, one against each long wall of the rectangular room. During Winter Over there are so few people that we each get our own room. I drop my small backpack and the rest of the cargo plane bagged lunch on one bed and peel off four layers of clothes: hiking pants, yoga pants, leg warmers, wool long underwear. I pull two ski beanies off my head, unwind my long braid of brown hair. I'm numb. That can't be good.

There is a mirror above the dresser. My clavicles are sharp. No boobs at all and a shadow beneath every single rib. My fingernails are blue. But then again, they often are. Which is its own special issue. Jesus. Me and all my *issues*.

I kneel on the other bed, beneath the only window in the cinder block walls. The view is mostly of the sides of other buildings, but those black mountains are closer. I can see the tops in the blue-gray-white sky.

I pull my T-shirt and yoga pants back on, and two of the four pairs of socks I'd worked into my giant NSF-issued boots, and crawl beneath the bed's wool blankets. My teeth chatter. My pajamas are somewhere in my two big duffel bags still being unloaded from the cargo plane. When I get my hands on those pajamas, I'm never taking them off.

There's a letter somewhere in those bags, too. Unopened. From a person—a guy—I've only just met, but who I might miss more than anyone else. Maybe it will stay unread.

There's a hum in the walls from the central heat. In the phone book–sized employee handbook the NSF gave us, I learned that waste heat from the generators in McMurdo's power plant heats glycol, which is pumped into the various buildings, and all that means to me is that Beard was wearing a T-shirt and no coat. So once I warm up, I bet it'll feel pretty nice in here.

Out of the blue, the noise of the warmth running through the pipes makes my heart hurt, because it sounds like the dishwasher at home. One of us always starts it as we're all heading to bed. At last, days of noise and cold and travel done, alone and quiet, I feel how far away home is. Mom and Dad are thousands of miles—oceans and continents and a hundred degrees of warmth—away. I roll over and face the empty bed across the room.

I may have made a terrible mistake.

- 2 -

San Francisco

140 Days Earlier

Snow is in my eyes. I blink it from my false lashes, but still it falls, first scattered, floating and then insistent, swirling: a blizzard. Our toes drag paths through the drifts, making patterns and circles. Our feet disappear beneath the white, but we keep on, sweating, absolutely boiling under ice-blue lights. Music, urgent as the snowfall's impetus, swells and races. I can't see past the dizzy cyclone, nothing but white, and still I point, prepare, whip my head around, and pirouette, turn, turn, turn—

"Harper!"

My name called from the darkness beyond the storm trips my concentration. I slip and fall. Hard.

"Oh, honestly," the voice sighs. Madame Simone. Pissed.

The music stops and the snow lets up.

I remain, stunned, on the floor.

"Ladies, if you were under the impression a pirouette would be any easier in a snowstorm beneath a hundred and twelve degrees of Fresnel light, I have no sympathy for you. I will not tolerate this laziness! Spot. Spot!"

From the audience she pounds the floor, her scare-the-crap-out-of-the-students stick probably bending, about to snap. So is she. Were the lights up, we would see the vein above her left eyebrow pulse. I glance at the backstage clock. Ten-fifteen. We've been at this for nearly three hours. I close my eyes.

"You're killing me! Killing your beloved *professeur.* I am physically dying! It is very simple: single, double, arabesque, plié! Clean, finish it, use the floor! Direct your energy down and up, from inside. Harper, stop turning those feet out! Use your hips. How many times must I say this? My God, it's like you've never seen a dance floor in your lives! Why must you torment me this way?"

The stage lights buzz and click in the snowy silence. Simone rents one of the smaller San Francisco State University theaters for our yearly *Nutcracker* (performed in November to get a jump on the season, and also it's way cheaper). Though compared with her studio, it feels huge to us. Especially now.

"Let us attempt to achieve competence this time, shall we? From Kate's entrance. And, ladies? I will not stop you again. If you bring shame upon yourselves and your families, I wash my hands of it. Music!"

Kate grabs my hand, pulls me up, brushes the snow from my rehearsal tutu.

"Oh my God," she whispers. "What the hell?"

We hobble offstage and regroup, rotate our ankles, stretch our feet. The music starts, Tchaikovsky's couldn't-be-less-subtle *Nutcracker.*

I rub my poor hip. "Be careful," I whisper to Kate. The stage is now three inches deep in coconut flakes. White and floaty, it doesn't melt. Smells like Hawaii. Looks like the South Pole.

Kate exhales, pulls up from her core, lifts her head, prepares, and runs lightly to center stage to start us again. I lean into the light and watch her from the wings.

Any yelling Simone does is definitely not directed at Kate. Endless extension, every turn precise, perfectly executed. Her pointe shoes make no sound, even landing jetés—I could happily watch her forever, even in this tropical snow, which Simone has always said we could never afford, but a bunch of parents donated the money for it this year. We've been jonesing for this night. What ballerina in her right mind wouldn't want to dance the "Waltz of the Snowflakes" with snow really falling, just like the San Francisco Ballet? It takes your breath away, synchronized ghosts moving through the blurry storm, stunning to watch—but clearly a giant pain in the ass to actually dance.

Kate is nearly ankle-deep in the coconut, the snowfall revs back up, and from the shadows, four of us wade through the slippery drifts to join her, our Snow Queen. I concentrate; muscle memory takes over. We watch each other and let Kate lead us in this most painful beauty. The burning in our legs and arms; the raw, open blisters on our feet; the blackened, missing toenails—they all go away. Our breath comes hard and fast, but we smile, sweat and snow in our eyes. We make it look like floating, flying. Effortless.

I turn out from my hips—shoulders back, arms strong—and let the melty joy wash over me. I land my turns. I don't fall. My heart races.

In all the world there is nothing better, no brighter joy, than this.

The music ends. We are still. Arms crossed, feet pointed, panting chests heaving with restraint, our smiles bright. Snow falls. Silence.

"Well," comes Simone's disembodied disappointment. "We'll try again tomorrow."

- - -

Kate and I sneak down the dark corridors of the science building, where I dump the contents of my dance bag—shoes, hairpins, makeup, medical tape, scissors, hair spray, Bengay, tights—to find the keys to my mom's office. She is a marine biology professor here at SF State and keeper of a mini fridge full of water and iced tea, and all kinds of delightful snacks.

"Oh, hurry, hurry," Kate moans. "I'm dying!"

"You are not, you big baby. Just hold on. . . ." I find the key and scoop my junk back into my bag, and we fall inside onto Mom's futon sofa.

"Thank God," Kate sighs. She leans over my lap to raid the mini fridge stash. "Chex Mix!"

"Gross." I drain a liter bottle of water in, like, ninety seconds, lie back against the whale-shaped pillow I sewed in third grade for a Mother's Day present, and open a bottle of iced tea.

We sit and breathe for a while in the quiet office, dark but for a sea star night-light and the ten-gallon aquarium bubbling on Mom's desk, guppies and mollies darting through waving grass. Maps of Antarctica and photographs of seals and penguins cover the walls. Kate searches for peanuts, tossing pretzels back in the Chex Mix bag.

"I know it's a pain," she says, "but 'Snow'—don't you *love* it?"

I nod, drain the tea, and open another bottle of water.

"Plus, if we get trapped in the theater, like if there's an earthquake or something, we can eat it."

"Sure."

"Harp," she says in her mom voice.

"Yeah."

"Come on. It's like running on ice. I'm amazed all of us didn't fall."

"I'm not."

"Oh jeez."

"Neither is Simone."

"Screw Simone."

"*Dude.*"

"No, seriously, she's insane! We get one rehearsal with it and it's off to the races?"

I love her for saying it. Still, her kindness doesn't help.

I look up into the eyes of Robert Falcon Scott. Explorer. Scientist. His black-and-white image in a place of honor on the wall above Mom's desk. He is our third cousin's aunt's great-grandfather. Or something, I don't remember. It's all cross-stitched on a pillow at home if I need to follow the genetics. His blood is Mom's, the reason for her life of science. His blood is mine, the reason I know I will not fall again.

In the photograph, my ancestor is standing on the Antarctic ice in 1912 at the geographic South Pole before a British flag planted in the snow. He is surrounded by his weary crew, all nearly dead but at last where they intended to be. Inscribed on the photograph's frame is Mom's personal version of Scott's do-or-die spirit: AUT MORIERE PERCIPIETIS CONANTUR. "Succeed, or die in the attempt."

"You are a beautiful dancer," Kate says. "You *are*." She chews in the silence. "Ashley Bouder!" she shouts. "Thank *God*! I couldn't think of her name; that would have driven me insane—New York, she's a principal, she falls *all* the time and no one cares—she's amazing!"

I shrug.

"Harp. You think Nureyev never fell? Yuan Yuan Tan?

Baryshnikov? Come on, that guy probably spends more time lying on the floor than he does dancing."

"That's because of the vodka."

She grabs my foot and shakes it. "Everyone falls."

What I want to say is, *You don't,* but I am a Scott. Self-pity is absent in the double helix strands of our do-or-die DNA, so instead I sigh. "Coconut is too expensive to practice with more than once. She wanted it perfect."

"Which is her own problem." Kate goes to the aquarium, sprinkles some dehydrated worms on the sleeping fish. "Just, if she gets on you about it, scream *Ashley Bouder* in her face. She'll *love* it. So listen—aside from your falling and ruining the entire rehearsal—really, how fun was tonight?"

I give in. "Amazing."

"Right?" She sighs. "Cross that off the life list: dance 'Snow' with *snow*? Done!"

She's right. She is.

"Okay." I yawn through my smile. "Ready?"

She catches my contagious yawn and stretches. We pull on sweats over our tights and leotards. I write a note to Mom on a Post-it and stick it to the aquarium glass.

Thanks for the sustenance.
P.S. Water your spider plant.
What kind of heartless monster are you?

I pour the last of my water into the parched soil of the struggling plant, root-bound in a clay pot my older brother, Luke, made for Mom probably also in his third-grade class— such a crafty age.

"Shall we?" Kate smiles.

San Francisco fog is never more beautiful than when we're boiling hot after rehearsal. I yank my knit hat off my head and shrug out of my hoodie.

"Don't," Kate says. "You'll get sick."

"That's a myth. Cold doesn't get you sick; germs do." The mist winds around the cypress trees and lampposts of SF State's rolling green campus, just a few blocks down and across 19th Avenue from the ballet studio and both our houses in the West Portal neighborhood.

"All right," she says. "Your funeral. Lie in bed miserable and miss the show. Miss graduation. Miss auditions. Just remember I told you so, dummy."

I pull my hat back on.

She smiles.

The Muni train rattles past, and we cross the tracks against the red.

She hugs me in the pool of streetlamp light at the bottom of her driveway. "It's a gorgeous dance. You're gorgeous in it. We're almost there. Okay?"

I nod.

"Coconut snow is slippery as snot. Everyone knows that."

"Gross. Why would anyone know that?"

"It's known!" She holds my shoulders. "Harp. It's Friday. We get to sleep in tomorrow!"

Sometimes it is hard to tell if she really forgets things or maybe doesn't listen in the first place.

"Class," I say.

"Not till ten!"

"Not *ours*. I've got kindies to teach."

"Ugh, Saturday *morning*? Since when?"

"Three years, dude. Sunday, too."

"Really?"

"Yeah."

"You just taught a class before rehearsal!"

"Those were the babies. Tomorrow's the kindies and first graders."

"Whatever. Simone can teach them by herself. *Sleep in!*"

The luxury. She knows I would if I could—teaching makes my own classes possible. I start the walk to my house, waving backward over my shoulder.

"Oh, wait," I call. "Breakfast! Nine sharp!"

"I'll sleep till eight-forty-five," she says. "Hey! Be careful. Walk in the light!"

"Got it, Mom."

"Good night!" She chaînés all the way up to her door, waves, and shuts it dramatically behind her.

- - -

West Portal hums with Friday night-ness. Loud, drunk SF State kids stumble in and out of bars. Neon lights in bar windows buzz lazily. Upstart little restaurants representing the cuisine of practically every member of the United Nations line both sides of the street. Date-night heels click on the gritty sidewalk. A Muni train clangs on the tracks and disappears past the library, beneath Twin Peaks' red-and-white Sutro Tower along the rails into the tunnel. My driveway curves up a steep incline to a narrow, two-story white stucco house crawling with night-blooming jasmine planted long before I was born, before my grandparents left the house to Mom, the only reason we're able to live in this beautiful, overpriced neighborhood. Our porch light burns a perfect circle for me in the foggy dark; I turn one perfect double pirouette.

The house is warm and smells of cinnamon and yeast and cream cheese in the oven—Dad up late baking. HarperCollins published his first cookbook a month before I was born, providing baby-naming inspiration for him, a lifetime of explaining "No, not *To Kill a Mockingbird*" for me.

I shuffle to the kitchen, drop my bag and myself on a stool at the counter, and wince, shifting off my painful hip.

"What are you doing?" I yawn. The guy gets up at four every morning. He can't be awake at eleven.

He shakes his head. "What are *you* doing? It's a million o'clock."

I rest my head on my arms. "Rehearsal. 'Snow.'"

"Ooh, really? How was it?"

I shrug.

"You were so excited! Didn't it work?"

"Yeah."

I untie my shoes and let them drop, pull my left foot into my lap and start working at the tape wound tight around the callused ball. My middle toes are black-nailed and fused together by dried blood and a weeping blister. Looks worse than it feels and totally worth it for the eight perfect rond de jambe turns I executed this afternoon before my fall in the snow rendered them meaningless. I pry the scabbed skin apart and watch Dad ease a sheet pan from the oven and set it gingerly on the counter. "If these things collapse one more time . . ." The sink is full of hardened dough disks.

"What is *up*?" I ask.

"I don't know," he whispers. "Yeast is being stupid tonight." The rolls on his tray are as big as my face, sodden with cream cheese frosting, and they stand tall and pillowy. He sighs. "I wish your mother would get up and taste these for me. I can't tell anymore."

Poor man. His own bakery, three cookbooks, and he gets stuck with my brother, Luke, who's allergic to gluten and nuts and dairy and just about everything else in life, and me, who won't eat anything, ever. It's pretty hilarious when people ask if, as a ballerina, I eat like a horse night and day. I have no idea who started this asinine urban legend, but I have personally been on a diet since I was, like, twelve. Thirty hours a week dancing, and still I cannot remember the last time I tasted a real cinnamon roll. I slide off the stool, lean in close to the frosting, and inhale.

"Yeah," I sigh. "Pretty sure you're good."

He will not give up until the rolls are perfect—I know. He is not a Scott by birth but took the name when he and Mom married. Because Scotts are badasses.

He plucks a big hunk from the center of the biggest roll and chews thoughtfully.

"Huh. All right."

It's actually not too scandalous he's still up, given that Thanksgiving, four or so weeks away, is the busiest time of the year for the bakery. You'd think it'd be Christmas, but Thanksgiving is really out of control. He wraps the rolls in a shiny blanket of aluminum foil and tucks them in for the night.

I make my painful way upstairs to get in the shower and soak my injured ass. And my pride.

"Hey," he calls. "You okay?"

"Yep."

"Because you're walking like you're a hundred years old."

"That's because I am. Good night."

"'Night, Benjamin Button."

I wave from the top of the steps and hobble off.

- - -

Oh my God, a hot shower is the greatest thing ever invented. I let the nearly scalding water run over my head and aching body, rehearsing the "Snow" choreography in my mind again and again. I'm perfect every time. Crap, it is going to be hard to wake up to teach in six hours—no, five because I still have geometry homework I have to do tonight. With rehearsals all weekend, it's sort of now or not at all. But I will, because Kate is right; we're so close. We're graduating in December, one of the main action items of The Plan.

The Plan has been in place since sixth grade. We've followed it religiously, and one fall isn't going to screw it up. We've been in ballet class together since we were three years old, devoted to it and to each other. Twelve years old is the magic hour for ballet—by then you either understand this is what you want for your life or you realize it isn't.

Our parents insisted that we must graduate from high school—real graduate, not GED graduate—which is ridiculous because there are girls who leave home to be apprentice company members all the time in their freshmen or sophomore years. They have tutors or are homeschooled and use their extra time to take private lessons. They have stretching coaches, and it makes me jealous. Even Kate's private school schedule is flexible enough to allow for some of that. But none of Simone's dancers have auditioned for San Francisco. And none of them, not one, has ever been as good at Kate. Everyone knows this.

So now Kate and I are Simone's oldest students, which makes us panic. A ballerina has only a precious few years to put her body through what it must do. We already feel old. Simone's students either fall away from ballet in middle school, when the lure of soccer or swimming or boys becomes inescapable, or they audition and leave for companies in other states. But never New York, never San Francisco, and always before most of them have even started their periods. While Kate and I slog through high school and dance with Simone. Year after year.

Our urgency, at this point, is palpable.

In the face of this unfair "diploma madness," Kate and I, after school one day in our sixth-grade year, made a pact. We used sewing needles for a blood oath and drafted our Magna Carta. The Commandments.

THE PLAN

1. Graduate from high school early so when we
2. Audition for the San Francisco Ballet, we are ready to go when we are both
3. Offered spots in the school or corps de ballet or even straight-up company positions, which would necessitate
4. Finding a cheap loft apartment downtown together that has hardwood floors and mirrors and barres on every brick wall so we can
5. Live forever in San Francisco and eventually be

soloists, maybe even principals, in the company and entertain our fabulous dancer friends and our families in our amazing loft—*being ballerinas!*

We don't bother including details such as how there is no such thing as a loft in San Francisco cheap enough to afford on a dancer's fifteen-dollars-per-hour salary, or the part about the second jobs we'll have to take just to have enough money to live, loft or no loft. We don't want to rain on our own parade. Aim for the moon and all that.

Kate and I are a rare breed—native San Franciscans. No one is *from* here; people like Dad abandoned their East Coast lives to move here because it is the most beautiful city in the world. And the San Francisco Ballet is the best ballet company in the world. It was the first professional dance company in America, and it gave the first American performance of *The Nutcracker*.

This is our home. This is our company.

Aut moriere percipietis conantur.

Auditions for new students, apprentices, and company members are on January 3. We'll have our high school diplomas mailed to us and our bags packed, ready to accept our company positions and start our ballerina lives in the loft on Market Street. Or Fillmore. Or Grant. Or at home with our parents until we're eighteen and can sign a lease. Details.

The hot water is gone. I step out of the shower and wipe fog off the mirror.

Fantastic. Already, a blue-green shadow covers a palm-sized area of my left hip. Hurts to even wrap a towel around me. But I do. And I floss and brush my teeth and comb the tangles from my hair, which falls, straight and dark, way past the bruise, almost to my knees.

I get in bed, and my heroes look down on me from posters tacked to the ceiling, San Francisco Ballet soloists and principals midleap, midturn, dying as Giselle, as *Swan Lake*'s Odette. And in the center, my own black-and-white portrait of Robert Falcon Scott in a fur-lined coat beside a supply sled at the geographic South Pole.

Mom has regaled us all our lives with the stories of the three main explorers, men who wanted so desperately to be the first in the world to reach the South Pole. Amundsen, Shackleton, and our Robert Falcon Scott.

Shackleton tried, failed, tried again, and was trapped in the shifting ice. It crushed his ship, the aptly christened *Endurance,* and he and his crew wound up in tiny wooden lifeboats, hiking mountains, and eating penguins for a year to survive and return home. He rescued his entire crew, but he did not cross the continent, the entire point of his expedition. Antarctica won. Mom speaks the least of Shackleton.

Our Scott was the heartbreaker. He and his crew struggled

against ferocious windstorms, suffered snow blindness, and reached the South Pole at last—to find Amundsen's Norwegian flag already planted.

"*The worst has happened,*" Scott wrote in his journal. "*All the day dreams must go. . . . Great God! This is an awful place.*"

I think he was wrong; Antarctica is not awful. Antarctica is Antarctica. Scott knew that going in.

Scott and his crew began the freezing, hungry walk hundreds of miles back to their base camp, dying one by one, until, at last, in a canvas tent, the remaining few men gave in. Scott wrote one last entry: "*Had we lived, I should have had a tale to tell of the hardihood, endurance, and courage of my companions which would have stirred the heart of every Englishman. These rough notes and our dead bodies must tell the tale.*"

So how did Amundsen march in, plant his flag, and escape with glory and his entire crew's lives intact? How did Shackleton and Scott make such faithful efforts and still fail?

Why do some people train all their lives to be professional dancers and end up performing interpretive "creative movement" at Renaissance Faires?

Mom worships Scott because he gave his life in his attempt and because he was, to the end, first and foremost a scientist. His insistence, in fact, that experiments and data collection continue as the team struggled to the pole slowed their pace and is possibly one of the reasons why they all died. Nobility.

Succeed, or die in the attempt.

I secretly love Amundsen. He knew how many dogs he needed to pull the sleds carrying food for the men—the dogs themselves dined on fresh penguin. He did not bring a huge, heavy supply of people food, because as supplies were consumed and the sled loads lightened, fewer dogs were needed to pull, so the surplus dogs were killed and eaten.

Precision.

Studying Amundsen's and Scott's nearly tandem journeys reveals what Amundsen would claim the rest of his life is the only truth of his success: *"I may say that this is the greatest factor . . . the way in which every difficulty is foreseen, and precautions taken for meeting or avoiding it."*

He had a Plan.

For me and Kate, the Plan is all we have ever worked toward since before preschool. Luck is bullshit. What people refer to as "luck" is actually opportunity meeting preparation. Opportunity will come if you invite it. If you are prepared. If you work your ass off and don't go to parties or screw around with classmates at the beach on weekends. If you babysit and teach Simone's beginning ballet students so you can afford your tuition. If you take extra high school classes each semester to graduate early, never eat cinnamon rolls, dedicate your entire life to what you truly love and put all you have into it, then there is no way it will not happen. It is, in fact, impossible that it will not happen.

It's nearly midnight, but I pull out my geometry notes. The

Plan will not be derailed by something as stupid as a failed math test. Amundsen in my will, Scott in my blood, I will plant my flag.

The odds of being the first person to reach the South Pole? One in one billion seven hundred thousand.

The odds of becoming a professional ballerina? One in 0.00532 percent of the world's seven billion population.

I like those odds. Those odds are not luck. To become a ballerina, it is understood you are taking on Antarctica. You've got to prepare accordingly.

And you must be willing to eat your dogs.

- 3 -

Antarctica

I SLEEP THROUGH MY ALARM, HITTING SNOOZE THREE TIMES before it makes me so mad I toss my phone onto the empty bed, and then I have to get up to turn it off, and my feet are freezing even in both pairs of socks I've got on. The blue cinder block walls even *look* cold. I remember where I am.

It's nearly six. Beard said six for dinner? Right? I never asked him where the dining hall is. I'm not hungry. But I pull on a few more layers and take my room key. Because I am here. So I should *be* here. Act like it.

Down the stairwell and through the empty lobby, I follow sounds of voices and find the dining hall, which looks a lot like SF State's campus cafeteria: round tables and people holding plates before a buffet of metal food trays. Dreadlocked white guys are in the kitchen, pulling pans from ovens, opening giant cans of fruit. I pick up a plate and put some lettuce on it. Cottage cheese, carrots. Hard-boiled egg. I pour a cup of hot water for tea.

"Scott!" Beard is at a crowded table. He waves me over and makes room beside him. "Charlotte," he calls across the table to a really beautiful woman talking to another shaggy guy. "This is your assistant, Scott!"

Charlotte rises from her chair to smile and reach her hand out to mine. She's maybe in her late twenties. Her hair falls in ringlets around her face, held back with a clip. She's the only woman at the table. The only black person in the room. "Harper, right? Ooh, like *To Kill a*—"

"No."

"Harper *Scott*," Beard Ben says, nodding.

"Yeah, Ben," she says. "We get it. Harper, I'm so glad you made it! How was the trip? Is your mom okay?"

I nod. "She will be."

"Have you called her?" I shake my head. "Come to my office after dinner. Call her so she doesn't worry or she'll never forgive me."

"You know her *mom*?" Ben asks.

"Harper, this is everyone. . . ." Charlotte railroads Ben as she introduces me to the five other guys at our table, mostly scientists, some support staff, all of whom Charlotte says I'll only see at meals because "I'm going to keep you busy every minute—you okay with that?"

I nod.

"So, Harper, your mom is . . . ?"

"Ben, I swear to God," Charlotte huffs. *"Ellen!* Ellen Scott, San Francisco, my thesis advisor?"

"Okay, but *Ellen's* never been here?"

Charlotte rolls her eyes. *"No."*

"So you're studying marine biology?" Ben asks through a maw of ice he's chewing like a handful of peanuts.

"No, I'm just . . ." I look to Charlotte.

"Oh," he says. "Micro, not marine?"

I stir my tea. I'm here now. The plane's gone—they can't make me leave for faking science credentials. I don't think.

Charlotte squeezes a lemon wedge into a bowl of yogurt. "Harper is the third high school student. She's my research grant assistant."

"You already have an assistant."

"Yes. And now I have two." She gives him an it's-none-of-your-business look.

I like Charlotte.

She leans toward me. "Vivian arrived on last week's flight and immediately caught a wretched cold. You'll meet her once she's out of quarantine. She's really smart. You'll like her. Not sure who's got the third—we'll have to investigate so the three of you can commit all your rascally teen antics!"

"Okay." Ben leans back. Eyeballs me. "So what was it, Scott? Someone die? Guy break up with you?"

"Ben."

"What?"

Charlotte full-on glares at him.

"Whatever." He shrugs. "You want to spend all winter babysitting, that's your deal. Have fun."

Charlotte hucks her lemon rind and clocks the side of Ben's head.

"What the *hell*!" he chokes.

Charlotte turns to me. "Harper, you'll need to learn to ignore Ben, and the other jealous members of his ilk."

"My *ilk*? Listen, there is no *jealousy*," Ben drawls. "I'm simply stating the *fact* that if a *Scott*, a *kid* not even studying science, is here in the capacity of a 'research assistant' when, like, hundreds of *actual* science students would kill for the opportunity, it is one hundred percent because you snuck in, and (a) you had some life-altering tragedy you think coming here will fix, or (b) some dude dumped you and you're on an *Eat, Pray, Love* journey or some shit."

The table is silent. There is a very strong whirlpool in my teacup. Charlotte reaches over and stops my stirring.

"Harper," she says, "if you've had enough of people referring to you in the pronoun sense and projecting their own life failures onto you, would you like to finish up and come with me to call your mom?"

Charlotte stands. I do, too, and we push in our chairs.

"Gentlemen," she says. *"Ben."* I follow her to the tray drop and out of the dining hall.

"Sorry about that," she sighs. She unlocks a door and holds it open for me. "Your plane was the last one. No more on or off The Ice until September. As of today, we're completely cut off from the rest of the world, which Ben should be used to by now—this is his third winter." She moves some papers off an office chair, sits me in it, switches a desk lamp on, and leans against her desk, which is piled with papers and files and a million ballpoint pens and highlighters. "Things close in; guys especially get territorial. It's a sausage fest."

I nod. "You really already have an assistant?"

"Harper. You're a Scott. They're going to be jealous, and they can screw off. You've got just as much right to be here as anyone. What I need your help with isn't dependent on some intense science-based education. I'm writing grants, too. I need data entry, organizing, nuts and bolts. Without the grants, I can't *do* the research. Okay?"

"You don't feel stuck babysitting?"

"Seriously, don't listen to a word that guy says."

"But it's true. I lied! I'm not into science—or research or anything!"

"People beg, borrow, and steal to get here; add lying to the pile. There were two legit science spots. You took nothing from anyone, and I need *your* help. Your stipend is less than theirs if that makes you feel any better."

"Really?"

"Yes! By fifty cents an hour, so cheer up! I love your mom so much. I can't believe she let you come."

"She wasn't thrilled."

Charlotte nods. "Winter isn't easy. Doesn't matter. You'll be brilliant. Might be just what you need."

My heart jacks up. "What did she tell you? Because I'm fine!"

"No one said anything to anyone, I swear. It was last-minute and not about science, so a person may naturally be curious—especially a scientist." She smiles. "But I'm telling you: all that matters is you're here and I need your help. That's all I want to know. This is the very last part of my thesis before I submit. I *need* you."

I nod. "Thank you. So much."

She's got aqua-blue crystals dangling from her ears, delicate birds tattooed on her small, bare shoulders. She is San Francisco incarnate: batik blouse, jeans, silver rings on nearly every finger; the clip in her curls is beaded, one a person could find for sale on a serape-covered folding table on Market Street.

"Where in San Francisco are you from?" I'm going to get wild and guess the Mission. Or the Haight. The cool neighborhoods.

"Outer Sunset. Forty-Fifth and Judah."

I smile, but my heart twists. I can see Forty-Fifth Avenue, the Sunset's wide streets, rolling gentle hills leading straight into the ocean, so beautiful it inspires poetry.

At the end of our streets is sunset; At the end of our streets the stars.

"Your mom let me build my own degree. It's taken me forever, but I'm nearly done—I'll be the first master of science in eco-marine biology the school's ever matriculated."

"Wow."

"Will you go to State? What do you think you'll major in?"

"I have no idea." Understatement of the century.

"Plenty of time for that. You're in the perfect place to think about it." She stands. "How do you feel about snowmobiles?"

"Um. Pretty neutral? I guess?"

"Because Vivian's not going to be well enough yet, and I've got to get some data I'm missing before the ice shifts. We can reach the rookery in forty-five minutes, and it may be your last chance to see it, so I say we go. You in?"

"Rookery?"

"Penguins! Weather's supposed to be gorgeous tomorrow, low thirties at least. Jet lag hates fresh air and sunshine, right? After your safety training, we'll get your gear and be back before noon."

She moves a phone to the center of her desk, writes the number for an outside international call on a Post-it, and moves to leave me alone in her tiny office.

"Charlotte?"

"Yeah?"

"It's good I came here. Right?"

She smiles from the door. "You'll know when winter's over. But I can tell you right now *yes*. You'll see."

"Thank you."

"Tell your mom I said hi. And try to stay up late-ish to get on a regular schedule. . . . Ooh, wait, perfect! It's movie night—did they tell you?"

I shake my head.

"Movie, in bed by ten, you'll be raring to go tomorrow." She glances at her watch. "Starts in half an hour. First floor, second room right after the kitchen. Follow the popcorn. It's special, to celebrate Last Plane Out. We used to watch *The Thing,* except last winter one of the guys found a hundred thousand microbial fossils in the ice, which is basically the plot of that one, so . . ."

"So what are we watching instead?"

She closes the door nearly all the way and sticks her head through to whisper, "*The Shining,*" then shuts it quietly behind her.

I'm pretty sure she's not kidding.

- - -

She wasn't. The freaking *Shining.* These people are insane; they laughed all through it. So then I dreamed of creepy elevator twins and didn't sleep. Jet lag is winning.

But I'm up at six, my bags are at my door (pajamas!), and I take a shower. The bathrooms are also dorm-like, rows of sinks and showers. I take my shampoo and loofah in a plastic caddy, and the first lesson I'm learning from The Ice is what a horrible water-waster I am. Antarctica is a geographic desert. McMurdo is a self-sustaining town alone in the world, so any water we've got is *all* we've got. My dearly beloved twenty-minute shower (Yes, shameful. Especially in drought-plagued California. Lesson #1: Learned. Antarctica is making me a better person already) has been reduced to five of bliss, which isn't long enough to rinse the shampoo from my heavy hair, let alone shave my legs.

But who cares because I'm not wearing tights today. Anymore.

"Harper!" Charlotte's cheerful voice and shave-and-a-haircut knock come through my dorm door.

She's in her red parka, tall boots, ski pants. "Ready for an adventure?"

The small McMurdo winter population also means there's no line for food. We just walk up and grab some toast and juice, and we're headed to Ben, the glorified hall monitor.

"Hey," Charlotte says to him. "Can you call fire and tell them we need a radio after safety?"

Ben is watching CNN on a tiny TV in his office by the building's entry door. "Uh, I don't know. Can you call them yourself?"

"Stop showing off for Harper. Tell them we'll be there before lunch." She turns to me. "Ready?"

Ben lazily dials some numbers. "And where am I to tell them you *ladies* will be off to?"

Charlotte pulls a ski mask over her head and helps me do the same. "Cape Royds."

"What?"

"The *rookery*. Don't have a hissy fit—can you just call, please?"

He sits there, seething, pissed at me. I have so much secret Antarctica Code to learn.

"Rookery, my ass." He mumbles something into the phone and pushes his knit cap off his nearly bald head.

"Excuse me," Charlotte says. "What was that?" Ben covers the receiver with his hand, overenunciates in a hoarse whisper.

"I said It. Is. Bullshit. This is my third winter. I haven't been to Royds once, and you're taking *her*? Pays to be royalty, I guess."

Royalty? Huh.

Charlotte heaves a huge sigh. "You know what, Ben? It also pays to not be a douche bag." She takes the receiver from his hand and hangs it up with a dramatic slam, way more satisfying than tapping the face of an iPhone. "I'll go myself." Then to me, "Ready, Your Highness?"

She leans her shoulder against the heavy door, and an icy blast of wind pours pain right back into my head. I will never get used to this.

She shouts, smiling into the cold, "You okay?"

I nod.

Charlotte is helping with this training, ten of us learning basic survival skills, should we become separated or lost on The Ice. Information I'm pretty certain I will never use, because I swear to God, I am never leaving the building again until September.

The sun is high and cold, casting short blue shadows on The Ice and mud between the corrugated metal of McMurdo's buildings. The group is laughing, loud volleys of talk echoing in the incredibly clean air. I'm a little light-headed, partly from exhaustion but maybe also from each absolutely fresh, cold breath I draw. Even with tractors and trucks nearby and all these buildings, this air is so remarkably pure it hurts.

A guy instructor joins Charlotte, and the rest of us are schooled about not falling to our deaths in deep ice crevasses, paying attention to black flags and orange cones, and always getting a radio if we're leaving the station. And then they blindfold us. We must learn to find home as if in an ice storm with no rope. Desert ice storms aren't about snow falling from the sky; they are about insane winds whipping across the empty, endless white, pulling up ice and sending it, burning, into a person's eyes. So with bandannas tied on our faces, one by one we flail our way to the small supply shed. Everyone makes it— except me. I am lost. Oh, the irony.

I can't go with Charlotte until I succeed, though, and so I try a second and third time and at last I stumble into the corner of the shed, and they ring a brass bell, celebrating that I did not wander aimlessly to my frozen death. Charlotte is thrilled.

"Class dismissed!" she calls through her ski mask and hood. "Equipment back in storage, and, Harper, let's go!"

I follow her back to the dining hall, where we grab carrot and cheese sticks and Charlotte eats a dinner roll. We drink black tea and jump around a little, warming our hands. She retrieves a backpack from her office, and, ignoring Ben's glare, we march back out into the cold.

At the fire station, Charlotte collects a radio transmitter from a guy in charge, she signs me out, and we hike a few yards to an open shed housing a row of snowmobiles. "Hang on tight, and we'll be there in no time," she promises. "Ready?"

We speed along the ice and snow away from McMurdo, around black crevasse flags, toward the sun. I turn my head against the back of her red parka and see, for the first time, the full height of Observation Hill, a long-dead volcano that is black and tall in the pale sky behind the station buildings. We are flying straight into the white, the ocean beside us our only landmark. I close my eyes. My heart races. Simone would be so furious if she could see this happening.

You'll break both legs! You'll break your back! You'll never dance again!

I open my eyes.

"You okay?" I barely hear Charlotte's voice sail past me.

"Yes!" I yell.

"Want to piss Ben off?"

I nod vigorously against her shoulder.

She steers the snowmobile inland around a stony rise in the ice to the front of a wooden building.

Shackleton's Hut. I know this because he'd wanted to use Scott's Hut at McMurdo Sound for an expedition, but Scott wouldn't let him. So Shackleton built his own here. Pissing match. In the snow. *Dudes.*

It's got a peaked roof and a stovepipe, a couple of windows. Piled behind the hut are big crates of random stuff covered with waxed canvas. Charlotte slows to a stop. We dismount and I stand in numb silence for a moment while the snowmobile engine sound is swallowed by the ocean's roar and freezing-cold stillness. My legs are cramping.

"This is my very favorite time of year." Charlotte stretches her arms across her chest. "Tourists are gone. Sun's still up. You did so great. Are you freezing?"

"Little bit."

"Jump around. Keep your blood moving. You'll love this."

The door is closed but unlocked. Inside it is 1908.

Shelves of tinned meats. Stiff clothes hanging from rafters, beds and blankets, antique research equipment on a wooden table beneath a snow-grimy window. We step into the center of this time capsule, virtually unchanged since the last of Shackleton's crew took refuge here, restocking their supplies to live long enough to make it off The Ice.

"Ben's an Amundsen," Charlotte says.

"He *is?*"

"Oh, sorry, no—not like you—he's a Peter Pan living for himself with no responsibilities who spends his entire off-season life traveling. I meant that everyone on The Ice is either an Amundsen, a Scott, or a Shackleton. They align themselves—Amundsens are typically the jocks, nonscientists like Ben who act like idiots and jump naked into The Ice to prove . . . whatever frozen balls proves. They all whine about how unfair it is that Amundsen *won*; he got to the pole first, but Scott gets all the attention because he's the martyr. And Shackleton didn't even get to the pole and yet he's the hero. *Why do they get all the reward even though they lost?* Like exploring Antarctica is a game. How is freezing to death a reward? It's so stupid."

Ballet is perfection of an art. It is not a competition.

Except when it is.

"All the scientists are Scotts, of course," she says. "So people are jealous you're an actual Scott. Ben's jealous you're here today because two summers and his third winter and he's never been to any of the huts, none of the graves—not the pole. Which is where everyone wants to go. Right?"

I shrug.

"Well, Ben wants to. And here, too. Scott's Hut is right behind the fire station—it's like three hundred yards, and he won't step into it. Idiot."

"Why hasn't he been anywhere?"

"Nobody wants to take him! Getting to the pole is something every scientist, every explorer on the planet wants to do, let alone some random jerk who just wants to 'win.' But unless you've got an assignment or a job at the South Pole Station, or you're support staff and there's a last-minute available spot and you've got a scientist willing to take you with—I mean, *I* could take him."

"No chance?"

"None in hell. The day I met that guy three winters ago, within the hour I arrived, he told me how great it was that affirmative action had reached The Ice."

"Oh Jesus."

"Yeah. The Ice is *white*."

Ballet is, too. Most tights and leotards are made for white skin; people have to dye them to match darker skin tones. And those same nonwhite dancers are constantly rejected on the basis of "wrong body type."

I am ashamed by proxy.

"What did—what do you say to shit like that?"

"Nothing. He said it right after I'd turned down his drunken offer to escort me to his room."

"Classy."

"He'll never get to the pole. His own fault."

"Have you been?"

She smiles. "Very best day of my life. True South." She steps to a window, gazing love-struck toward the pole for a long while, then back to the hut. "Look at these blankets. Folded! I don't think they've been touched. Isn't it beautiful?"

Maybe it's the jet lag or the cold, but in this moment, it really is. Beautiful. Sacred? Like being in a church. Like in the ballet studio before class ... alone, waiting. The floors are wood—rough—but it's such a big open space, except for Shackleton's small bedroom. High ceilings. Push these beds and tables against the walls and it would be perfect for a balls-out series of grand jetés across the floor.

I shut my eyes.

"Scott was kind of mean to Shackleton," Charlotte says quietly, studying a pair of laced leather boots. "They were on The Ice together once, Shack got sick, Scott kicked him off the crew, sent him home. He was jealous the men trusted Shack more. Natural leader ... Why am I telling you? You know all this."

Not all of it. The light through the windows bathes the hut, and its perfectly preserved hundred-year-old contents glow.

There are unlit lamps that are fed, Charlotte says, by a carbide acetylene generator above the door. I have no idea what that means. Except that Shackleton was clearly very smart.

"You're a *reluctant* Scott? Right?" I say.

She tips her head to the beams in the peaked ceiling. No dust. No cobwebs. "Yeah," she says. "In my heart of hearts . . . I like to think I've got some Shackleton in me. I think everyone wishes that. 'For scientific research, give me Scott; for swift and efficient travel, Amundsen; but when you are in a hopeless situation, when there seems to be no way out, get on your knees and pray for Shackleton.'"

She's paraphrasing Sir Raymond Priestly, a geologist who narrowly escaped dying with my Scott.

I love the light in this room; it is quiet, electric, *waiting* alive-ness.

"All right!" Charlotte says, breaking the spell. "Penguins."

We step out into the ice air, and the wind is carrying sounds, like floating to the surface of water, waves against the ice and rocks. Wind. Long, low voices and higher, shorter calls. Charlotte grabs her pack, and we walk toward the Ross Sea.

Thousands of smooth little black-and-white penguins. And their *eyes*—

"*Blue* eyes?" I whisper.

"Black," Charlotte says quietly. "The white ring just makes them look blue."

They're maybe two feet tall and smaller, milling around, climbing rocks, and calling out to one another. Tuxedoed little kids playing in the snow.

"Adélies!" Charlotte sighs from inside her fur-lined hood.

I've never had any kind of affinity for penguins, despite

Mom's love of all things Antarctica. The walls of our San Francisco house are full of paintings and photographs of whales and seals and penguins. But now here, so close, there is a rising lump in my chest.

"This is the end of breeding season," Charlotte whispers. "And tourist season, thank God, so I can get in there without a bunch of random people standing around, freaking them out. Those piles of little rocks . . ." She points to clusters of smooth gray stones among the black crags. "Nests. Two eggs at a time, parents take turns feeding in the water. The babies have nearly all finished their molts, but there may still be a few. . . ."

Oh my God. There is a cluster of parents and babies, chicks in various stages of maturity, not twenty yards from us. Miniature white-chested, red-beaked babies hang with the grown-ups, and there is a tiny, fuzzy gray-flocked angel; its head is smooth, his body a pouf with legs. It waddle-runs to a parent, who bends its head to the baby's, and they have a conversation about something.

There's a makeshift wire wall contraption set up in the rocks, just a two-foot section with a gap in the middle. The penguins investigate it, walk through the space, and then ignore it.

"That's a scale," Charlotte murmurs as she unloads her pack. "It sends aggregate stats for the whole group back to the station. They don't know we're going to put them all on Atkins. Little fatties." She's got ziplock bags of test tubes, lidded petri dishes, tweezers, some superlong Q-tip things. She pulls off her mittens, snaps on a pair of latex gloves, unfolds a small blue tarp, and arranges it all in rows. "We've tagged a bunch of them. I need some samples of poop and maybe a feather or two if I can get them before my hands freeze. They're very curious. Just stay still and quiet and wait; they may decide to investigate you."

I forget to be cold, to be anything *but* still and quiet. You know those coffee table books of photography, and there are images of places on Earth and animals, and they don't seem real, like it's all Photoshopped marvelous? This is real. These breathing, moving . . . I am never this touchy-feely, but . . . *souls?* They *live* here; this is their *home,* these black rocks and white ice, this dark, undulating sea beneath the upturned bowl of intense blue sky.

I can barely breathe. My heart hurts more than my head.

Charlotte walks carefully toward, then into, the group. She turns and beckons me forward, but I can't move. Her red parka and giant snow boots move carefully among the flight-less birds. They regroup and follow her, ignore her and talk to her. They are not afraid.

She kneels in the midst of them all, holds one on her knees for a moment, looks at its tag, swabs its foot and its beak, and lets it scuttle away to shake its feathers and head, annoyed, but still it likes her being here—you can tell. Charlotte collects some poo, watches the babies run around and slip on the icy rocks. She scoops a bit of sand into a bag. Makes notes on a folded paper.

And then one of them leaves the group. He . . . she . . . who knows? He is walking toward me. I don't blink. I don't breathe.

He is an adult. His body is sleek and shines in reflected-snow light. The ring of white feathers around his seeming ice-blue eyes makes them brighter in his perfect black face. He stretches his neck to the sky, unfolds his wings, and levels his gaze at me. His family calls to him, someone in the group does, and he turns and runs to them. He stops and looks over his shoulder at me, then rushes back into the rookery's warm embrace.

I exhale. My face burns. Tears are frozen there, and they hurt.

Charlotte makes her cautious way back to me as the colony separates and swims around her retreating form.

"What do you think?" She smiles, stashing the samples and notes in her pack. We stand and watch the Adélies together.

"They're leaving in a few weeks," she says, her face lit by the pulsing sun. "The babies will finish molting, winter comes, and they migrate all together."

"Like emperors?" I can't imagine these sweet birds, the dads huddled together in the freezing inland wind, balancing their egg-bound babies on their feet while the poor females make the icy trek to the ocean. I've seen *March of the Penguins*. Those guys are nuts.

"No, not at all," she murmurs, still intent on the rookery

antics. "Adélies follow the sun. When it sets for winter, the Ross Sea freezes, the continent size nearly doubles. They walk with the ice as it forms, hundreds of miles, to always be at the water to feed. They walk straight into the horizon, following the sun so they've always got this sliver of a glow in their sight. Then, when winter's over and the sun rises, the pack ice melts and they stay on the shore and let the sun bring them right back to the rookery. It's magical. I love them so much. Follow the sun and you'll always be where you're meant to be."

She pulls her mittens back on. "You still okay?"

I nod.

"Harper, you need to live this place for all it's worth. Do you understand? Every moment you're here, you need to be a lover of life. You need to think like a scientist."

"Like—think in questions?"

"Yes! Turn what you think you know over and over. See what's underneath. Let yourself be surprised."

"All I ever am is surprised."

She puts her mittened hands on the sides of my hood. "Okay, then remember: 'Science is nothing but perception'— that's Plato. He was all about getting out of the cave, seeing life from a new angle, in a new light, letting things move all they want. The ice we're standing on is shifting as we speak. We're not where we were five minutes ago. Be here while you're here. Understand?"

I imagine Earth in space, Antarctica at the very bottom of the axis. Gravity is holding us as we walk upside down, keeping the blood from rushing to our heads, the ocean safely at the shore. If there ever was a place to see things from a new perspective . . .

The Adélies are hushed, their faces turned up to the sun.

"I understand," I tell Charlotte. "I do. I will."

- - -

We return the snowmobile, give back our radios, and fight the wind to pull open the station door—dark and unfathomably cold. There's another guy at Ben's desk to sign us in to the dorm, thank God.

"I'm going to shower and hit the hay. You all right?" Charlotte says from inside her parka, already halfway up the stairs with her pack full of data. She calls over her shoulder, "See you at eight, bright and early! Meet me at my office then or at seven-thirty for breakfast. Sleep well!"

There are voices from the dining hall, and at once I'm hungrier than I think I've ever been in my entire life. I pull off my parka and mittens and grab a plate.

There are mashed potatoes. Dehydrated, probably, but still. Soup and corn bread and green beans, cheese and butter—it all looks amazing, and my stomach tightens. I fill my plate with salad. Splurge with Parmesan cheese. An apple for dessert.

It is late. Most of the tables are empty, and I fall into a chair by myself and destroy the food. I drink hot tea. My hands finally start to tingle and warm a little. I lay my head on my arms.

"Hey," a voice says quietly near my ear.

"I'm up," I mumble, half asleep.

A guy in an apron . . . half apron, tied around his waist like people on cooking shows wear them. T-shirt, jeans.

"Hey," he says again, and smiles. "You need one."

He offers me a tray of cinnamon rolls.

I can't stay here six months. I miss home so badly I could cry—what is this guy doing with cinnamon rolls? He's just standing here, holding the tray at my face.

"I thought there's no milk or eggs in winter. What's in these?"

"We'll run out for certain, but your plane brought the last of the freshies. We freeze them or use them till they're gone. Take one."

He's Irish. Scottish? I'm awful—it's one or the other, one of those accents that give legitimacy to Hollywood movie spies and lean, muscular international criminals who go around committing treason and espionage with their strong jaws and dark curls and—Are his eyes really that green?

"Go on," he says. "You must be starved, gone all day."

The rolls look nothing like Dad's, but they have lots of melting frosting and they're warm. Straight from the oven.

"I'm sorry," I sigh, and I am. "I'd love to, but . . . wait, how did you know I was out all day?"

"Watched you go this morning. Are you gluten intolerant?"

"No."

"Diabetic?"

"No."

"Allergic to perfection?"

The cinnamon and cream cheese are killing me, they smell so good. I swallow and shake my head. "Sorry."

He puts his hand over his heart, dejected. *"Really?"*

"Thanks, though."

He takes my cold left hand in his, shakes it. "You're Harper. Scott, yes? High school grant student? I'm the third! Astronomy. I got stuck with a Beaker who never wanted an assistant but got assigned me anyway, so I'm sort of also work study in the kitchen. Aiden." He pulls my fingertips closer to his eyes. "Your nails are blue. Should you go to the infirmary?"

I pull my hand back, stand, and pick up my plate. "They're always blue. I think I just need sleep."

He blatantly takes in my bony frame. "You're sure, then? Not just one small bite?"

I want to eat them all. I shake my head once more.

"All right," he says. "Coming to breakfast?"

I nod. He smiles.

"I'll save one for you."

I drop my plate in the dirty dish tub, climb the stairs to my room, get my shower caddy, and take a seven-minute shower. Because I'm frozen and tired, and the whole shower thing is on an honor system anyway. It's not like they've got timers on the showerheads. I don't think. I need to ask Charlotte.

I pull the blackout shades over the window. I should unpack. I should also call Mom and Dad again, but I can barely lift the blankets of the unmade bed to crawl in and finally close my eyes, let alone go find Charlotte and ask to use her office phone. They'll live. This bed is so comfortable I can't believe it; what am I lying on here, a million kittens?

In the dark, quiet hum of the heat rushing through the pipes, I close my eyes and hear the Adélies, their bossy, barking words. I hear the crashing waves and the snowmobile's engine skimming the ice away beneath the sun, straight into the wind all the way from the rookery. Perfect penguin feet, sleek and fuzzy bodies so graceful. Elegant. Shackleton's cabin, just as he left it. Blankets folded. Cream cheese. Cinnamon and powdered sugar. Home.

In a drawer, the unopened letter waits patiently to be read.

- 4 -

San Francisco

"GOOD MORNING, ANNA PAVLOVA," DAD SINGS AS I STAGGER IN the kitchen door, boots off and bag dropped beside them. He's already been to the bakery and back, never not in a kitchen. "How were the kindies?"

I sigh happily and fall into my seat at the table, right on my bruised hip. "Argh, my ass is totally broken! I actually just had the first graders, but my kindies are amazing. They're picking up the steps so fast, and they just want more—more turns, more travel patterns." I rub my poor, broken body. "I've got an hour, and then I've got the kindies to teach before rehearsal, so let's get this show on the road!"

"I'm here! Feed me!" Kate calls from the door, collects a hug from Dad, and drops her bag beside mine.

"Perfect timing," Dad says. "What would you like in your crepes and how many?"

"Strawberries and as many you can fit on the plate, please." Okay, so people like Kate are where the urban legends come from. Racing metabolism or something. She pours a glass of juice for Mom, who shuffles in, still half asleep, kisses the tops of our heads, and sits.

Dad puts my Saturday oatmeal in front of me: steel cut, blueberries, bananas, raspberries. I hug his neck.

Kate's plate is heaped with crepes. "How are we going to survive in an apartment on our own when we're used to this spoilage?" She sighs.

"We'll live on Cream of Wheat and carrot sticks," I say. "And Dad will come make us breakfast every Saturday. Right?"

"Absolutely not. You people are on your own."

"Don't talk about it," Mom wails from behind her juice glass. "I can't think about you not being home, and speaking of which, did Luke go out?"

Saturday breakfast happens only once a month. Dad does his 5:00 a.m. check-in at the bakery, then leaves it in the hands of his staff every first Saturday so we can all eat together. Mom and Dad are militant about it; we may not get to eat together during the week, but our monthly morning together will happen come hell or high water.

"I'm here, sorry!" Luke hollers right on cue from the front door, cold air and some guy following him in. "This is Owen, friend of a friend from school. Okay if he stays? Hey, Kate."

Kate waves. Kate is probably the only reason Luke ever shows up to monthly breakfast. Which is hilarious for two reasons: The Plan precludes any kind of distracting fraternizing with boys until employment is secured, and also, dating her best friend's brother? Too much awkward for one lifetime. It's not going to happen. He needs to let it go. Poor guy.

It is Luke's one Saturday off from the bakery, too. He works weekends and after school with Dad, between classes at SF State, where he is majoring in Living in a Van Down by the River, working toward a degree in mythology and comparative religion, an education perfectly suited for a career in decorating cupcakes with fondant.

"Nice to meet you, Owen. What would you like in your crepes?" Dad calls without turning around.

"Oh. Um . . . hi, thanks so much, I'm . . ."

"Just do it all, Dad, thanks. Hey, Mom." Luke tosses his backpack on the sofa, rubs Mom's shoulders, and takes a clean plate from the dishwasher for this Owen person, and they sit opposite Kate and me at the kitchen table, where Mom pulls her robe around her and sits up.

"Owen," she says, extending her hand across the placemats. "Lovely to meet you. You're an SF State student?"

"Yeah, yes. Great to meet you, too." He's a total Luke guy: probably nineteen, jeans, hoodie. He's Chinese, taller than Luke, and leaner. Hair a little long around his face, but not in a sloppy way. He pulls off the hoodie, revealing lean, muscular arms in a faded SF State T-shirt.

Kate is wide-eyed.

"What're you majoring in?" Mom presses.

"Well, biology. I was premed. But—"

"That's wonderful! I'm amazed I haven't run into you in the science building."

"Well, I'm—sort of—I'm taking a gap year."

"Really. To do what?"

"Well . . ." He's got really good posture for a guy Luke's age. He moves his hair off his eyes.

Holy . . . Kate nudges me under the table.

Look at those eyes, she mouths, not at all discreetly. I nudge her back. So dark. Insanely long lashes.

I'm suddenly aware of how postclass sweaty I am. Jeans, threadbare class leotard, no bra. My hair is probably coming loose. Jesus. I reach behind me into my bag for a hoodie, pull it on, and zip it up.

"Mom," Luke sighs. "Enough with the CSI."

"All right, fiddle-dee-dee . . . But you *like* school, Owen?"

"I do."

"And you'll go back?"

"Of course."

"Good for you." Mom smiles. "We've begged Harper to apply. . . ."

"*You've* begged," Dad corrects from the sink.

Aaaand the humiliation begins. I become intently focused on the oatmeal in my bowl.

Mom shakes her head. "An education is something you'll always have; it changes who you are even if you major in something you don't end up working in. No one can ever take knowledge away from you. Critical thinking, a breadth of intellect and new ideas, challenging yourself—right, Owen?"

Owen turns his face across the table to mine, giving me the perfect opportunity to openly ogle his eyes. "I absolutely agree," he says. Then: "Oh, *Harper* . . . like *To Kill a—*"

"Nope," everyone else says in unison.

Kate extends her hand over the fruit bowl to Owen. "Hello," she says, "I'm Kate. Harper's friend." He takes her hand and smiles.

Dad finally sits down, scraping peach slices off his plate and into my oatmeal.

"Dude," I whisper. "Enough!"

"You need vitamins," he nonwhispers back. "So, Owen, whereabouts do you live?"

"Funny you should mention that!" Luke says. I push the peaches down under the fifteen other fruits in my bowl. Owen is watching. He doesn't look away. So I do, back down at my bowl.

"Owen lives in the Presidio," Luke says. The Presidio is the forested hillside near the base of the Golden Gate Bridge, and it is dotted with gorgeously restored World War II barracks, now renting as homes. "Owen works at LucasArts," Luke adds.

"Ohhh, Star Wars!" Mom says dreamily.

"Yes!" Luke beams. Mom and Dad are self-proclaimed

"midichlorian-blooded Gen Xers." They were born with light-sabers clutched in their baby fists. They named Luke after the Jedi. Luke Falcon. Not just for Robert Falcon Scott, but *Falcon* as in the *Millennium Falcon*. Seriously.

"You work on the movies, then?" Dad asks through a mouthful of crepe.

"No," Owen says. "Games. Star Wars games."

"Video games?" Mom says.

"Yes!" Luke is all antsy, smiling his face off. "Isn't that cool?"

Kate leans on her elbows toward Owen. "Which games have you worked on?"

"Um. *Republic Commando*?"

"Oh," she says. "So you do the art or the story?"

Kate has never played a video game in her entire life.

"Well, it's all part of . . . I'm level design."

"Wow . . ." She leans back in her chair. "That's amazing."

This conversation is amazing(ly ridiculous). Owen seems embarrassed, though good-naturedly playing along. He leans forward, not to Kate. Toward me.

"So, not *To Kill a Mockingbird*?"

I shake my head. Could I not have splashed some water on my face, worn a nicer leotard? And why do I even care? He smiles. At me.

Okay, and the smile (poster child for orthodontics) has got a seriously competitive edge with his eyes for most striking part about his unbelievably handsome—*Oh my God, what is wrong with me? I need to get out of here.*

"Owen works in the complex Lucas built at the Presidio."

"Gorgeous," Mom sighs. "Can you see the Golden Gate?"

"When the fog lifts," Owen says. "The whole south side of the building is windows, and the commissary is all glass. We're sitting, eating burritos, and the Palace of Fine Arts and the Golden Gate are right there. . . . It really is beautiful."

Kate looks like a drunken bird close to falling off a branch.

"Level design," Mom hems. "That sounds very . . . involved?"

"Mom!" I say. "They haven't announced their engagement— what's with the third degree?"

Owen laughs, chokes on orange juice, and smiles gratefully at me, which nearly sends me out the door, and Luke whacks him on the back.

"Oh, honey, here . . ." Mom and Kate thrust napkins at the poor guy's face.

"Thanks, sorry . . . ," he croaks, still smiling.

"So when you return to school, what kind of medicine are you working toward?"

Owen cuts his crepe very neatly with a knife and fork.

"Mom!" Luke whines.

"It's just a question!"

"No, it's okay," Owen says politely to Mom. "I can't honestly say what will happen in the future. But I know right now, I love making games."

She nods.

"Okay," Luke says. "So here's the thing. . . ."

"There's a thing?"

"Yes," he says, and exhales. "I got a job."

Dad frowns. "You *have* a job."

"Yes, I . . . got another one."

"Two jobs?"

"I got a job with Owen. At LucasArts."

Dad sticks his fork in a grapefruit. Leaves it there. "Really."

"Yeah."

"Doing what?"

"Games!" he says. "Making games! Star Wars games!"

Mom and Dad just sit there. I can hear their wheels turning: *Video games = bad! But Star Wars = good! And . . . what about school? Tragedy!*

Mom looks pale. "You're leaving school?"

"No!" he says. "No, not at all. I'll just be game testing! Part time."

Mom nearly faints with relief.

"But so . . . ," Dad says, "you're . . . leaving the bakery?"

"Well. I mean . . ."

"I can tell you that even part time he'll be salaried," Owen pipes up. "And he's eligible for our health insurance, which is insanely good. If that makes a difference."

What is this guy, some kind of parental maneuvering wizard?

"Kind of does," Mom says.

"You know how to . . . test things?"

"Dad," I sigh. "He's spent fifteen years sitting around in his boxer shorts, playing *Halo*. I'm sure he can test the hell out of a game."

Again, Owen laughs.

I suppress a smile.

Kate gazes at him.

Luke shrugs. "True."

"Huh," Dad says. "That's . . ." He wipes his eyes with his napkin.

"Dad," Luke says. "Are you crying?"

"No! I'm . . . No one sculpts fondant like you. I'm just thinking about how everyone's going to miss your Yule logs, is all. Christmas."

This is not a play for sympathy—the man is sincerely the mushiest, most full of often-embarrassment-inducing love any of us has ever met. Mom's a close second.

Kate, Mom, Luke, and I, even Owen, all breathe a collective and honest "Awwww!" and I lose my mind for a second and smile at Owen, then pretend it was meant for Mom, and then I'm back to staring into my nearly empty oatmeal bowl.

Will this meal never end?

"I don't start for a month," Luke says. "I'll be at the bakery all through New Year. I can't even move in till, like, the middle of January."

"Move in?" Mom says.

"Oh. I mean . . ." Luke shifts in his seat, messes with the grapes on his plate. "Owen shares a house with some other Lucas guys. In the Presidio—they *walk* to work! One of the roommates is moving out in a few weeks."

Now Mom wads a napkin up on her face.

"You guys! I'm nineteen years old. I can't live at home forever!"

"Nineteen isn't old!" Mom sniffs.

The Nutcracker overture plinks from my phone. Thank God.

"That's us!" I say. "Classes to teach, choreography to perfect!" I toss back the rest of my water while Kate grabs our bags and puts her plate and my bowl in the sink.

"You have to go?" Luke whimpers.

"Don't be a baby," I say close to his ear.

"Thanks for breakfast, Dad," Kate says. She hugs him and Mom and holds the back door open for me while I refill our water bottles at the sink.

"Leave everything. I'll do the dishes when I get back," I tell Dad, who will rinse and stack everything even though it's my turn.

"Bye, Kate," Luke says, well-rehearsed casual.

"Later, Luke. Nice meeting you, Owen!" Kate calls, leaning also way too casually, but still gorgeously, in the doorway.

"You too." Owen smiles.

"Oh, Harp, wait!" Dad says, jumping up and running to

the freezer. "Here." He tosses me a bag of ice. "Put that on your butt!"

I shove the ice in my bag, turn Kate, and steer her out the door.

"Nice to meet you, Harper!" Owen calls.

Humiliation: complete.

- - -

We drink water and walk through the fog, hips turned out, arms strong, necks stretched, long strides up and down the house- and tree-lined streets, to the steps of Simone's West Portal Ballet. Our second home. I love this studio more than any place on Earth; floor-to-ceiling windows look out over West Portal Avenue and the houses and hills beyond. The floor is gorgeous, spring-loaded wood, and polished monthly. Barres line the side and window walls; an upright piano sits in the corner. Fog rolls past the windows and reflects in the opposite wall of mirrors, which Simone covers with sheets when she feels like we're "gazing at ourselves too much."

On the top step, I give Kate my bag and sit on the porch to stretch. "I'm waiting here. . . . Want to watch my class?"

"Not today." She yawns. "Think I'll nap in the dressing room and dream about my husband."

"Cool. And who would this be?"

"My breakfast boyfriend! *I am in love.* Luke needs to bring friends home more often. Wake me for class?" She lugs both our bags through the door.

"Hey!" I call.

"Yeah?"

"Addendum thirteen."

She grins, her beautiful face lit up, and disappears into the studio.

We're so close. I will drag her across the finish line if I have to. No matter how cute that guy is.

I try a few battements and pliés at the porch rail. The bruise is huge, hip still sore, but functioning.

At last, who I'm waiting for comes racing down the sidewalk, chased by her mother. A little dark-haired tornado in a pink leotard that used to be mine bounds up the steps.

"Harp!"

"Willster!" My Willa throws her six-year-old arms around my legs, grabs her elbows, and squeezes me tight, presses her face against my hip.

"I feel your bones," she whispers.

"Yeah," I say. "Well, I feel yours, too." And I tickle her elbows till she screams.

"Willa!" her mother, Hannah, pants. "Take your sweater!"

Hannah is mom's teaching and research assistant. She also waits tables at the Beach Chalet, our favorite restaurant in Golden Gate Park, near the ruins of the Sutro Baths, right on Ocean Beach, which means tons of good takeout and also that Willa needs a lot of babysitting. Pointe shoe money for me.

"Harp!" Hannah calls up the steps. "Thank you! Late, late, late as always. Baby, give Mama a kiss. See you tonight!"

Willa blows her a kiss, and Hannah's off to catch her Muni train.

"Whoosh!" Willa says.

"Whoosh," I agree.

She hugs me again, pressing the bruise.

"Ack," I say. "You got my big bruise."

"Oh no, what happened?"

"Slipped at rehearsal. On the *snow*!"

"Ohhh, is it pretty?"

"You'll love it. Wait till you see. Ready for class?"

"How do I look?" she asks, as she does every time.

"Like Margot Fonteyn. Let's hit it."

- - -

Simone gave the babies and little kids to me three years ago, entrusted me with introducing the music, the posture, the lessons of "Everybody needs to stop talking now and put your arms here. Got it? Hands *above* your head, not down your tights . . ." My teaching began as a favor to her, as her patience for the little kids had stretched to ribbons. But now it is a favor for me. Because ballet is expensive, prohibitively so. Teaching the baby classes makes my classes possible. Simone and I barter my tuition.

And last year, after months of watching Willa watch me teach Saturday class, one day the music started and I had my ducklings all set for warm-ups, and Simone walked Willa in wordlessly. She moved some kids out of the way, put Willa's hand on the barre, and left. Willa was ecstatic. So was Hannah; she never could have afforded even one class, and Willa loves it so much.

I toss Willa's bag in the dressing room beside Kate, already asleep on the sofa, and Willa and I shout hello to Simone up the stairwell that leads to her private residence. Willa admires herself in the mirrors, and I see that, despite washing my hair, I've still got snow in it. Snow and glitter are the herpes of the ballet world—we may never get rid of it. Willa plucks out the bigger pieces, and I give her a little preclass barre.

"Miss Harper!" my kindies scream at the tops of their tiny but powerful lungs as the herd comes galloping up the inside studio steps. They wrestle themselves free from their mothers and dads and nannies and grandmas and run to me, crash into my legs, and grab me around my knees, but I am prepared, holding on to the barre for dear life. Three years and still every single class begins this way. Only someone with a tiny black heart could resist, could not love this. Love them.

"All right!" I yell above the din, dragging them off my limbs. "We are *ladies.* Get to the barre, port de bras. *Dépêchez-vous!* Now!" And they scatter to their assigned places. The parents and grandparents and nannies smile and wave and take off for forty-five minutes of Starbucks or jogging or wrangling their other kids.

The little kids get only one performance dance each year,

and it's in *The Nutcracker*. They are angels, wearing white tutus and silver garland halos and real feather wings left over from 1972, when some friend of Simone's donated them from his company's costume stash. They were old then and they're ancient now, but they are soft and real and lovely, even if yellowed and dripping feathers.

My kindies love the costumes and the candles and the tree, even though half of them are Jewish and one is Muslim, which I keep telling Simone is kind of a good reason to maybe look into doing a show not so blatantly . . . well, Christmasy. Like, we could do a solstice-themed concert of variations—Vivaldi's "Winter," stuff like that. Simone just laughs.

"*The Nutcracker* brings in half my yearly revenue. As soon as there's a beloved, traditional Hanukkah ballet people clamor to buy tickets for, I'm all ears. Maccabees in tiaras, bloodshed on the snow . . . No thank you. Now, climb up into the attic for me and bring down my plastic reindeer!"

So I work my little angels. I urge them to strive for as much perfection as they can muster. Today's class is especially game. They put their all into it, arms strong, feet mostly pointed, determined little faces, and by the end, they are breathing hard. They bow and flop on the floor, flushed and worn out. The parents and nannies will be thrilled—a guaranteed early bedtime.

They hug and kiss me goodbye, and when they're gone the stillness is delicious. I'm kind of pooped myself. Twenty minutes till rehearsal.

Seriously, have I mentioned that I cannot wait for graduation?

"Harper." Simone is in the doorway.

"Did you see? They're ready, right, Willa?" Willa nods. "Monday and Wednesday better bring it, because these are some ferocious Saturday angels."

Simone frowns. "I don't want them *ferocious.*"

"You know what I mean. They're on it! We got through the whole thing twice without stopping."

"I saw."

"Aren't they great?"

"Very nice. May I see you in my office?" She turns and walks.

My stomach flips.

"Are you in *trouble?*" Willa whispers.

"I don't know," I moan.

I duck into Simone's tiny office beside the dressing room—a glorified closet, tutus of a million colors hanging from the rafters above her desk, candy-colored fruit ripening on low branches, sparkling sequins and glitter.

I decide to make a preemptive strike, and also I'm so nervous I can't keep my mouth shut.

"I was concentrating," I say. "It's just the snow is really, really slippery, but I know that now and I won't fall again, ever. I swear. Okay?"

She frowns. "What?"

"*What* what?"

"I was going to say your dance with the babies—it is a beautiful picture. They love you. That is why they try so hard."

"Oh."

"You get work out of them I never could. So now, when they are older, they will not drive me half so crazy as you and your snow friends."

I nod.

"You were made for this," she says. "Born to it. Tell me about summer. Have you given it more thought?"

I mess with the strap of my leotard.

"Because they need to know by the end of the year," she says. "The twentieth. To be registered for spring."

"Madame, I don't—"

"Just think. Some more."

"I have, so much, and I—"

"For me," Simone says.

Ugh, cripes. She pulls that one out only when she's truly desperate. Which is nearly never. I sigh.

"Okay."

"You understand."

"Yes."

"Think. *Hard,*" Simone says.

"Yes."

Kate pokes her rumpled head in. "Hey! You were supposed

to wake me up! Time for class!" she grumbles, and stomps off to the studio.

Thank God.

Simone folds her hands.

"What's your father putting in the scones this week?"

"Um. Pear?"

"In a *scone*?"

"It's wintry."

She shakes her head. "Americans."

Dad brings her a baker's dozen of whatever she likes every Saturday on his way home, I think out of gratitude for letting me teach for tuition.

She rolls her eyes. "All right," she says. "Half dozen, a few plain croissant."

"Got it."

I turn back to the dressing room, and she calls, "Harper."

"Yep?"

"It is a rare opportunity."

"I know." I duck out to the dressing room to set Willa up with coloring books and her blanket, then back to the barre beside Kate.

"She still at it?" Kate whispers.

"Still at what?" Lindsay, two years younger, our Nutcracker for three years running because she's so tall and we currently have no boys in the entire school, whispers—loud.

"Lindsay, *God*!" Kate hisses. "You don't have to shout!"

Lindsay's eyes widen.

"Nothing," I tell her. "It's nothing."

"Simone's on her to go to England," Kate blabs. "She wants Harp to do the teacher training this summer."

"Royal Academy?"

I nod.

"Wow!"

"No, not *wow*. It's completely insulting."

"How is it insulting?"

"Because it *is*! She's essentially saying, 'Hey, give up the one chance you have to audition for companies to be a dancer, ever, and spend a year in London learning how to teach other people to dance instead.' I'm a dancer. I'm *not* a teacher."

"Okay," Lindsay says. "But are you also a lover, not a fighter?"

"Leave me alone."

"Why is it one or the other? You *do* teach—"

"Babies! For tuition!"

"They worship you! You don't like it?"

"Yes, I do. I love *them,* but that's not—"

"How much would it cost?"

"Nothing," Kate says, her spine curved over her legs, forehead touching her knees. "Simone's sending her. A year in London, full-time training to be a Royal Academy teacher. For *free*."

"Harp." Lindsay frowns. "Really?"

I nod.

Her mouth is agape. "Why *not?*"

"I think she may even get a stipend, right?" Kate says. "Didn't Simone say living expenses?"

I take my leg off the barre. "What are you doing?"

"What?"

"What's with pushing the Simone agenda?"

"I'm not!"

"Kate."

She looks down. Reties her shoes.

"Kate."

"What?"

"I would never do that. You know I would never ditch you. . . . Come on! The Plan! I could give a crap about London; we are dancing for San Francisco in January. Got it?"

"It's just . . . I mean, an entire career, all that training, England—for *free?*"

"Kate. I'm with *you.* I'm not leaving you. January third. You and me. Right?"

She nods.

"I wish Simone wanted *me* to teach," Lindsay sighs.

Simone sweeps into the room. "Left hands on the barre, port de bras!"

"I've already said it to her a hundred times," I whisper to Kate. *"I'm a dancer. No thanks."*

Kate smiles.

Sort of.

- - -

When class ends, I pull Kate back. "Once?"

"Yeah."

I run to the crowded dressing room for my iPod and Willa, so she can watch. Lindsay sits on the floor and lets Willa lounge in her lap. I start the music.

Our San Francisco audition solo pieces are brief, only two minutes to prove to the director and choreographers why they need us in the company. I choreographed Kate's; she did mine. We dance them both consecutively, together, fourteen years condensed into this perfect one hundred twenty seconds.

Lindsay and Willa applaud wildly. We give exaggerated reverence, wave to our fans.

"I wish Simone would let you go to the Grand Prix," Lindsay says. "They've moved it to November, last Saturday. . . ."

"Contests are stupid." Kate sighs, sliding to the floor for a last long stretch.

"You know you'd go if she let you."

Simone's studio is a *ballet* studio. Hard-core Royal Academy of Dance ballet syllabus, not tap, not jazz, not hip-hop, no cheerleader-esque competitions. There are no tacky plastic trophies lining the walls.

YAGP is the Youth America Grand Prix. And Lindsay is

sort of right; all of Simone's students—maybe even secretly Kate and I—would die to go. But students must be sponsored by and represent their school, their instructor—and Simone refuses. She balks at any competition. *Ballet is perfection of an art. It is not a competition.*

The YAGP prizes, though, are not only medals and trophies. Directors from companies all over the world judge a ton of age groups for scholarships to schools and for apprentice spots, even company positions. For some people, it is the only chance they'll have to be seen. The auditions happen in cities all over the world; the finals for the scholarships and jobs are held in New York. Every year, girls beg Simone to take them, and the answer they get is her yearly lecture about love and truth and scaring the crap out of us.

"A true dancer auditions for the company they most love, the company they will make better and be made better by. This is not a football draft; this is dance, and you had better love who you are dancing for, because you'll give your entire youth and a good portion of your life and health for a very few short years of this love. It had better mean something."

Kate and I were ten the first time we heard this speech and had reveled in the feeling that we'd had it right all along. We'd always known this truth; Simone's confirmation only intensified our devotion to The Plan. To the San Francisco Ballet. And to her.

"We know what we're doing," I say. "Right, Kate?" Her forehead is resting on her knees. "Kate."

"Yeah. Sorry, what?"

"Nothing." I smile. "Get your stuff," I tell Willa, "and we'll hit the road."

Lindsay and Willa hobble to the dressing room together, Saturday sore. It's like Simone's out to get the weekend for being frivolous, so she puts us through more than just our paces. I love it.

Kate stands. "Slumber party tonight?"

"Soon as Hannah gets back. I'll be home by, like, five?"

"Perfect. I can sneak in a nap." We gather our junk from the dressing room, say goodbye to Simone and Lindsay, and zip our hoodies for the misty walk home.

I try not to be jealous of Kate's nap schedule, do my best to convince myself that an afternoon of making crafts with Willa from empty toilet paper rolls and pipe cleaners and white glue mixed with glitter will be just as restful as sleeping.

I am a terrible liar. Especially to myself.

- - -

"Honey, I'm home!" Kate calls from the kitchen door.

"Bedroom!" I yell back, home from babysitting and just out of a wash-the-day-off-me shower.

I hear Kate take the stairs two at a time.

"What is *up*, Mary Poppins?" She flops on the bed beside me. "No one home?"

"Mom and Dad are at dinner with some biology department people. Luke's spending the night at a friend's."

"Ohhhh, an *Owen* friend?"

"Hey. Addendum thirteen."

"Yeah, yeah."

I pull on sweats, and Kate pulls the pins from her class bun and unwinds the hairnet, releasing a shining cascade of swinging auburn waves, silky and thick, perfect hair for ballet. Or shampoo commercials. She grabs a brush from my nightstand and works it through the waves, off her flawless, porcelain face.

"Your mom out tonight?" I ask.

"In," Kate sighs. "With a dude."

"Sorry."

She shrugs. "Eh."

Kate's parents divorced forever ago. It's hard to remember, even for Kate, because her dad was never home even when he and her mom were married. He's an international airline pilot with no imagination who decided to have affairs with flight attendants, which Kate says her mom sort of knew but pretended not to. And she was never home much herself; she's a corporate attorney in an office in Twin Peaks. But when it turned out that Kate's dad had an entire other family in Seattle ("He couldn't keep it on another continent?" Kate sometimes complains. "How about 'Don't shit where you eat'?"), her mom couldn't pretend anymore, so she divorced him and got a huge child support settlement, which pays for private school and ballet lessons. As many as Kate wants. So something good came of it.

"Who is it tonight?" I ask carefully.

She shrugs. "New one, never met him. But check this out: my dad wants to come to *The Nutcracker.*"

"No way."

"With his *wife*. And the *boys.*"

"Oh my God."

"I know! Like any of them gives a crap about seeing a ballet. Or seeing me. Or seeing me *in* a ballet."

"How old are they now?"

"I don't even know—ten? Twelve? And super eager to come sit through two hours of dancing, I'm sure. It's been at least five years since he's even called, and if I have to read one more Christmas letter about 'The Boys' . . . 'The Boys are on the soccer team.' 'The Boys entered their goats in the 4-H fair.' 'The Boys are the greatest alternative to a daughter I ever could have asked for!' Kill me now."

"Oh, Kitty-Kat," I sigh, and lie beside her on my bed. "He's a douche canoe. What does your mom say?"

"That she's not going to any performance *he* comes to, so I'd better let her know which show she needs to avoid because she's got a lot of potential plans lined up for that weekend, including a Napa winery women's retreat her hot-yoga teacher is leading, which I think is a thing where they ride in a van and drink a lot and shop at the outlet stores, and that if she misses it just because Satan and his spawn insist on showing up, she's going to be *devastated*."

The fog is suddenly golden, and my room is hazily aglow.

"We're almost there," I say. "We're so close. January and we'll be San Francisco Ballet company members, rehearsing for a living. We'll be *apartment* hunting!"

She nods. Turns her face away.

"Are you crying?"

"No."

"I blame my dad. He's got everyone all weepy! Cripes! Do you need a tissue?"

"No."

I hand her the box from my bedside table, and she takes it. Sits up.

"You are the best friend anyone could ever have," she says. "*Ever.* You know that, right?"

"Well, obviously."

"No, Harp, seriously. You are the very best friend I could have ever hoped for."

"*You* are! Come on, what's the matter?"

She shakes her head. "I'm not. But you know I love you, don't you? You're my sister."

"You're mine, too, sister from another mister . . . just like your brothers from their Seattle mother."

"Gross, don't even talk about them!"

"It's not their fault, poor little suckers."

"Harp, I'd be so screwed without you."

She looks so tired—not just our usual exhausted-but-happy. Lately she looks completely wrung out.

"Did you get a nap?"

"I wish. I can't sleep anymore. At all. But I know what would help," she says hopefully.

"Brownies coming up! You have to help me shave the chocolate."

"See, this is why no one else should ever bother baking. *Shaved chocolate* . . . will you eat one?"

Her poor eyes have such deep shadows beneath them.

"Sure," I say. *"One."*

"Good enough."

We also make popcorn, and we watch *The Turning Point* for the millionth time and laugh and laugh. Because how the hell, with eight hours of training and classes and then three more hours spent performing on any given day, do filmmakers think a professional ballerina would have time for the sexual hijinks and tumultuous interpersonal relationships and tantrums these women spend all their time indulging in? The real story (constant rehearsal, bleeding feet) would be excruciatingly dull, I guess.

Exhibit A: Kate and I are in bed, asleep, by nine.

- 5 -

Antarctica

A WEEK IN ANTARCTICA AND I'VE FIGURED OUT THAT SHAVING my legs in the sink beforehand gives me more of the allotted five minutes of shower time to just stand and let the hot water wash over me, warming me up for the day. Charlotte says five minutes is luxurious; in the summer, when there are twelve hundred people at McMurdo, you get three minutes if you're lucky, and there are long lines for food.

My body has acclimated to the cold a little more since our day at the rookery and Shackleton's Hut. The heat in this main building is great; in fact, when I mess with the thermostat in my room, it's sometimes too hot. Like almost every one of the other two hundred people here, I'm walking around in jeans and T-shirts. It's getting way too cold and dark to go outside. The sun will set in a couple of weeks and not rise until August. Charlotte says I should get outside while I can; she says the sky is more beautiful each day as winter nears, but the freezing head pain the air gives me is not so beautiful. Also, we've got plenty of work to do in the lab, and the mysterious Vivian is still out sick.

The lab is small, all tables and file cabinets and microscopes and beakers and mini fridges for samples and a desktop computer nearly buried beneath a pile of paper and folders and Post-it notes. So far Charlotte does a lot of sighing and microscope-looking and note-taking and math analysis, and my job is to organize all this information she's culling. I transcribe notes and organize boxes of files and input statistics and run computer-calculated algorithms that mean nothing to me, but a ton to Charlotte. And to the Adélies. So I am meticulous. Most of what I do goes into these super-involved grants Charlotte writes to keep the research going when she's gone after the winter.

"It's taking years of research to prove to the NSF that the shit we're dumping in the ice isn't good for the ice, or the animals. So I'm here on a grant, contributing to the problem to show them that the problem exists."

Global warming has caused open water where there used to be ice, so the Adélies are having to walk hundreds of miles farther to follow the sun. Also waste and pollutants from McMurdo seem to be partly to blame for some jacked stuff called HBCD in the wastewater treatment, flame-retardant chemicals found in the tissues of birds and fish, and Charlotte's especially worried about the Adélies because it screws with their thyroid function, which messes with their metabolism and brain development. It's preserved by the cold and stored in their fat, she says. It is all completely foreign to me. And oddly totally enthralling. And heartbreaking.

She gives me tasks, explains them once, and we work without talking, solely dedicated to getting at least McMurdo's part in this mess fixed. She's smart and enthusiastic, and, while we're working at least, my mind is spared from wandering to home. To ballet or to Simone, to Kate ... Just numbers and data and her nice, floaty work music, which is yoga-studio-massage-sounding stuff with whale calls mixed in. Late in the day, it makes me sleepy. I've taken to drinking caffeinated tea. Lots of it.

This Friday morning I trek to the dining hall at seven, where, every day since the morning he plied me with cinnamon rolls, Irish/Scottish Aiden comes out from the kitchen to wipe his hands on his apron and offer me some extra thing to eat, some treat he's made or found frozen in the giant McMurdo walk-in shed.

"Harper Scott!" he says with a smile, like every day. "Want to take a walk this afternoon?"

"Sorry," I say for the hundredth time. "Working."

"You've got to get out. It's gorgeous! Maybe tomorrow?"

I nod.

"Look what I've found behind a side of beef!" He's made a

bowl of orange Jell-O with canned pineapple slices suspended in it. Winter food, with no planes to bring in fresh vegetables or fruits, is starting to reveal its essential kitchen sink–ness.

"Thank you," I say, maneuvering wheat toast, three paper cups of hot tea (one for Charlotte, two for me), and a banana. That dark hair falling all in his face . . . I'd think the kitchen would make him wear a net or something. "I'm vegetarian," I say, "so Jell-O's kind of not my thing . . . but thank you."

He frowns into the bowl. "Jell-O's got meat in it?"

"It *is* meat—gelatin is connective tissue. Mostly from pigs."

"Oh," he says. "Huh. You coming for lunch? You and Charlotte?"

"Sure."

"All right, then." He smiles. "Good—we'll make a plan to go out walking soon, yes? We've got to stick together!"

"Against what?"

"The *grown-ups*!" he whispers, and falls dramatically back through the doors to the kitchen. I hear his voice as I walk to the lab, "Did you know Jell-O is *meat*? Is that true?"

In the lab, a girl in jeans and a huge wool sweater sits on a lab table stool, earbuds in, huddled over a cluster of Bunsen burners, cleaning them with Q-tips.

"Harper, look—Vivian's alive!" Charlotte cheers from behind a fort of boxes, settled down in a heap of files in the overstuffed armchair she keeps beside the only window—not very lab-like, and also how does furniture like that get to

Antarctica? "At last, now you two can be my research wonder twins. Harper, Vivian, she's an immensely smart biology
student, and, Viv, this is Harper. She's going to save us from
ourselves. Those burners are looking amazing, by the way."

Vivian looks up and pulls out one earbud. White girl, no
makeup, close-cropped brown hair, and huge blue eyes. She
extends a hand over the table, and I fumble with the paper
cups. "Oh, perfect!" I say. "Would you like some tea?"

She yanks her hand back. "Get that away from the
equipment!"

Charlotte looks up. "Vivian," she says quietly.

Vivian shakes her head. "*Please,*" she says. "Please keep
scalding-hot liquids away from the very expensive and sensi-
tive lab equipment. If you wouldn't mind."

I give a cup to Charlotte, who crosses her eyes at me.

"You're biology, too?" Vivian says pointedly.

I look instinctively to Charlotte.

"Harper's here to help with the grant writing, stats—*you're*
my research guru."

Vivian nods. "So when are we going to the rookery?"

Charlotte frowns. "Oh, Viv, I'm so sorry—you were passed
out and exhausted. I didn't want to wake you. I had to go at
Last Plane Out before they black-flagged the road, so Harper
and I did just a quick turnaround. I swear, we'll go again when
the summer staff comes."

"Oh," Vivian sighs. "Okay. Did you get it all?"

"Yes! Thank God, we got everything. It's all labeled, sealed, ready to go. See, Harper's already saving us!"

She nods and turns back to me. "So, not biology—what kind of science do you study?"

"I'm . . . all kinds," I stammer.

"Luckily, there's possibly too much work for even the three of us to ever plow through before winter ends, so enough with the chitchat, ladies," Charlotte says, tossing a box of data my way. "Onward!"

Vivian shoves her earbuds back in and bends over her work.

The rest of the day passes in silence. Charlotte for her usual concentration, Vivian for what I fear is pissed-off resentment, and me for trying to not make anyone else mad at me.

At five-thirty, Charlotte stretches, picks up our empty tea cups, and yawns. "We forgot to eat lunch!"

Vivian pulls out an earbud. "What?"

"Friday!" Charlotte says. "Who's going out tonight?"

I look up from the notes I'm transcribing. "Sorry?"

"To the—Oh my God, I was going to say bars. Your mom would kill me! Sorry. Have you been talking to her?"

"Not really, no."

"You should email her. Do it tonight, okay?"

I nod.

"You bring a laptop with you?" I shake my head. "Just use

the one in here, then, anytime you want. Make sure you stay in touch with her. Promise?"

"Yeah."

"Vivian? You still talking to your parents every night?"

Vivian nods.

"Good girl. Hard as it is to be away from your family, you being here is way worse for them. I guarantee it. And I'm legally in charge of you not dying, so you know. Call home."

"Okay," I say, "we get it—Hold up, there are *bars*?"

She's changing her shoes under the lab table. "Three. I can get you in."

My eyes widen. Vivian shakes her head.

"I'm kidding. Do *not* tell your parents I said that. I just go to hang out. I don't even drink."

"Sure . . . ," Vivian drawls.

"I don't! Not lately—stupid party when I first arrived. Someone started the whole shots business, and I got so sick. . . . Horrible for your liver. Just don't do it. So gross."

Not to pigeonhole Vivian's bookish temperament—I'm sure still waters run deep—but I doubt Charlotte's got anything to worry about with the two of us.

"There's tons of other stuff to do. There're, like, ten different game nights, a book club . . . We used to have a bowling alley, but that closed. . . . Ooh, movie night!"

"No thank you."

"It's not always *The Shining*. Come on! Oh, there're two gyms if you want to work out?"

Vivian, earbuds back in, is packing up.

I shrug. My poor, unused muscles scream their heads off in protest.

"Okay. Well, take the weekend and explore. There're classes you can take, really neat history of exploration and biology of The Ice, volleyball, a basketball court. Sun'll be down soon, too, so we'll have the party for that. Ooh, and Midwinter Formal!"

"Formal . . . like a dance?"

"Did no one tell you any of this? Oh, Harper, please tell me you brought a dress?"

I wince. She stands and tosses up her hands.

"It's Antarctica!" I wail. "What are we talking about, a *dress* dress? Like prom?"

"You're a Scott; it's *his* Midwinter celebration! How do you not know this? It's a formal! Didn't you read any of the manual?"

"There was nothing about cocktail attire in there, just articles on hypothermia."

"Oh, good grief!" she sighs.

"Good night," Vivian practically shouts over her music, then waves to Charlotte, and the door closes behind her.

Charlotte smiles apologetically. "We'll work on her," she says. "She's very serious."

"I noticed."

"And a rule follower."

"Sure."

"Hey, Harp?"

"Yeah."

"Really good work this week. I don't know what I'd do without you. You are a true Scott—born to Winter Over!"

- - -

In the dining hall, I fill a glass with ice and water, which I toss all over myself in surprise when someone touches my shoulder.

"Oh God . . . sorry!" Aiden says. He starts wadding up paper napkins and pressing them all over my neck and shoulders.

"Okay," I say, taking over. "Got it, thanks."

He's laughing, but not unkindly. "I'm *really* sorry. That's not right. . . ."

"It's fine."

"You didn't come for lunch."

"Working. We forgot." I have no boobs to speak of so I very rarely bother with a bra. And now my T-shirt is wet. I toss the napkins and cross my arms over my chest. "Nice seeing you again," I say. "Have a good one!" And I run away through the obstacle course of tables.

"Hold on!" he calls. "I've got something for you!" He catches me at the door and puts a foil-wrapped package in my hands. "For later."

"Okay, thanks." I rush to the stairs to end this *Girls Gone Wild: Antarctica* episode, but he calls out once more.

"Harper Scott, you going out tonight?"

"No."

"Well, come with me now. Let me show you something!"

He pulls me by my hand into the kitchen. I shift my free arm to cover my chest. He takes me past prep tables and people cooking, and back near the freezer to a sink beneath a small window. He fills a cup at the sink.

"This is what happens to hot water in thirty-degree-below-zero air. Watch. . . ." He unlocks the window, shoves it open, and tosses the water out into the orange street-lit air.

A sparkling cloud of ice explodes from the cup. Powdery shards of frozen water float and dissipate. Aiden smiles, probably just as amazed as he was the first time he saw it happen.

"Wow," I breathe. A person cannot deny that magic. Or Aiden's sincere reverence for it.

"I'm off work," he says. "Are you?"

"Yes."

"What're you up to now?"

"Bed," I say, arms crossed, still mortified.

"No! It's not even eight-thirty. Really?"

"I'm so tired. . . ."

"Want to go to movie night? Just started."

"No thanks."

"Really?"

"Next time, for sure."

"Coffee house? No smoking, no booze."

"I don't know. . . ." Seriously, the whole front of me is soaked. Can he not tell I'm squirming? Maybe not because, to his credit, his eyes never leave my face.

"Library? It's right by the laundry and the weight room. Lots of . . . books? Or . . . oh, we could make stuff. You hungry?"

I don't think I've ever not been hungry.

I feel so bad. This poor guy—three teenagers on the entire continent, and he's the only one not currently sulking in his room or humiliated by accidental participation in a wet T-shirt contest. "Honestly, I really will be more fun soon. I'm just still sleepy. Not caught up."

"Ohhh," he says. "Right. California?"

"San Francisco." Dad is forever quoting Sartre, this French playwright who was always clarifying that he was, in fact, not French; he was *Parisian. We are not Californians,* Dad says. *We are San Franciscans.* Makes it sound like we're monks, but I know what he means.

"San Francisco! I've been there, on holiday. Lovely. Want to go take a walk? Outside?"

"Outside in the dark? Where it is so painfully cold, as you have just demonstrated, water instantly freezes?"

"It's beautiful out! There's a moon, not a single cloud, and no telling how many nights like this we'll have before the sun's gone. We're here! Let's *be* here! Where's your friend?"

"Who?"

"Vivian. I saw her this morning. What's she like?"

"Um. Not sure."

I make my way back through the dining room, and he follows.

"Harper!"

"Yes."

"You've left my night open, so I'm making alternate plans. There's a radio in your room?"

Is there? "I don't know."

"Look in the drawers and such. I've heard people leave things behind to lighten their loads. Turn it on in half an hour. Station 104.5."

"I will," I say from the stairwell. "I promise."

"Good night!" he calls. Relentlessly cheerful.

I take a hot shower and wash my hair, ten full minutes until I think of the Adélies and turn it off, guilty. No one else is anywhere around the bathrooms or in the hall. They're all at the bars, I guess. Silence. It is beautiful.

In my room I put on my flannel pajamas, comb my wet hair, and lie down. Out the window, McMurdo's lights make the sky hard to see. I get up and pull open the desk drawers, careful to ignore the letter.

Aiden was right. A small radio is in a bottom drawer, along

with three strings of Christmas twinkle lights all connected, not even tangled. There are some stray tacks in the walls.

I plug the radio in and tune it to 104.5 and Kurt Cobain is singing *Heart-Shaped Box*. I climb all over both beds and the chair to string the twinkle lights along the perimeter of the narrow room, where the walls meet the ceiling. I plug in the lights, turn off the desk lamp—heaven. Just enough to take away the shadows and warm the blue-gray color, still dark enough to sleep. I unwrap the foil package.

Cinnamon roll.

I put the radio on the chair beside my pillow, crawl back into the millions-of-kittens bed, and pull the blankets to my chin.

"Well, good evening, McMurdo. Aiden Irish Spring Magically Delicious Kelly with you on a beautiful Friday night on The Ice. (Okay. Mystery solved. Not Scottish.) *Here to remind you that climbing Observation Hill while drunk is not only illegal, but also stupid. So let's not have any repeat performances like those of last week involving two people whose names I won't mention, but they rhyme with Dave Connor and Jack Dolan. You two nearly got all our Ob Hill night-hike privileges revoked, which would have really pissed me off, as I'm trying to convince a certain lady to embark on said journey before winter's here for real. So don't screw it up for the rest of us.* (How is he so familiar with people already?) *All right. That's business done. Now to some music for your moonlit Friday night. This one's for the aforementioned lady. Welcome to McMurdo; welcome all of us fingys to The Ice; welcome to the*

rest of our lives. *It will never be the same, now we're here. And to the lady: I'm especially glad you're here."*

A song begins.

"Some Flogging Molly for you. This is a ballad called 'Drunken Lullabies.'"

It is not a ballad. It's a hard, fast Irish rock song.

There were no emails waiting for me when I wrote Mom and Dad tonight. Nothing from Kate or Luke. Or Owen. No one.

I'm okay. It's okay.

I fall asleep beneath the twinkle lights, radio on.

- - -

Might as well follow the sun.

"Let's go," I tell Aiden the next morning over the silver bins of toast and blueberries. He's back in the galley kitchen, whisking eggs to scramble.

"Where?"

"The mountain," I say.

"It's a hill."

"Yes. Let's go."

"You found a radio."

"Maybe."

"I'm . . . Can you wait a couple of hours till I'm on break?"

I look around. Hardly anyone in the dining hall. "Okay. Meet me at nine. Sharp. I'm ready."

"Nine o'clock, yes. Okay. At the desk."

"Yes." I drink a glass of iced tea, fill a bowl with oatmeal, and sit alone to eat. I don't read. I don't listen to music. I just eat. By myself. It's something I'm not used to doing, and I think it's a good skill to learn.

"Screw it," Aiden says, striding toward me, pulling off his apron. "Everyone's hungover. No one's coming to breakfast. Let's go."

Awesome.

He runs to his room for his cold-weather gear while I zip my own parka and wrestle into the mittens. Ben is at the desk, leaning on his elbows.

"Going somewhere?" He yawns.

"Observation Hill."

"Not alone, you're not."

"No, I'll be with her," Aiden calls as he rushes toward us, pulling on his own huge parka.

Ben rolls his eyes. "You've got to get supervisor permission. Kids."

"Yep," Aiden says, and produces two legal-length printed documents, both signed in pen. "Found Charlotte in the lab; she's cool with it," he tells me. Sure enough, he's got her signature there on my permission slip. I didn't even know there was such a thing. I really should read the employee manual.

Ben stamps and shoves both papers in a file.

"Ready?" Aiden smiles. He pushes the door and holds it open, and a blast of cloudy light and that freezing wind hit me directly in my forehead. But I've taken a few preemptive Advil. So the cold can screw off.

"Okay?" Aiden asks over the wind.

"Yes." At the fire station we collect our radios and tell them where we're going, and we're off.

I follow Aiden's footsteps on a path of muddy tire tracks, past black and red flags, through the buildings of McMurdo, and finally beyond, to the base of Observation Hill.

"At the summit we'll be at seven hundred fifty elevation."

"Okay."

"We're at seventy-nine now."

"Oh."

"Just might give some people a headache, I mean." Perfect. Piggyback headaches are the best. We start the gradual ascent. "Do you do a lot of hiking in San Francisco?"

I'm already huffing a little just keeping up with him. "No," I breathe. "Not really."

The Advil I took is no match for this wind. He can tell.

"Did you know the Vikings' image of hell wasn't fire at all? It was ice. Hel with one *L*."

I stand and breathe the pure, sharp air.

"Hey," I pant, "haven't you only been here, like, a week longer than me?"

"About that."

"How do you know so much?"

"I've been trying to get here for a really long while. Been reading up. Winter Over blogs. Books. Like that."

Standing still makes breathing easier, but invites the cold so quickly. The Vikings were onto something.

"I'll tell you a secret," he says. "Hiking? It's just *walking*."

And so we walk. Up the hill. There's no actual climbing beyond the elevation. It's just a trail; it switchbacks and rises pretty quickly, and I keep my head down, one foot in front of the other, for nearly half an hour, so that I do not see where we're going until we're there.

And then we are.

The wind whips cold and McMurdo lies below the mountain, a Lego town with Matchbox vehicles. But beyond the station . . . if I had breath left, it would be taken away.

The Ross Sea, cobalt blue today and choppy, the sweeping curves of ice and snow, a dome of endless white-blue sky. Skuas, penguin egg–stealing brown birds, float on the current of the icy air over the water. All the world is white and blue and gray, still, so strange and resplendent that I'm getting the Adélie feeling once more, the ache of overwhelming beauty I've only ever felt while standing backstage in the dark, watching my little kids, watching Kate, myself ready in the wings—until, at last, the music starts. Gradually, quietly swelling and then the cue, the one note signaling movement, into the light, *now, go, turn . . .*

"You're not a scientist."

A statement, not a question, loud over the wind. "No."

"But you're a Scott."

"Yes."

"You here for school?"

I shake my head.

"Didn't think so."

"You're astronomy," I say.

"The winter skies here are supposed to be insane," he says. "But I wanted to come even before I cared about that. I think most people have lives that keep them, more or less . . . anchored. And some others don't. But the world's spinning, and anchorless people tend to fall to the bottom . . . here."

"You have no *anchor*? What are you, a world-weary sea captain? You're seventeen! What about your family? School?"

"Life's too big to stay in one place forever. After university, I can see being here every winter, spending the rest of the year seeing the world. I mean, the *whole planet*. All of it."

Charlotte's voice is in my head. *Peter Pan living for himself with no responsibilities.*

"Come see this!" Aiden says. He is up on the highest ledge, rocks and sand in the snow, standing beside a tall wooden cross.

Mom's got a framed photo of this cross on her bedroom wall; it is featured in the final chapter of every book ever written about Scott. It is the nine-foot-tall memorial the search party erected when they found him frozen with his last three men. It is engraved, I know, with their names, and with the last words of Lord Alfred Tennyson's "Ulysses": TO STRIVE, TO SEEK, TO FIND, AND NOT TO YIELD.

Aut moriere percipietis conantur.

Months after Scott and his three remaining men succumbed to The Ice, the expedition crew who found the frozen bodies could tell, based on the positions the men were lying in, that Scott had been the last to die. The search crew built a cairn of snow over the tent, made a cross of rough wood to place on its top, and let the Ross ice shelf be their grave.

After a century of storms and snow on the ever-moving shelf, the bodies now lie beneath maybe seventy-five feet of ice, thirty miles from where they died. It is thought that in two hundred years, Scott and his men will reach the Ross Sea and float away, suspended in an iceberg.

I think of their dark, sleeping forms, maybe holding each other for warmth. Or comfort. Perfectly preserved in clear, aqua-blue-and-white ice, forever floating in the freezing blue-black sea.

"Aiden," I say into the icy wind. "Do you want to go to the pole?"

"Absolutely. The minute I'm legal next year, I'm coming back to be there the second the sun's up."

My heart sinks. *Next year.* "Okay," I say. "But what if you wanted to go *this* year?"

He turns to me. His face hidden in a balaclava, all I see are his green eyes. "I'm sure you've got a sight more sway than most. *Scott*. You keep your head down, put in your hours, be helpful every moment someone needs you. Charlotte can help, and I'll talk to my guy. Let the sun rise, and you'll see."

With my mittened hand, I trace the names of the men, of my ancestor still suspended in ice, somewhere beneath the years of snow, of shifting white and water, waiting to drift forever alone in the endless ocean.

"I *need* to get there."

"Then you will."

It is nearly impossible not to believe him.

I breathe in the sea, the birds and the sky and the ice and snow, and exhale.

- 6 -

San Francisco

"ANGELS, I NEED YOU ALL TO PEE RIGHT NOW. I DON'T CARE if you don't have to. Think about nice, cascading waterfalls, and let's go!" I gather my angels before anyone puts on tights. Opening night, my Saturday kindies are performing, and I'm more nervous for them than for myself.

"Harper?" Willa says. "Do I have to go? Because I went before we left."

"Yes," I call over the din of preshow backstage chatter and music. "Everyone pees!"

I get all eight kids rotated through three stalls in record time.

"Okay, we've all peed, right? Everyone?"

"Yes!" they screech.

We wash our hands, laugh at the crazy Dyson hand dryers, and hustle back to the dressing room. Simone strolls into the chaos as I'm tugging tights over the first set of dimpled knees, and she kneels on the floor to help.

"Are we ready?" she asks the angels, who nod shyly. I don't blame them. Simone is scary/striking in a sparkly silk skirt and blouse, silver hair pulled slickly up in a perpetual ballet bun. "They've used the restroom first, correct?"

I nod, struggle with a snug waistband on one angel and hitch up sagging ankles on another. Years of this and still she checks up on me—did we use the restroom first? What the hell! She's dealing with a professional kid wrangler here.

"Harper." Willa is at my ear, tights on, tutu fluffed, halo on, white feathers in her bun.

"Yes, babe?" I whisper back.

"I have to pee." She blinks at the floor, hands tucked behind her wings.

I sit back on my heels. "Willa, are you freaking *kidding* me?"

"Sorry."

Simone shoots me a sidelong *look*.

"We just got back from the bathroom; she's nervous!"

I grab her hand, heave the heavy dressing room door open, and nearly clock Kate, hurrying back in. Brow furrowed.

"You okay?"

"My dad never picked up his tickets. Not coming."

"Oh, Kat. Maybe he's just running late?"

She shakes her head and shrugs. Smiles brightly. "Good news. Didn't want to see him anyway." She looks down at Willa. "Potty?"

Willa nods.

"Kate—"

"It's all right," she says. "I don't care. See you in a minute. . . . Go. Hurry."

The whole bathroom routine, part two, with my heart clenched tight for Kate—I hate her stupid dad. I rush Willa through the Dyson, and we're back in two minutes.

"Okay, ladies," I tell the angels. "I've got to get myself ready." I run to my bag and pull out the giant comforter Mom lends me for shows. Coloring books, crayons, paper dolls. I spread the blanket in a corner and corral the angels onto it. "No one moves off this spot until I come get you, right?"

Finally, at forever last, the music starts. They pipe it to speakers mounted over the makeup mirrors, and we all shut up. Kate squeezes both my hands, which are freezing, my fingertips blue. Kate rubs them vigorously, kisses my knuckles, dashes back to the mirror to put some last-second glitter in her hair, straightens her tiara. I make sure my eyelashes aren't going anywhere and line my angels up once more—they open the second act. I lead Willa, who in turn leads the wobbly-whispery line snaking around the dark backstage, maneuvering around props and stage crew, and I put my finger to my lips. They all nod. Fluff their feathers. I send them out and hold my breath. They blink in the lights. Turn to me in the wings.

"Plié," I whisper. "Arms up, second and straight and point..."

They wake up. They dance. Oh, they remember! All of it! My face hurts; I'm counting silently through the smile that's nearly breaking my face. They are *so good*; my chest aches, they're trying so hard, and in what feels like ten seconds, they bow. It is over. They run quietly to me, and I hug them all, each one, and send them off with the stage manager because *snow—it is time for snow.* . . . Oh God, I am terrified.

- - -

We wait in shafts of light in the wings, holding sweaty hands before our entrance, watching Kate soar and turn and be beautiful in her spotlight. Ballet is a petri dish crammed full of the jealousy-inducing bacteria of physical appearance requirements with incredibly narrow parameters, and competition for very, very few employment opportunities. But even the most jealous heart could not deny the truth executing a perfect triple piqué turn into a beautiful tour jeté right in front of us. Kate is what we aspire to. She is perfection.

A hand rests on my shoulder, which scares the crap out of me. Lindsay.

"Harp," she whispers, "two piqués and a sauté or three and two?"

"Two and a fouette," I whisper back.

"Oh God..."

"Don't think," I insist. "Just dance. No hesitating. Right?" She nods but looks ill.

The music floats and swells, our cue. We run lightly to our places.

Lindsay catches my eye. I cross mine at her. She is pale. But she smiles.

We dance.

The stage crew is really going for it. The blizzard falls, sheets of white, and though we're sweating in the boiling lights, this snow is magical. An icy chill sweeps my bare shoulders. Simone's choreography is a well-matched union of the traditional Balanchine and her own; it uses the entire stage and does not let up. We turn and leap and balance all our weight on the strength of our feet, our toes, every muscle in our legs. Our backs and cores are lifted, engaged, and the audience is silent as years—thousands of hours—of training for these eight minutes and forty seconds go by. The music is urgent; it fills my head and heart, and I turn out from my hips, the snow falls, and The Plan, school, any worry or thought of anything in the world—*everything* else—disappear.

- - -

Kate and I change backstage, grab Willa, and meet everyone at the Beach Chalet. Kate hands the cabdriver a wad of bills, and the three of us climb out beside Ocean Beach, sea spray salty on our lips, and the wind whips Willa's hair around her face.

Kate's and my rhinestone-studded performance buns are still intact, and she is ethereal in a filmy silver slip dress and fishnet stockings. Even Willa's got a dress on, one of mine from the childhood stash. "I can't believe you're in *jeans*," Willa says. "This is a fancy night!"

"I've got my fancy silky!" I shout into the wind, turning to model the pale blue satin blouse I found brand-new at Goodwill. "And I'm bejeweled!" Faux emerald-cut aquamarines shine at my throat. Willa shakes her head.

"Hold hands!" Kate laughs and pulls us across Great Highway through a break in the steady stream of Friday night traffic. We run from the sandy sidewalk beside the ocean to the edge of Golden Gate Park, and finally up the steps of what was once the Sutro Baths but is now the Beach Chalet.

From the cold mist into the warmth of the lobby, I stop and pull Willa near me to stand and marvel. In 1925 this was where Ocean Beach swimmers changed into and out of bathing suits. Willa fogs up the glass case that houses a miniature replica of Golden Gate Park. Tall windows face the sea, and the walls are alive with bright murals of San Francisco.

"Harp," Willa whispers. "Can we go?"

"She's doing her thing, babe." Kate smiles. "Harp, if you love San Francisco so much, why don't you marry it?"

"Maybe I will."

"Fantastic. We're starving. See you up there," she says, scooting Willa up the steps two at a time.

The stair rails are sea creatures carved from magnolia wood and worn smooth beneath thousands of visitors' hands. Arched doorways open to Golden Gate Park and to the mosaic-tiled stairway leading to the dining room.

But my very favorite part of this room are the words painted carefully in lovely script, looping around images of seagulls in flight curving above one archway, *Fair City of my love and my desire*. A love poem to San Francisco.

"What are we looking at?" a voice beside me asks.

"The words, it's poems . . ."

Owen.

Owen?

"What are you—are you eating here?" I stammer.

"Yes!"

"Oh, we're here, too. Luke's upstairs, and my parents—"

"Yeah," he says. "I came with."

"With who?"

He frowns. "Luke. To the show."

"What show?"

"Um. *The Nutcracker*? He asked if I wanted to, and I did. I was just parking the car."

My throat is suddenly dry. Luke pisses me off sometimes. This is a family thing—what the hell!

"I have to tell you. I've never been to a ballet before, ever, and—"

"It's just a school show. A recital."

"Oh. Well, I was all set to be bored. No offense."

"Sure."

"But then you're there dancing and—it wasn't . . . *pretty?* Not the way I thought it would be."

"Okay . . . thanks?"

"I just mean . . . *ballet.* Tutus and tiaras and all that, but we were sitting so close, two rows back, and all of you were . . . *sweating.* I could hear you breathing, and your *legs* . . ." He drifts off, looks at the floor.

But I like this. What he's saying. What I think he's getting at. "Our legs what?"

He shakes his head. "Muscles."

"We're not supposed to be breathing that loud."

"No, it wasn't like panting, just—you were *working.* I'm so glad I got to see it."

"Well, that's . . . I'm glad you liked it."

What is happening? He saw the show and he's wearing a jacket? A jacket! A nice tweed jacket and jeans! Not in a hipster way—in a really good way! And his hair is out of his eyes again. . . . Oh God . . .

"It was really beautiful," he says. "You were amazing."

I nod. "I know. We all watch her, even when we're onstage together. She's our guru."

He frowns. "Sorry—who is?"

"Kate."

"No, you—I said *you.* *You* were. So good."

My hands are sweaty. "You didn't see me."

"I didn't?"

"I'm in the chorus."

"Yeah."

"We're all wearing the same costume. You can't see anyone *but* Kate. It's okay. That's how it's supposed to be."

He looks up again at the words on the wall. "I've been here so many times, and I've never read any of these. Poems, really?"

"Parts of them. This 'Fair City' one is Ina Coolbrith. She was California's first poet laureate. People say she had a torrid affair with Mark Twain." The second the words are out of my mouth, my face burns pink. *Torrid affair?* I'm the worst!

But Owen nods. "Hot," he says. "Poet sex hijinks."

I smile against the back of my hand—*I think I might pass out; seriously what is going on?*—and he walks across the tile floor and stands at the archway to the park, beneath my favorite words of all. George Sterling's:

> At the end of our streets is sunrise;
> At the end of our streets are spars;
> At the end of our streets is sunset;
> At the end of our streets the stars.

Only the last two lines are painted here, and if I were to ever get a tattoo (ballet sacrilege!), it would be those words.

At the end of our streets the stars.

I love this poem. I love this beautiful city on its hill surrounded by the sea. Our streets do end in the ocean, in stars.

We stand together, reading.

And then Owen says, "You entered from the right. Your right, audience left. You stayed mostly on that side, but then after the circle thing, you were down toward the audience on the left corner, and then you were stuck in the back for some of the jumpy part, then to the right for all the toe stuff. And those turns—you're kind of amazing at turns."

Luke is forgiven.

- - -

Candle and lamp light warm the dining room, and Dad waves us—me walking slightly behind Owen so we're not coming in *together*—to a table beside the wall of windows, which, in the daylight, would afford an amazing view of the ocean. Tonight, the bamboo shades are drawn so it's cozy, nice just knowing the ocean is there, close enough to hear the waves crash.

"Oh my God!" Kate pulls me near to whisper so loud I'm sure the people in the kitchen and all the drunkies at the bar hear her. "*Owen!* Did you know he was coming? Why didn't you tell me?"

I shrug. "Talk to Luke; they're joined at the hip apparently." I work my best feigned annoyance.

I sit beside Willa, across from Luke and Kate and Owen.

Okay. He looks like a young Bruce Lee. Jet Li? His arms are all lean and cut—holy crap, that sounds super racist.

I'm not saying he's a martial arts guy; those are just the first famous Chinese actors coming to mind when I imagine being pressed to describe him to someone in a way they might know who I was talking about, to paint the most accurate picture of his really black hair and those eyes and how long is my inner monologue about this dude going to go on and have I said any of this out loud?

I take a long swig of water. Kate is smiling, leaning into a conversation with Owen, and Mom and Dad and Hannah raise their glasses to Kate's and my last *Nutcracker* with Simone and to the start of Willa's years of being angels and mice and soldiers and, maybe one day, Snow.

Willa reaches up to my shoulder and tucks my black bra strap back under my blouse.

I kiss the hair-spray-sticky top of her head.

Across the table, Owen smiles. At me.

My water is empty, and so I swallow Willa's entire glass, take her hand, and push back my chair.

"Let's go potty, babe."

"I don't need to."

"Really? You sure?"

She nods and dips a hunk of bread into a puddle of olive oil.

"Well. Okay. Be right back."

"I'll go with you!" Kate jumps up and steers me by my elbow through the crowded dining room, down the stairs, and into the ladies' room.

"I'm having a stroke," she says. "We've been talking non-stop. Did you *see*?"

"I'm on it." I smile weakly. "Bridal shower's being planned as we speak." I lock myself in a stall.

"He watched the show! He came and sat through an entire ballet recital, and he *liked* it—or at least says he did. He is a stunning specimen of manhood. I could *die*."

I step out and join her at the sink, my stomach burning. Boys falling all over Kate is nothing new, but she's never been so giddy in return. She leans close to the mirror to rub gloss on her lips. "Do you think Luke will actually go through with moving out?"

"I'll believe it when I see it."

"He better," she sighs dreamily. "Because then we can go over to say hey to him, and oh gosh, look who just happens to be home, too. . . ."

I'm grateful she's thinking about something besides her dumb dad. But this may be even worse. "Hey," I say. "Addendum thirteen."

She hugs me hard and brushes some glitter from my forehead.

Back at the table, the food has come. "Harp," Willa whispers, "what is this?" She's got scallops on her plate, skewered on what look like lavender stalks in bloom. I hold one to my face and inhale. Yep.

"It's just a flower," I say. "It's a thing now. People make

lavender ice cream, lavender honey. I don't think you'll taste it; it's just for the smell. And to be pretty."

She frowns. "It's like perfume soap. Fish and perfume aren't delicious." I laugh, wrap my arms around her, and squeeze her tight.

"I got the scallops, too," Owen tells Willa. He holds his lavender up and slides the scallops off, cuts the flower stems short with his knife, and hands the bouquet across the table to her. "You were a really beautiful angel."

She smiles shyly at him and puts the flowers in her water glass, punch-drunk. "Thank you," she demurs.

Oh, Willa—not you, too.

Kate starts back up with Owen, flirting hard like she's out to save her own life. She is stunning in that dress, and Willa and I watch the show until—"Here we are!" A line of servers swoop in to whisk away our empty dinner plates and put delicate chocolate sand castle cakes before each of us, even Luke—because they are flourless chocolate, dusted with crushed almond "sand."

"Ohhhh . . . ," Willa breathes, the disappointment of the fancy scallops forgotten with the first bite of dense, heavy cake.

"I will go to my grave trying to replicate this," Dad murmurs, eyes closed.

"Harp," Mom says, leaning forward around Hannah and Willa. "Just try it. It won't kill you. Seriously, this is the best thing in the world."

Smells so good. But I can't screw it up this close to the end—no, the *beginning*—the start of our lives, the entire point of our existence so carefully crafted every day of every year for so long.

It is nearly here.

I see Owen watch this exchange with interest.

"I'll have it later," I tell her. "I'll take it home, I swear."

And I do. In the kitchen that night, I wrap it in foil with a note reading, *HARPER'S! DO NOT EAT!*

Tonight's snow is the best I've ever danced. I felt it. Fourteen years and I'm ready. *We're* ready. *No thinking about Owen or Owen with Kate or Owen at all* until the safety of January, when, SF Ballet contract in hand, I'm going to eat this entire sand castle of chocolate, all of it, because it will be my reward.

"See you after auditions, little chocolate minx!" I whisper.

- 7 -

Antarctica

THE SUN IS GOING DOWN THIS AFTERNOON, APRIL 25. IT WILL stay dark until late August, and tonight there is a party. A dance to celebrate or say farewell to the sun or something. This is not the Midwinter Formal, but Charlotte says it is nuts and mostly everyone drinks themselves into oblivion. The condom bowls are being refilled daily.

"Be there for sunset. It's gone at one-forty-three; do *not* be late. Both of you. Promise?"

It's only ten in the morning, but we're taking the rest of the day off. Charlotte's pinning her curls up off her face and pulling her shoes back on. "Stupid feet keep swelling," she says. "The heaters are on too high. Sunset! I'll see you out on The Ice, right? Viv?"

Vivian shrugs but nods as she lugs a box of beakers to a cabinet.

"Harper? Sunset?"

"Yes," I say, "of course." I smile in the half daze I've been in the last few weeks. I think the heaters *are* on too high. "Charlotte."

"Mm-hmm?"

"When do planes start going to the pole? Can they go before Winter Over is . . . over?" I laugh quietly to myself. Vivian sighs.

Charlotte strides to me, holds my face in her hands, and looks into my eyes. "You're eating, yes?"

I nod.

"Staying warm? Taking vitamin D?"

"Yep." She studies me.

"I don't know." She frowns. "If you're not more with it on Monday, I'm sending you to the infirmary."

"What?" I whine. "Why?"

She shakes her head. "I promised your mom. You've got to be careful. *Never look a Winter Overer in the eye*—you know why people say that?"

I shrug.

"She's got it," Vivian pipes up from across the lab.

"Not necessarily," Charlotte says.

"Oh my God, what? I've *got* something?"

"T3," Vivian says flatly.

"What the hell is *that?*"

"You don't want to know," Charlotte says. "Just stay hydrated. Get some exercise . . . and you've got to socialize. I'm not kidding. You *have* to."

"I *am*!" I wail. "I go outside all the time with Aiden. What is T3?"

It is true; I walk outside with him in the afternoon. Sometimes.

"Take a class, get in the Ping-Pong tournament—there are a million ways to have fun here." She turns to Vivian. "I know it's hard when everyone's drunk and stoned all the time, but the three of you—Vivian, have you even met Aiden? Why aren't you all hanging out together?"

"I'm fine, thanks," Vivian says.

Charlotte is not convinced. "I'll see you both on The Ice, and then we'll eat a few gallons of chocolate, okay?" She hugs the top of my head with her hand. "Okay?"

I smile up at her. "Yes."

"Good! Viv, you're done. Stop working, please . . . and make sure the lights are out, will you? I'm going to shower and change into clothes that make me look female. I'm sick of walking around here looking like an Antarctica five."

"Antarctica five?"

"An Antarctica ten is a Mainland five. Men are pigs. See you at sunset. Do not be late. Do. Not." And she's out the door.

Vivian sits on her lab stool for a moment, her hand absently on a microscope.

"Hey, Vivian."

She looks up.

"What's T3?"

Vivian shakes her head, puts her earbuds back in, locks the microscope away, and hefts her backpack onto her shoulder.

"What are you listening to?"

She pushes the door open. "Lock up, will you?"

"Hey!" I call. "Are you going? The sunset?"

But she's gone.

I would never have gone to the rookery if I'd known it was going to cause this ridiculous Sharks and Jets rumble—no, not a rumble; it's just cold indifference. I wish Charlotte would tell her to knock it off.

I wish I still had Kate.

I turn out the lights and run to a take a shower, pull on my warmest layers, and lie down on top of the blankets to take a mini power nap before the sun does its thing. I'm drifting in the kitten bed . . . until a knock wakes me.

"Hellew . . . ," the Irish cadence sings. "Harper Scott?"

I heave myself up. "It's open!"

His smile peers around the door. "Perfect! You're dressed. Let's go!"

"It's not for hours. I'm sleeping!"

"Oh, but the show beforehand is *not* to be missed. Come along." Aiden sits on my chair and waits while I pull my socks and boots over my shower-warm feet. He looks around my empty room.

"Nice holiday lights."

"Thanks. Someone left them."

"Radio working well?"

"I'm your biggest fan."

He picks up the books on my desk. "Using the library? Good!"

I nod. The library *is* awesome. Worn-out ski-lodge carpeting, shabby sofa. Lots of coffee table books about the explorers and, of course, a million science texts. Dog-eared fiction paperbacks people bring from the mainland and leave behind.

"Kübler-Ross. *Tao Te Ching.* Light reading for the darkest, coldest, most isolated place on the planet."

I shrug.

"Don't you like lady books? I always see they've got plenty of those."

"Lady books?"

"The ones about ladies going shopping and eating sweets when their fella drops them."

"Uh . . . am I the first female human you've met? Where are you getting your lady info?"

"Hey, nothing wrong with lady books! They're better than the . . . What is this?" He picks up the top of the stack. *"On Grief and Grieving."* What in the world are you grieving?"

"Let's go."

"You've got everything on? It's nearly twenty below."

"Got it."

He sits and looks me over. "How're you feeling?"

"You know what? I'm feeling T-three-licious. Let's *go*!"

At the door, he hesitates. Looks real cagey. "If I show you something, will you not say anything to anyone about it?"

"Not if you're committing a felony."

He opens his red parka, not an easy feat once it's on and zipped.

"Ohhh!" I squeal.

"Shhhh! See, that's what I'm talking about! Shut up or I'll get in trouble!"

"Whose is it?"

"My guy," he whispers. "The 'supervisor' who doesn't even know my name. I'll put it right back, but today's supposed to be perfect. We're not missing this chance. This is the smallest telescope with any power I could fit under here. Let's go."

At the stairs, I stop us once more. "Hey," I say. "Come with me." We troop up to the third floor, and I knock on a door I'm pretty sure is the correct one.

"Vivian," I call.

"Do we have to?" Aiden whispers.

"She would love this," I hiss back. "She's still so mad for the Great Penguin Betrayal, I need to make her not hate me!" I knock again. "Vivian!"

Maybe this is the wrong room. I press my ear to the door. A man's deep voice is speaking. Modulated, conversational. Maybe she's got a TV in there. "Vivian?"

The voice stops. "What?"

"It's Harper. And Aiden!"

Pause.

"What do you want?"

"Well," I call, "we're going to watch the sunset. Come with us?"

"It's not for another two hours."

"Yeah," I say, hopeful. "But Aiden's got"—he nudges me hard with his shoulder—"a thing for later, a surprise that's going to be amazing. Please?"

The man's voice starts back up.

"All righty!" Aiden chirps. "We're off, then!" And he's halfway down the hall.

I knock once more. "Vivian?"

Nothing.

Aiden stands at the stairs. "Scott," he calls. "She's fine."

Why is this making me so sad? I give up and join Aiden in the stairwell.

"Are we going to get arrested for this?"

"Probably," he says brightly.

At the main door Ben's rearing to go with preloaded snark. "Little early, aren't we, children?"

"Have a good one!" Aiden smiles and holds the door wide for me. "Kill him with kindness," he murmurs as we step out into the icy wind. "Or just kill him, eventually. I hate that guy."

Even through the now familiar cold-induced head pain, I laugh. It's so nice to hear my inner thoughts spoken out loud—and with an Irish accent. "I kind of hate him, too," I admit. "But I feel bad for him."

"What for?"

"He wants to go to the pole. Charlotte says he never will."

Aiden sends his green eyes skyward. "If he truly wanted it, he'd have gone by now. I hate people wailing and lolling about, 'I can't do this, that's too hard.' My gran always says, 'Just shut your yap and do it, for God's sake!' Get a better attitude, make some friends, and get on a damn helicopter. He got himself *here,* didn't he? That's the hardest part, and the rest, pardon my saying so, is not too effing tough. This way."

He takes my mittened hand and pulls me toward the fire station.

"Where to?"

"Trust me?"

I let my hand stay in his. But not without thinking of Owen.

"Yes," I say. "So far."

We sign out, pick up radios, and follow the flags along the familiar path to the Ob Hill hike, past everyone else gathering on the flat expanse of ice near the main buildings, the sun very nearly set.

"Should we be doing this?"

"Trust me." He smiles inside his hood.

At the start of the trail, he moves in front of me. We stay

on the flat road, and now I know where we're going. Charlotte is right. The early-evening sky couldn't be more perfect, just about twenty below zero, only a few pale clouds around the lowering sun. It will be beautiful. I've not been out in such dark yet—too cold—but I understand this is special. And the hike—uphill walking—keeps us warm.

Happily, I see that other people are also heading up the hill, red parkas dotting the path to the top, but we take a detour, back to the base of the mountain, where there's only snow, and quiet, and us.

A ten-minute walk, and we're standing in Scott's Hut, shelter for his first trip here, sailing his ship, *Discovery*—not to get to the pole, but to explore The Ice. This was the trip Shackleton was on and got scurvy, and all the dogs died—but Scott gathered a ton of information about the penguins and seals and the ice. They stayed in this hut for a while, before losing *Discovery* to the crushing ice, and they all had to be rescued.

Not unlike Shackleton's Hut at the rookery, it is made of wood and perfectly preserved, though not so full of personal objects. There are tables, mostly, and crates and boxes labeled DISCOVERY EXPEDITION. Hundred-year-old dog biscuits.

"You're a *Scott*," Aiden says in the quiet of the hut. "That is so amazing."

"Yeah," I sigh. "We'll see."

I close my eyes and breathe, try to feel my lineage, feel

Scott's courage, his refusal to give in, moving through my veins.

Rose-colored beams of the sun's sinking rays come straight through the windows and spill in rows on the wood floors.

"What is it you're grieving?" he asks again.

I touch the thick glass window with my mitten. Outside, the reflected light off the snow is blinding even in these very last moments.

What the hell.

"You know what?" I admit. "I am mourning the loss of the love of my life."

"You're *seventeen*! That is insane."

"It's true."

"That's why you're here?"

I shrug.

"Scott. Honestly."

"I am completely lost."

He shakes his head.

In the last sunlight, we climb Observation Hill once more, with about fifty other McMurdo people. Citizens of The Ice. Our red parkas are moving dots winding around the face of the mountain until we stand together at the windy summit, near the cross for Scott and his crew.

To strive, to seek, to find, and not to yield.

Everyone stands in groups, and we face the sun. No one speaks and I understand why Aiden insisted we climb.

Our goggles briefly off, we watch the last burning sliver of light sink into the sea, and at once the sky is a million swirling waves of iridescent pink and orange, purple and blue, clouds lit from inside, glowing. My eyes sting because I'm not blinking.

"What is happening?" I whisper, reaching, without thought, to hold on to his arm. We are so tiny, even the mountain is dwarfed beneath this unreal color and light.

"Nacreous clouds," Aiden says close beside my hood. "Polar stratospheric clouds. They're so high and the air is so cold that they follow the curve of Earth. They're lit from the sun below. It's set for us but still reflecting light into the clouds."

Paint spilled into a glass bowl sky, lit from beneath.

The colors are the underside of an abalone shell, deepening, shifting above our upturned faces, not the green and blue of the aurora australis—that comes later, Charlotte says—but shimmering.

And then it is dark.

The cold is a whip-crack pain in my head.

"Can you hold out just a while longer?" he asks.

In my giant parka, I nod.

Most of the other people are gathering to hike back down the mountain, and Aiden reaches surreptitiously into his parka. The glorious clouds are moving swiftly on the ocean wind, sweeping the black sky clear, revealing . . . oh my God . . .

Stars suspended in its depth, infinite points of light—*this* is stardust. There is not a bit of sky untouched, not pricked with diamond light.

Aiden sets up the very small tripod and telescope he has borrowed without permission. "Okay," he says. "Here you are."

I pull my goggles aside once more and aim my gaze through the lens, straight into the burning light of a billion stars, so close my eyes can barely focus.

"My astronomy professor is always on about how stars are rebirth in the form of light," he says. "Molecular clouds of dust collapse—they die beneath the burden of their own gravity—and from this death, stars are born. It's how the universe began, carbon and nitrogen and oxygen—we're made of the stuff of stars."

In an instant, for the first time in months, my heart unclenches.

I wish Owen were here. I wish he could see this sky.

At the end of our streets the stars.

I will find my way beneath these stars; the stars my Scott, all the explorers, used as guides to navigate the unforgiving, endless ice and sea. The stars will steer me.

"Aiden," I whisper. "What is T3?"

I hear him smile. "It's a thyroid thing. The brain sort of . . . reassigns chemicals it normally uses for itself to your muscles."

"Because of the dark?"

"Because you're *cold*. Your brain's trying to keep your body warm and alive. Sacrificing itself for the good of warmth.

"And then what happens?"

"Uh . . . well, your brain loses some of its . . . what is the . . . cognitive sharpness? You're dull. Forgetful. You'll have the *Antarctic stare*."

"How do you know all this?" My voice feels too loud for the perfect frozen stillness.

"Because," he says, "I read the manual."

I cannot afford to exist in a fugue state. I've only got a few months to unravel the ruins of my life.

- - -

The party is raging. Charlotte was right—is right. Aiden and I get separated in the crowd hurrying back from the ice and snow to the warmth of Building 155, and she pulls me into a tight parka-full embrace. "Harp, I looked everywhere for you! Did you see it? Wasn't it the most unbearably beautiful sky you've ever stood under?" She holds on to my elbow, and we practically fall into the entry hall. The wind is whipping up icy bits of snow, and the darkness is nearly black. But inside the lights are blazing, music is blasting from speakers in the rafters, and everyone is apparently totally hammered already. Except Charlotte, who doesn't drink, and Aiden, who claims Irish babies drink whiskey from sippy cups, but he hasn't had the opportunity yet to sneak any tonight.

"Charlotte," Aiden calls above the music, moving through the crowd, clutching cups above his head. "Are you *drunk*?"

"Oh my God, *no*," she says. "I love sundown. I'm under the spell of winter! Have you seen Vivian?"

We shake our heads.

"She made it to sunset, but I haven't seen her since. Keep a lookout, okay?" She turns to Aiden. "Does your supervisor know where you are?"

Aiden nods.

"Okay. Walk Harp to her room, will you? And, I'm not kidding, look for Vivian. Buddy system. Especially on party nights. Got it?" And she is gone, into the darkened dining hall, where a spinning disco ball has been installed in the ceiling. There's a long table with a ton of food, hors d'oeuvres, and yes, a chocolate fountain.

"Hungry?" he asks.

I nod.

"Okay. Here's what I think: I'll stash the scope, we get out of our gear, grab as much food as we can carry, and let's have a picnic!"

"Where?"

"We'll figure it out. Okay if I don't buddy-system you to your room?"

"I'll live."

"Excellent! Meet back here in ten!"

The music is incredibly loud and sounds as if we're at a rave.

In my room, I yank my cold gear off, hang it to dry, and pull on my warmest yoga pants, T-shirt, and hoodie, and I meet Aiden in party central, where we pile all the food two trays will hold.

"What do we think?" he says. "Library? Hide in the kitchen?"

Both occupied.

"Oh!" I say. "I know!" and I pull him up the dorm stairs.

"Oh, Scott, come on!" he groans as I march down the hall to knock on Vivian's door. "She's obviously not interested!"

"Vivian!" I say. "It's Harper!"

The man's deep voice again. This situation is getting creepy—is it a book on tape? What is up?

"Viv!" Aiden calls. "Come on out. Harper's not giving up. It's just the three of us here. Let's be young and crazy!"

I smile gratefully.

On the other side of the door, the man's voice is silent; the lock slides and clicks. "You two will be in so much trouble for getting drunk," Vivian says through a one-inch opening.

"Oh, lighten up!" Aiden smiles. He leans his shoulder against the door and eases it open.

"I'm sleeping!" she yelps, pushing back to no avail. It's like *Cops: Dublin*. Aiden pushes the door wide and steps into the room, and Vivian, head to toe in flannel, dives beneath her covers. Aiden switches on a small desk lamp and makes himself comfortable in a chair. "I'm calling Charlotte!" Vivian says.

"Did you watch the sunset?" Aiden asks her.

She glares.

"Look!" I smile and step inside. "We've got food!"

"I already brushed my teeth."

"So brush them again!" Aiden sighs, tossing pieces of scone down his throat.

She glares. "You *are* drunk."

I sit gingerly on the foot of her bed. "Vivian," I say. "Tell me stuff. Charlotte says you're used to the cold. Are you from Alaska?"

She frowns hard. "St. Paul."

"Oh, Minnesota!"

"St. Paul."

"Right, but that's—"

"St. Paul."

"Hey," Aiden says, stealing blanched green beans from my plate. "I think she's from St. Paul."

"Oh, wait, yes . . . I'm San Franciscan!"

Silence. This girl is a tough nut to crack.

"We saw the stars from Ob Hill. Aiden borrowed a telescope. . . ."

"Shush that," Aiden hisses. "Don't go advertising."

Vivian sits up. "Borrowed or stole?"

"My supervisor is a git," he assures her. "It's already back in his office, tucked in safe and sound."

"Astronomy?" she asks.

A volley! It's practically a real conversation.

Aiden nods. "I'm already accepted to National University of Ireland at Galway. They've got this wicked new astronomy research center. God, I can't wait! So if this guy's going to be a dick about it, I'm on my own. Beg, borrow, or steal."

Vivian narrows her eyes at him.

"I said borrow! And bonus, I get to learn to cook and be a radio star."

"Hold up," I say. "You're *learning* to cook—currently? We're eating that stuff!"

"Under direct supervision. This is Antarctica; it's the wild frontier!"

"Oh my God," Vivian sighs. "If you two are finished eating on my bedspread and staring at me, I would love for you to leave now."

"Well, thanks for hosting." Aiden smiles, gathering paper napkins and both trays. "This was fun—we're the Three Musketeers!"

"See you Monday?" I try cheerfully.

She levels a withering glare as we back out the door, and we hear the chain lock slide into place.

Aiden carries the trays and walks me to my door.

"So," he says. "That went as well as could be expected."

"I think she liked it. I think she's warming up to me!"

He smiles. "You're quite the optimist, aren't you?"

If he only knew.

He walks the hall backward, waving.

"Aiden!" I whisper-shout.

"Yes."

"Thank you!"

Not even six o'clock, but I'm so tired I brush my teeth and fall into bed, dreaming hard, all night through, that I am swimming in color, in ice-cold nacreous clouds.

- 8 -

San Francisco

TUESDAY IS VETERANS DAY, NO SCHOOL AND NO TEACHING, JUST pointe class in the afternoon, so I sleep in, wake up lazily well past eight, and stretch, still glowing from Sunday night's final, sold-out *Nutcracker*.

House to myself, Mom at her office, prepping lectures; Dad and Luke at the bakery; Kate at home, hopefully still sleeping. Her Sunday Snow Queen was especially breathtaking, her extension and jump height into the stratosphere, and her mom came and loved it—but she brought her stupid boyfriend along, which kind of ruined it for Kate. That and the fact that her Dad, predictably, never did show. No call, no text, nothing.

Her parents suck so much.

I lounge around all morning, walk to the beach, and even attempt a nap—but there is an electric current running in my veins because *everything is happening*. The Plan. It is happening.

I put my hair up, dress for class, and go an hour early to

rehearse, because this audition will be the best two minutes of my life if it kills me.

"Hey!" I call up Simone's stairwell. "I'm here to practice!" And in moments I've got "Appalachian Spring" in my earbuds, pointe shoes on, and a delicious long stretch in my hamstrings, my lower back, my arms, neck, shoulders. If this were my house, I would sleep here in the studio. When Kate and I have our apartment, we won't put rugs on the floors. Hardwood, freed up for dancing at all times. I fall forward, forehead touching my knees, and when I look up, Simone is standing in the doorway. I pull my buds out.

"Hi!" I breathe.

"Give me your soutenu, into the sauté arabesque. Let me see."

"Now?"

She nods.

I toss my sweater and iPod on the piano, walk to the center. Prepare. Turn out, arms up, turn and jump with height, plié.

"From the beginning."

"The whole thing?" I ask.

"Let me see."

"No music?"

"Let me see."

"Can I get a drink first?"

"From the beginning."

I rosin my shoes, cross to center. Begin. I give her the

entire dance, one hundred twenty seconds to demonstrate to the artistic director of the San Francisco Ballet why they need me in their corps, in their professional training program, in their company.

I finish and stand, breathing hard, before Simone. Her pink scalp is flushed beneath the cloud of carefully swept-up white hair.

"You work hard on this," she says.

"Yes."

"I see your heart. In this. In class. Every day."

The heart she claims to see suddenly pounds. This woman is not touchy-feely. Ever. Any mention of a heart is only ever as an organ when she's screaming at the younger girls to quit eating the Doritos they sneak into the dressing room: *You want to give yourselves heart disease and cellulite, go do it in someone else's studio!*

I nod.

"This is your very best."

I can't help smiling. "Really?"

"Isn't it?"

"Yeah," I breathe. "Yes. I think so."

She nods. "When do you graduate?"

"From school?"

"Yes."

"December," I say. "Middle of December."

She nods.

"Kate and I."

"And what are your plans in that case?"

"In what case?"

"After graduating, what will you do?"

This woman. She makes me insane. She knows The Plan nearly as well as Kate and I do. Everyone does; we blab about it nonstop to anyone who'll listen. "Well," I say, "San Francisco auditions are only two weeks after that, so no thoughts on the interim, really. . . ."

She frowns at me. "Besides the auditions. Have you thought about London?"

"Still thinking." I smile.

"How about college?"

"College?"

"After high school."

She stands there. And I stand there, sweating and breathing. What the hell is she going on about? *College?*

"Well," I fumble, "I mean . . . we're graduating early because the auditions are in January. Maybe we'll start rehearsing right away with the company for the spring shows. Wouldn't we?"

Her face changes. Softens. She studies her watch and steps to the wall of windows. Fog is rolling in again.

"Come with me," she says, turning to her office.

My stomach is jangly. She sits at her desk. I sit in the chair before it. The jewels of tutu fruit above our heads close in, the room suffocating in sparkling tulle and ribbon.

Something isn't right. She looks . . . sad? Defeated.

Oh my God.

All the teaching nonsense, college . . . she's sick. She's *dying.* She wants me to take over the studio. No wonder she's so worn out lately. How could none of us have noticed? I'm so self-absorbed! She's been suffering silently right before our eyes, and all we've cared about are auditions and snow and—oh God, my mind is racing. I can't catch up. How long does she have? Was *The Nutcracker* her last recital? Is that why she was so especially dressed up for opening night . . . ?

I reach across her desk and take her bony, papery hands in my sweaty own. Hers are so cold. "Madame Simone . . ."

"Harper." She squeezes my fingers. Holds them fast. "Darling girl." She draws herself up, inhales. "It's been a long time. I should have spoken to you. I've wanted so badly to see your body do the things it needs to do; turnout, dear heart, extension—these things cannot be *learned.* They are either in you or . . . You work the hardest of anyone. I know that—everyone knows that. This shouldn't come as a surprise, Harper."

I lean forward. "Sorry . . . I'm not . . . What are we talking about?"

"You are an inventive choreographer. I've never known a student so in love with dance, and you should never, ever stop. You are a wonderful teacher, a gift to the ballet. If every student had even just a tiny fraction of what is in your heart . . ."

I take my hand back. "You're not sick?"

She frowns. "Excuse me?"

"You aren't *ill*?"

Her eyes close. She massages her forehead and reaches again for my hands, which are now colder than hers and firmly in my lap.

"I don't understand."

"Yes, you do."

I swallow. Hard.

"A career in dance can mean many things. Come to London with me. Teachers with your natural ability are rare. You are especially singular; students will fall over themselves to be trained by you. Or if I cannot convince you, you can dance at university. An education is invaluable. I wish all my girls would go to school." She inhales. "I've waited far too long, selfishly. I'm telling you now while there is still time to make a wise decision, so you do not pin all your hopes on one moment that will do nothing but disappoint you. Your love is evident," she says. "But, darling, sometimes the ballet does not love us back."

Don't. Please.

But she does. Words we've heard all our lives, words I've spoken myself to hopeful, crestfallen parents of eight-year-olds, but now why is she saying this to me? Am I still sleeping? Because her voice is hollow, underwater, this definitely could be a really screwed-up dream *nightmare*. I need to wake up, wake up, wake up. . . .

It is more than being thin and the right height. You must have a high foot arch with a top bump; long, hyperextended legs; stretchy Achilles tendons; short torso; long neck and arms; a small, round head; 90 degree turnout from your hip rotators, not your knees or ankles, giving you a foot stance of 180 degrees; you must have natural facility and musicality; you must you must you must—

"I don't understand," I say again.

"Harper. I have done all I can for you; all *anyone* could do. 'A Pavlova is no one's pupil but God's.'"

"You make that up?"

"Balanchine. Even he knew the truth."

"Well," I say. "Those must have been some pricey lessons."

"What's up, ladies?"

Kate's voice is freezing water tossed in the warm bed of my stupor. Madame Simone's mouth straightens to a tight line. Kate's small head on her short torso supporting a ninety-degree turnout leans into the open office door.

"Happy Memorial Day!" She smiles.

"Veterans," I whisper.

"What was that, dear?" Simone asks gently.

"Not Memorial Day." I stand and push the chair in. "Are we done?"

"Harper . . ."

"Okay." I walk past Kate, into the crowd of girls arriving for class, put my iPod in my bag, and then, because I don't know what else to do—I go into the studio. Stand at the barre. Stretch.

Miss Hayward, the pianist who has played for us since we were three, shuffles in. Sits at the upright and opens her sheet music.

Lindsay comes in. The rest of the class follows. Kate takes her place beside me.

"Get some sleep?" she asks, yawning.

I nod. "Lots."

"What was Simone saying?"

"Nothing."

Simone walks in. Claps for silence. Music begins.

"First position. Demi-plié. Grand. Demi—Lindsay, get your clutching talon off that barre. For God's sake, it is there for balance. It is not your crutch to hang on to. Plié, relevé, tendu, and other side. Very nice."

The ninety-minute class is at once interminable and over in an instant. We give reverence. I find my sweater on the floor, pull boots over my pointe shoes, grab my bag from the dressing room, and take the stairs two at a time. Out onto the sidewalk, cold sunshine in my eyes, I find I have to think hard about which direction I must walk to get home, where I crawl into bed and sleep until morning.

- - -

When my grandma died, my grandpa lasted a couple of months, then followed her. Luke was seven; I was five. Once Grandpa went, Mom was a wreck. Slept, didn't work, barely noticed any of us at first. Not a fun time around our house.

So after the funeral, Dad sat Luke and me down. He had this book, which I now know was this famous Kübler-Ross *On Grief and Grieving* thing where the five stages of grief came from: denial, anger, bargaining, depression, acceptance. Dad promised us that Mom was going to be okay, and Luke asked, "When?" and Dad smiled and said, "Okay, let's see if we can guestimate...." And he pulled out this hand-drawn poster board chart.

He'd written the names of all five stages of grief and a kid-friendly description. No help to me—I couldn't read yet—but he drew faces for me, old-school emojis. They were pretty good. And he told us we were to pay attention to Mom, help her, and be good for her, and that as she moved from one stage to another, we could put a checkmark and a foil star beside the ones she'd passed. When she got to the final one, acceptance, that's when we'd know Mom was okay.

It totally worked. Lucky for Dad. And us. The chart gave us something to do. We were creepy little anthropologists: *How do you feel today, Mama?* As soon as we noticed a consistent expression of new sadness (*Bargaining! Anger!*), we'd run to Luke's closet, where we had tacked up the chart with pushpins, and cross off another hurdle. Affix another star. Sure enough, acceptance was it. She woke up. Started grocery shopping. Went back to work. Back to herself.

And so now, I go on, no idea how to proceed, so I just ... do. I keep going to class. As if nothing is different. I avoid

Simone before and after class, tell absolutely no one about her asinine *Sometimes the ballet does not love us back* speech, and obsess over that grief chart. Because I feel myself checking off stages as I ignore voice mails from Simone, make excuses for not hanging out with Kate, rehearse my audition solo, and dance harder and for more hours than I ever have before in all my life.

Which is stupid because first of all, there is nothing to grieve. No, I'm not Kate—who the hell besides Kate is? But I'm *good*—no one, in fourteen years, has ever said otherwise. Also, I see myself! There are mirrors and videotaped recitals. I *see* myself; if I were flailing the way Simone is insinuating, I would see it—everyone would. It isn't true. She is not telling me the truth.

But why? Is she saying all this because she wants to retire and sees how the babies listen to me? If she ropes me into becoming Royal Academy–certified, I could teach without her here, and she could go off on an old-lady cruise and leave me to keep the studio going, funding her retirement and my doom? Is she sabotaging my confidence so I'll blow the San Francisco audition and have nowhere else to go but stay with her forever and be her lackey? My God!

But then what if ... maybe sometimes I turn out with my feet, not my hips, but that's more a habit, not a physical inability. The auditions aren't for six more weeks. I could find a stretching coach, Pilates after class and on weekends. I could schedule some private lessons. I've still got time.

Yes, and piles of cash waiting around to be spent. And there are dance teachers all over the city sitting by the phone, waiting to be booked now, in the height of *Nutcracker* season.

Hopeless.

Stage four: depression.

I trudge home from ballet the Tuesday before Thanksgiving now deep in it, this mourning, and push the kitchen door open to call hoarsely, "Hello?" No one. Mom at school, Dad and Luke at the bakery.

I toss my bag up the stairs and nearly have a heart attack when the quiet is broken by "Harper!"

Owen. Sitting on our sofa. Great big, giant headphones on his head, pulled aside so he can hear me when I clutch my chest and scream: "Don't! Do that! You—don't scare people! God!"

"Sorry, I'm sorry!" He pulls the headphones all the way off and gestures with them. "Didn't hear you come in."

I hold on to the stair rail, breathing and willing my heart to not pound itself to death. I could have fallen down the stairs and killed myself. I shoot eyeball daggers at him.

He is still so beautiful. Jerk.

"What are you doing? Where's Luke?"

"In his room. He's on the phone with Lucas human resources. Social Security, tax stuff. I'm just waiting."

"Uh-huh."

"Then we're going to get coffee."

I nod.

"Hey," he says. "Come with!"

"No. Thank you."

His smile fades. "Really?"

I'm suddenly aware how half-naked (leotard, tights, and boots) and how very sweaty I am. Even after walking home through the fog, my face is certainly still bright pink from class, hair coming undone. I tuck some loose strands behind my ear and cross my arms over my flat chest.

I turn and start up the steps.

"Then maybe another time? Coffee? Or tea. Water. With lemon? Alone. I mean, without Luke? With me?"

Oh my God, why is everything in the world happening at once, and what exactly *is* happening?

Too much.

"Thank you," I call. "I can't. Ballet."

"Well, yeah, I meant *after* class. Or before."

"Sorry." At the top of the steps, I grab my bag, run to my room, and shut the door.

My phone buzzes. Kate.

Oh, nothing, just turning down an invitation to have coffee with the guy you're in love with. What're you up to?

My heart clenches.

No one would understand more, no one would be able to tell me to *Screw Simone! She's insane! Don't listen to her!* better than Kate.

I let it go to voice mail. She's given up texting; I never respond. She's stopped coming over; I'm never home. I can't burden her with this. We can't both be jacked for the audition.

There is a knock on my door, The Jedi sticks his head in.

"Hey. Would you please answer Kate's calls?" Luke says.

"What?"

"I'm trying to talk to my new boss, and she's texting and calling the whole time! I'm, like, 'Hold on a sec' to my *new boss,* so I can switch over and tell her to cool it!"

"Sorry."

"Why aren't you?"

"*Sorry!* Phone was off for class, I'll call her right back. I swear."

"Fine." He stands in my doorway. Leans in it.

"What? I will!"

He frowns. "Sad the show's over?"

I shrug. "Job definitely happening, then?"

He nods. "Are they mad?"

"Who?"

"Mom and Dad. Are they mad I'm leaving?"

"What?"

His head drops back against the door. "They're so pissed."

"Oh my God, of course they're not! You got a job—you didn't get caught running a meth lab. What is wrong with you?"

He bends and messes with his shoelace. "I feel bad. Maybe I shouldn't move out."

"They'll survive."

"They cried!" he says, miserable.

"When don't they? They're tenderhearted. We're *supposed* to grow up and have a life—they want that. It's just . . . Dad's Dad, and Mom's been a mom longer than she hasn't."

"What about the bakery?"

"What about it?"

"Will he be okay?"

"Luke. You're for real worried everyone's lives are going to fall apart if you move six miles away?"

"Oh, man . . ." He puts his head in his hands.

"Luke."

"What?"

"Knock it off," I tell him.

He shakes his head.

"They were just surprised. They'll live."

"I don't know," he says.

"Yes."

"What do *you* think?"

"About what?"

"Me moving out."

"Besides that my ultimate fantasy in life has just come true?" He looks so sad. "Luke, I'm kidding—I'll miss you being down the hall. But I think, on a clear day, if we stand on the roof, we'll be able to see your house. We can wave to each other."

He steps in and sits on the edge of the bed, all serious. "If I could make up a job, I mean, like, my *dream* job—this would be pretty close."

I sit in the blue chair Mom bought at the Salvation Army and helped me reupholster last year when I said I had no place to sit and tie my shoes. "I know."

"I mean, the ultimate would be making, not just testing. . . . Owen *designs levels,* I can't even imagine . . ." He's all misty in the euphoric picture of it: sitting all day in front of a computer, typing code.

"Sounds dreamy."

"Yeah." He nods. "I'd feel like I'd be using my degree already."

"Well. Sure. Comparative Religion is all about shooting guys and leveling up."

"Dude, the *stories* . . . Lucas is all about the hero myth; religion's all about it, too. . . . I could use all that to make games."

"Good."

"I feel like you guys now."

"What guys?"

"*You.* Mom. Dad . . . you. Doing what you love for your life. Dad loves food; he bakes in his sleep. Mom knew her whole life she was Jacques Cousteau. You and Kate have known since you were babies you're ballerinas, and you're about to go off and do it for real, and I figured I'd spend my whole life decorating cupcakes and wishing I'd majored in something useful that I also liked doing, but all I've ever really loved is video games. And Star Wars."

"You don't love the bakery?"

He thinks. "I mean, I'm good at it. Without trying. So I like it that way. I like that it's helping Dad. But . . ."

"It's a luxury."

"What is?"

"Doing what you *love* for your job. It's just random chance."

I cannot believe the words coming out of my Antarctic-explorer-do-or-die mouth.

Simone has planted doubt. My Scott blood is infected with doubt.

Luke frowns. "I don't know. I used to hate going to all your recitals, but I think I get it now. It's sort of . . . your only option. What you are. What you put *all* your energy, your whole *life* into. No backup, so how can you fail? Right?"

Two weeks ago these words would have made my heart soar. Now I'm squirming.

He gets up, hangs on the door, and says, "I'll say this once, and if you ever tell anyone, I'll deny it. But I applied to Lucas because of you. You don't take no for an answer. You work harder than anyone I know."

I drop, miserable, onto my unmade bed, face buried in a pillow.

"Harp!"

"*What?*"

"I mean it. You're my Yoda."

He closes the door behind him.

I sit up and find my phone.

"Kitty-Kat," I say when she picks up, "we're going to the beach. Rehearsal in the sand till even the water can't knock us off balance. Put on a sweater and look out your window. I'm coming up the steps."

Do or do not. There is no try.

- 9 -

Antarctica

THE MCMURDO DOCTOR PUTS ME ON A SCALE FIRST THING
and tsks.

"Did you weigh this much when you had your application
physical?"

I shrug.

She looks at my chart again. "Ohhh, I see. *Scott*," she says,
and tosses my file on her desk. "Those irresponsible, bloodline-
obsessed . . . Climb up."

I hop onto the table in my cotton gown. She listens to my
heart, shines a light in my eyes, looks at my teeth, and pulls her
wheeled stool to sit before me.

"Harper, I'm a little confused. You've got an incredibly ath-
letic build. The muscles in your legs and arms are quite"—my
calf tenses in her warm hand—"ropy. But then you're also
pretty skeletal. What's going on?"

I shrug.

"Okay. Well, here's the thing. Even inside this building,

your core temperature is going to be ten to fifteen degrees lower on The Ice in the winter. You've got the gaze, you're lethargic, you're not eating. Either you're depressed, or it's T3. What do you think?"

"I think . . ." I'm trying to be honest. I don't want to feel this way. "Could it be both?"

"For sure. One piggybacking on the other. Do you want to talk about it?"

"Not really."

She puts her hand on my bony knee, snatches it back. "Ugh, see?" she says. "That's not—your poor joints. Yikes." She shakes her head. "I'm writing you two prescriptions. You follow the instructions for the next two weeks. Come back then, and we'll see what's what. Do we have a deal?"

I like her. No lecture. Not bad. She gives me her card.

"Clinic hours are on there. Mine are in blue. Don't forget— two weeks from today. There are two hundred people here. If you don't show up, I'll know where to find you. Got it?"

I trudge off to breakfast, where Aiden sticks his head eagerly out the porthole in the kitchen door. "How was it?"

I hand him the two prescriptions.

He frowns. "I could have told you this," he says, and hands me back the paper that reads, *Gain at least ten to fifteen pounds.* But the other note makes his face light up. "The greenhouse! Oh, Harper, you're my connection! Get me some lettuce and cherry tomatoes, and I'll propose marriage on the spot!" He folds the paper, hands it back, and says, "Wait—I've got something for you." Foil-wrapped cinnamon rolls.

"Take them to work," he says. "And don't share."

- - -

The lab is warm, the New Age massage music is going, and Charlotte nearly tackles me when I open the door.

"What did she say? T3? I could be a doctor; I should have made you bet me cash. T3, right?"

"What would you do with cash?" I sigh, handing her the prescriptions and sliding onto a lab stool. The McMurdo stores sell only cigarettes, booze, McMurdo T-shirts, and postcards. For about fifty million dollars each.

"Ha! I was right! Oh, Harp." She kneels at my feet and takes my cold hands. "You'll be okay. I promise." She reads the prescriptions. "Oh my gosh—greenhouse! I wish I could go with you."

At her table, Vivian looks up.

"I don't even get what that has to do with anything," I grumble.

"It's amazing. It's the light and the warmth. They've got a hydroponic garden because, you know, no soil. They grow a few lettuces and things between flights with freshies. Allison's running it this year. She's really smart and nice—biologist from the East Coast somewhere, I think? Total hippie. You'll die." Says the woman wearing the macramé hemp belt and Birkenstocks. "What's in the foil?"

I unwrap three huge cinnamon rolls. Vivian shocks me by accepting the one I offer. Charlotte plucks one from the foil and attacks it.

"You getting emails to your mom on a good schedule?"

I roll the foil into a ball.

"Harper."

"I've been busy."

"Oh my gosh. How long has it been?"

"You mean since the first one I sent? Which was a really good one?"

"Yes."

"Um. Six weeks?"

"Harper!"

"I haven't felt good! And I can only email from your office or in here, and once I'm in my room, I just want to go to sleep. . . ."

She gets up and rummages through a metal cabinet, tosses wires and empty boxes over her shoulder until she retrieves a laptop, a kind of old one. "It'll get Wi-Fi. You need to be sending them mail daily. Did the doctor talk about that?"

"No."

"Okay, listen to me. You too, Vivian. It was nearly impossible to persuade the NSF to let underage people on The Ice, everyone drunk and crazy and especially in winter. I understand it's ridiculous, but I would have died to be here at your age, and I think it's an amazing program, and we have to prove it's possible by having you people learn some stuff and also *not die*. Viv, you write your family, don't you?"

"Every Sunday."

Kiss-ass.

"I send both your parents my dorky Daily Update, but, Harp, they need to hear from *you*. And hearing from them will help with this." She puts the prescriptions on the table before me. I fold them into little triangles.

"Have they mentioned me not writing?"

"Not yet."

I nod.

"Okay. So. Communicating with family. Eating. Let's not die. In the name of our brave forefathers, in the name of the Adélies, let's not lose our minds here, okay?"

I smile. "I love the Adélies."

She sits in her chair. "They're so beautiful, aren't they?"

Across the room, Vivian huffs.

I can see the ice, their little faces, as if they're three feet from me now. The waves on the ice, the rocks . . .

"Harper."

I snap to attention, my gaze fixed on the middle distance. Good grief.

Charlotte sighs. "Oh, babe—you've really got it. When do you start the greenhouse?"

I unfold the prescription. "Um . . . this afternoon."

"Okay. Take the laptop. It's a thousand years old, but it works. Use it. And, Vivian, if the office and lab are locked, you can use it, too. . . . You know where Harper's room is, right—*Oh my God,* I have the answer!"

Vivian and I exchange an uneasy glance.

"You two are sharing a room. This is perfect."

"What?" Vivian practically chokes.

"Help each other out! You'll get to know one another, I'll feel better knowing you're never alone, and, Harp—this'll pull you out of T3 for sure. Ooh, and you can share the laptop!"

"I have a laptop," Vivian says darkly.

"She's got a laptop . . . ," I echo weakly. "And I treasure time alone. . . ."

"That is the last thing either of you needs," she says. "You're fading on my watch. You're *my* responsibility. Whose room is bigger?"

I raise my hand and sigh. Charlotte is immovable.

"Okay!" She beams. "Now, go get me another two or three cinnamon rolls, and we can get to work."

- - -

Charlotte is right about one thing: The greenhouse is amazing.

It has rows of tiny sprouts and the misty, clean scent of green leaves and water. It's warm and humid, and I instantly love it.

"Harper!" Allison calls from behind a mass of vines. "Right?"

I smile and offer her my hand, but she moves in for a full-body hug instead. "Oh—oh gosh," I stammer. "Okay . . ."

She's wearing denim overalls (Antarctic farmer!), and a clip secures her blond hair. She holds me out and gives me a once-over, looks into my eyes.

"I'm starting to feel real self-conscious when people do that," I say. "Are my eyes doing a cartoon pinwheely thing?"

"Poor thing. No, it's just your gaze we're all looking at. If it's unfocused and, you know, a little all-over, it's not a great sign."

"Oh. Okay. So how's my gaze?"

"Unfocused. A little all-over."

"Fantastic."

"The good news is," she says, brightening, "it's nothing we can't fix! Cold's doing a number on your brain, but with all this warmth and oxygen, it'll learn to tell the cold to knock it off." Among the rows of sunlamps and budding green leaves, there are hammocks swinging empty. Five of them.

"Anyone can come in anytime and get a tune-up, but I'll keep one set aside special for you. Doctor's orders."

I smile.

"How are you liking it so far? Having fun?"

I nod. "Except for . . ." I gesture around my eyeballs.

"Good!" she says. She's near Mom's age and reminds

me of her. Except blond. And softer in her overalls. And shorter—Oh, who the hell am I kidding? I miss Mom so much, any lady who is nice to me is going to make it worse.

I choose the hammock farthest from the door, ease myself into it, and close my eyes.

This is even better than my millions-of-kittens bed.

I swing a little and breathe the clean, warm, living air. It's weird to realize it's been weeks since I've seen a plant. Grass. Trees.

"I'll be in and out. Call out if need me. You mind a little music?"

"I'd love it," I murmur.

From the speakers mounted in the corners of the ceiling come familiar notes on familiar instruments.

"Vivaldi," Allison says. "*Four Seasons*. The lettuce seems to like it. That okay?"

I know it as *Music for center floor pointe work*. My chest tightens and burns.

"It's nice," I say.

I close my eyes and breathe through tears. I push against the floor and swing gently with the orchestra, back and forth. Back and forth.

Where is Kate? Is she rehearsing with the company? Is she in class? I should be beside her at the barre, watching her straight spine, following her lead in giving an arabesque more extension, right up to where it hurts and then a bit more past that, and holding it just a little longer than feels possible. Is Simone mad I'm not in summer intensive classes teaching the kindies? . . . Oh, my kindies. Willa. Will Lindsay expect as much from their tiny backs and limbs as I do? Or not enough? Will she lose patience and be mean to my babies? How could I leave them for this cold?

"You're not to think about things that way or you'll never make it back," a man's voice says, close.

My eyes fly open, but I lie still. How much of that did I say out loud?

"Allison?"

I hear her nurse shoes softly clip-clop to me. "You okay?"

"What did you say?"

"I asked, are you okay."

"No, before that."

She shakes her head. "You're half asleep." She puts her hand on my forehead and smiles. "Warm," she says. "Good!" And she's back down the rows of plants.

A man is sitting on a pile of ice at my feet. Beard stiff with icicles, face raw and blackened with soot, layers of wool and canvas outer gear. Old-fashioned.

My breath is shallow.

"Robert," I whisper. "Robert Scott?"

He shakes his head. "But *you're* a Scott. Correct?"

"I am. Are you Amundsen? Roald, like Dahl. Right? He's named for you."

"Sorry?"

"The writer—*James and the Giant Peach? Matilda?*"

"No, I meant, sorry, I'm not Amundsen. Not Scott."

"Oh." My throat is dry. "Shackleton."

"Yes."

"*Why?*" Oh God, that sounded awful. "It's just, Amundsen . . . I know every step he took to get there. I've studied. . . . And I *am* a Scott, so why not . . ."

He shrugs. "I am not here unbidden."

"*What?*"

He just sits there, looking at me.

Of course. We who sank in the sea, who have the wrong hips and feet.

My voice is barely audible. "Are you my Ghost of South Pole Past?"

He twirls his finger loosely around his head. "T3."

"No one mentioned hallucinations!"

"You're really going to need to eat something," he says. "Be with some people."

"Oh my God, if one more person says that . . ."

"And why haven't you been writing to your family? Kate? Owen?"

"I will."

"I mean, this computer business . . . if I'd had some of that, who knows how things would have gone down? My wife surely wouldn't have had to worry I was dead so often. . . ."

"Okay!"

"Harper, you need me?" Allison calls.

"No, sorry . . . sleepy!"

Shackleton frowns. "Keep it down."

I breathe deeply. Exhale. Just the T3. This will stop. I'm fine with it. It's fine. I turn over in the hammock to face him. "All right," I whisper. "Impart your wisdom."

He holds up his hands. "Just did. Eat some food. Talk to people. Even as we watched the ice crush *Endurance* and pull her down into the water, my men played football. They put on some plays. When I hired my crew, one of the first questions I asked every single candidate was *Can you sing?* But that's just to keep away the . . ." He gestures to his head once more.

"Yeah, got it."

"As for the larger issue at hand . . . I understand your instinct, coming here. And for what it's worth, I think it was an excellent decision."

"You do?"

"Absolutely."

I nod. "Well, thank you. I know how badly you wanted to get there."

He frowns. "Get where?"

I frown back. "Uh . . . the *South Pole?*"

"No," he says. "See, that's where you're losing me; I don't understand this overwrought determination to make this solely symbolic pilgrimage. So you talk someone into giving you a seat on a helicopter—what is that? Suddenly you're a ballerina again?"

"It's not just symbolic! Hardly anyone, barely any humans, ever get there. If I can do that, I'll feel . . . I can do anything."

"How so?"

Oh my God, this *guy*. "Because!" I whisper-wail. "So many people want to get there so badly all their lives, and they *never* make it."

"Because they're not meant to."

"Because they haven't tried hard enough!"

His snow-blind eyes laser-beam me. "You were right to come. Especially winter. When the storms are here, you'll see. There are no landmarks anywhere. Just empty open white. Nothing but possibility. A blank canvas. Best place to stop following the wrong path and make a brand-new one."

"I loved my path," I whisper. "I don't want anything else."

"Yes, I know," he says. "Why are you giving up so easily?"

"I'm not *giving* anything up. I never had it! There's nothing left to surrender. I worked my entire life. I did everything I was supposed to."

Shackleton shakes his shaggy head. "You kids. One disappointment, one misstep, and you lie down and cry about it. Throw the baby out with the bathwater."

"What *baby*?"

He puts his freezing hand on my stockinged feet. "Look

at these disgusting things. You ruined them and enjoyed every second of it. Correct?"

I nod.

"Did anyone *make* you do it? Why dance every single day, every day of your life? Who was forcing you to do that?"

"No one."

"Because why?"

"Because . . . it's everything. It's all I am or ever want to do or be. Nothing makes me happier. I *love* it. I love it."

"Don't you miss it?"

I put my head in my hands.

"You need to be here to figure out why you heartlessly stopped being a ballerina. What did ballet ever do to you to make you abandon it?"

"It doesn't love me back!" I hiss at him, sitting there calmly on his ice, beard still frozen in the humid air of the greenhouse.

He sits back. "Well, there's your problem."

"What?"

"Entitlement. No person, no thing—not Antarctica, not the universe, not ballet—is ever obligated to love us back. True, honest love for a thing is because you love it, with no expectation or want of reciprocation. You love ballet?"

I nod.

"Why?"

"Because . . . I *do*. Why did you keep trying to get to the pole again and again?"

We sit for a while. Vivaldi fills the silence.

Shackleton leans toward me. "Harper Scott," he says. "Did you eat your dogs?"

In the hammock, my heart thumps. I nod.

"Me too," he whispers.

I pull my left foot to my knee, my hand over one scarred heel. "I was ten. Simone said my heels weren't right for pointe shoes. There was extra bone; she told my parents it would screw up my feet. I begged them until they let me have the surgery. Cut the bone off so my feet would work in the shoes."

He nods. "That's pushing the river a bit. Don't you think?"

"No."

"Still you love to dance?"

I nod.

"Well," he says, "you've just solved your problem."

"Which one?"

"All of them. You know what to do."

"No, I don't! I'm not worthy of ballet. I'm not made for it. My body's not *meant* for it. . . . I'm too old. It's too late."

"You're meant for it."

"No, it's—You don't understand. I'm seventeen years old; it *is* too late. I've wasted my entire life for the love of something I can never have, and now I don't have any idea who

I am. But I thought, if I came here, if I get to the pole, I'll know—it will come to me."

"What will?"

"The answer!" My eyes sting.

"What do you miss, most of all, besides dancing? What have you given up—what do you regret?"

"Willa," I whimper instantly. "I miss my kids."

Shackleton smiles.

"What?"

"You miss teaching them?"

I see right where he's going and he's *wrong*. "I miss *them*."

He sighs.

"Harper Scott. The Ice is not to be conquered. It is just ice. You know what to do. Follow the sun. And for God's sake, pay attention."

I struggle to sit up in the swinging hammock. "What does that even *mean*?"

"Do *not* give in."

I close my eyes.

Still lost.

"Harper?" Allison's hand is on mine. "Hey," she says. "Why the tears?"

- - -

I zombie into the dining hall. I'm hungry. And sick of it. Why am I still starving myself? I'll never be a ballerina. That ship has sailed—and been swallowed by The Ice. I pick up a plate and fill it with the remains of the last of the lettuce until August. Or until Allison's crop comes in. I pour dressing on it, *not* lemon.

There is a basket of bread. All kinds. I take a multigrain-looking one, slather it with butter, and instead of water, I pour a glass of milk. Low-fat, not skim.

Take *that*, T3.

Charlotte walks in, sees me, and darts straight to my table.

"How was it? Did you love it?"

I nod, my mouth full of balsamic-dressed iceberg lettuce. "You can go in anytime, you know. Allison said so."

She scrunches her nose. "Was there anyone else besides you?"

"No."

"See?" She sighs.

"What?"

"It's more for people who . . . How do you feel?"

I shrug. "Hungry."

"Good! Ooh, listen—move Vivian in tonight, okay?"

I shovel more salad and keep chewing.

"Take the rest of the day off. Okay? Harper?"

"No, I've got a ton of data to get through. I'll just finish—"

She puts her arms around me for one tight, strong hug. "Tomorrow. You're going to be okay, Harp. You'll be glorious."

That is debatable. I watch her go and I stand, toss my plate in the wash bin, and walk into the kitchen.

"Aiden!" I call. He turns from the wash sink, suds up to his elbows.

"Hey!"

"I need your help."

- - -

"Have you ever *used* a computer?" he says later, in the warm Christmas light of what is for the next few hours still *my* room. "See this thing that says, 'Connect to network'?" He clicks it. The Internet pops up.

"You fixed it!"

Aiden rolls his eyes, gets up, and sits on the second bed. "How're you feeling?"

"Tired." Shackleton's *You know what to do* rolls around in my head. "Annoyed."

"Even after the greenhouse?" He finds a new pile of library books I've borrowed. "Still mourning?"

"Yeah, I'm pretty pissed forty-five minutes in a hammock didn't cure me."

"Sorry."

"No," I sigh. "I am. I'm a boring broken record of . . . boringness. You tell me things now."

"What things?"

"All the things. Where in Ireland do you live?"

"Have you been?"

"No."

"But you know the basic shape?"

"Of Ireland? Sure."

"Okay. I live at the bottom."

"Oooh, near Dingle?"

His eyes widen. "Dingle, yes! Did I tell you that?"

"No. My mom watches this travel show on public television, *Rick Steves' Europe*—Rick is hilarious. He's always talking about going to Europe 'through the back door,' which I'm not sure he gets what that means. . . . But he *loves* Ireland. He's done so many episodes there, and I've seen the one in Dingle a million times. I can't believe you live there!"

Aiden is laughing. "Oh God, Rick Steves. Practically every American I've ever met has got a *Back Door* guide with them. Rick put us on the map."

"Is there still the music festival? In the churches, all the pubs?"

"Every autumn."

"Do you play an instrument?"

He nods. "Fiddle."

"Really."

"My whole family does. I miss that, definitely."

"Will you go back after college? To live?"

"Absolutely not."

"You like your family? Your parents?"

"Love them. A lot."

"But you won't go back."

"I would never have left if I stayed any longer. They're perfectly happy there, and I was, too. I've got three brothers. We know every inch of every field and street, and there's not a neighbor whose house we've not eaten supper at. There are the girls we grew up with we're supposed to marry and have a gaggle of kids with, and the schoolmates we drink and play music with in the pubs every Saturday, and I did. It was hard to leave. But it wasn't meant for me. I'll visit, but I was always . . . straining against it. You know?"

I don't. I've never strained against my life. I've stretched into it. Yearned for it and loved it more, even as I lived it.

At the desk I stare at the screen. Sign into my mail account. Eleven new messages.

Mom. Mom and Dad. Mom. Kate. Luke. Mom. Owen. Owen. Owen. Owen. *Owen.*

"That's a lot of Owen," Aiden says close to my shoulder. "Relative?"

I close the laptop. "Friend."

"Huh. Prolific."

I shrug—and gasp as a sharp pain shoots through my left shoulder, straight into my neck. I reach up and grab the burning spot.

"Whoa," Aiden says. "What's up?"

"I don't know," I moan. "Stabbing, awful pain . . ."

"Where?"

"Where I'm *rubbing.* Oh my God, it hurts. . . ."

"All right, don't shoot the . . . person trying to help. Hold still."

His hands move to the painful shoulder, and I instinctively move away. "I'm fine," I say. "It's okaahhh. *God,* what is wrong with me? I'm broken!" Another bright flash of heat pulses near my neck.

"Sit still," Aiden says kindly. "Tell me if this hurts."

He moves my hundred pounds of hair aside and puts his hands on the muscle, gently pressing his warm fingertips into my skin.

"Gah, okay, ow!"

"Breathe. Just let me do this—"

"It *hurts!*"

"Yes, you've established that. Shut up, and let me help you!"

I whimper pitifully and clench my toes while he massages my shoulder, and the pain explodes, then gradually subsides.

"Are you breathing?"

"Yes," I snap, and exhale because I have not been breathing.

"Wow," he says, low. "You've got some muscular . . . muscles."

The pain is dull.

"Mmm."

"You work a lot of free weights?"

"Mmm."

"What could possibly have your poor shoulders so tense?

You're neck's all jacked up, too." He kneads my gristly muscles slowly. I breathe.

Wind is sending icy snow past the dark window. Snow will always be Kate dancing. My heart breaking again, and again, and again.

Does Owen wonder why I haven't written back?

Aiden moves his hands under the shoulder of my T-shirt. I flinch.

"Sorry!" he says. "Sorry . . ."

"No, it's okay, I'm . . . thank you."

"Harper."

"It's fine! Feels better. Thank you."

"I didn't mean—"

"I know. I'm just . . ." I stand up, immediately get a head rush, and Aiden sees it happen. He takes my arm and sits beside me on what will be Vivian's bed. I put my head on my knees, and I try so hard but can't keep the tears from springing out of my eyes. "Sorry," I tell him. "This is so dumb. I'm tired of being in pain."

"How long has it been like this? Have you seen the doctor?"

"No, *this* kind is new. I'm just—sick of myself. Feeling sorry for myself." I grab a hair tie and wrestle my hair into it.

"Well, if it helps, your neck may be really screwed up, but you've still definitely got the best posture of anyone I've ever met."

"Great, thanks." I pile my hair into a giant mass on top of my head.

"What do you want to do?"

"I don't know. I'm driving myself insane."

I rub my neck and my hair falls, spilling down my back. So heavy.

Outside the window, the blizzard is more insistent. I climb over Aiden beside me on the bed, march to the door, and yank it open.

"Aiden? You coming or not?"

- - -

The haircut lady looks like a grandma who's still determined to keep it together with lots of makeup and a way-too-skimpy tank top. She's sitting in the makeshift salon across from the laundry room, lights on, reading a two-year-old *People* magazine. The old headlines make me suddenly nervous. Aiden holds my bare hand. No mittens.

"Hello!" he says. "Open for business?"

Haircut looks at her watch. "Sure," she says, and tosses *People* aside. "Who's up first?"

Aiden looks at me. Huge, encouraging smile. He squeezes my hand.

Butterflies.

"Me." I sit in the chair before the mirror. She looks us both up and down.

"You the kids?"

We nod.

"I'm Deb," she says. She hefts my hair up and snaps a plastic cape around me. "What are we doing? Trim? Few layers?"

"Cut it off," I say to her face in the mirror. "Please."

"Which part?"

"All of it."

Aiden is sitting in a plastic chair. His eyes are wide.

"Honey," Deb says, "you're going to have to be more specific."

I frown. What could be more specific than *cut it off . . . all of it*? If she doesn't start soon, I'll lose my nerve. I move my fingers over my scalp. "Close. Nothing left."

"Shaved?"

"Well, *no,* but . . ."

"Cropped?"

"Yes," I say.

"Close."

"Yes."

"Like a *boy*?

"Sure."

She sighs and lifts the heavy length of my dark hair in both hands. Shiny. Straight. Nearly long enough to sit on. She shakes her head. "What is your name, sweetheart?"

"Harper."

"Harper. You need to take a minute. Give this some real thought."

"I have. If you don't want to, I'll end up doing it myself in my room with sewing scissors, and it'll take forever. Deb. Please?"

She sits on the spinny stool beside my chair. "You think on it some. Come see me next week."

"Please."

She zeros in sternly on the reflection of my red-rimmed eyes. "You break up with a boy?"

I shake my head.

"Sure you did. Come here to get away from the mess? You listen to me; this is not the way to do it. Not off The Ice and especially not on it—end up looking like what's-her-face in *Rosemary's Baby,* and plus, didn't they tell you eighty percent of your body heat escapes through your head? You're lucky to have all this; no hat could keep you as warm as hair will. Pretty, too. You talk her into this?" she asks Aiden.

"No, ma'am."

Deb picks up a plastic comb, steps back to sweep it through the full length of my admittedly beautiful hair. "I'll tell you something else, too; you're here and he's not. It's done. Won't matter to him either way.

My eyes are starting to sting. "I have to."

"Oh, come on. Says who?"

"I only grew it because of him. For him."

In the mirror, Deb's eyes narrow. Aiden perks up. "How long was your hair when you met him?"

"Shoulders. Trimmed but never cut since."

Deb sets the comb down. "How old are you?"

"Seventeen."

"Takes decades to grow hair this long. What kind of deal are we talking—arranged marriage? Not allowed to cut your hair, walk three steps behind him?"

"No," I say hoarsely. "I wanted to. I loved him. He wanted it long so I could pin it up. Wanted me skinny, took all my time, took my money, my parents' money—and now he doesn't want me. I'm not good enough."

"How so?"

"Body's not right. Not good enough."

"He *said* that? Your *body*?"

I nod.

Aiden is slack-faced in the mirror, hanging on every word.

"Where were your parents during all this?"

I shrug. "I loved him."

She weighs my hair in her hands, exchanges the comb for a brush. She works it all into a low, dense ponytail, holds it tight, and brushes it smooth. "You're telling me the truth? This was just for *him*."

I nod.

"Men are asshats," she says. "Boys are worse." She eyeballs Aiden behind her in the mirror. "No offense."

Aiden nods. "None taken."

I fold my hands beneath the cape. "It was my own fault. I knew who he was the whole time, from the very start. I knew, but I loved him, and I thought I could make him love me, but nothing worked. Not starving, not growing all this hair. None of it mattered. Years and years for nothing."

Deb watches me cry for a minute, pulls a tissue from a box beside her hair dryer, and puts her hands on my shoulders. "I know this dummy," she says. "I married him. *Twice*. He's a dime a dozen and, true fact, he's an idiot. You're lucky you got away from him, and your folks should've never let you near him to begin with."

"I love him," I say again.

She puts the brush down. "You going to come crying to me tomorrow when you wake up and wish you hadn't done this?"

I shake my head. She turns to Aiden.

"You'll be with her when she does? 'Cause for sure she will."

Aiden looks to me. "Harp?"

"He'll be with me."

Deb picks up a pair of clean silver scissors, hacks off my ponytail, and holds the severed hair, three feet long, up into the fluorescent light.

"Well," she says, brightening. "Some nice cancer patient will have a gorgeous wig."

Free haircuts are one more delightful McMurdo perk. Aiden puts a twenty-dollar tip in her jar, takes my hand again, and pulls me out into the hall.

"Was all that true?" he asks.

"Come with me? I want to feel the cold," I say. "On my head."

"No, you don't."

"I do," I insist. "I really, really do. Please."

"Was all that true?"

I nod.

We run to the entry hall. Ben *lives* at that damn desk. He stares at me. At my head.

"What did you *do*?"

I lean into the door with my shoulder, push with all my might.

"Hey!" he shouts. "You can't—"

The blast of icy wind is so sharp it burns. It sweeps Ben's voice aside. I step out into it, into the dark, just to the landing of the steps, Aiden behind me, neither of us wearing cold gear. Immediately it is in my skin, inside me. I am frozen and I love it. I step down onto the snow. No clouds. Beyond the station lights a million stars, more than I ever could imagine.

I am so light. My neck is free. Aiden stands before me, puts both his hands on my head and moves his fingers through my shorn hair. He says something the wind carries away.

"What?" I shout.

"Your eyes are *huge*!" he says next to my ear. "You are so beautiful."

He pulls my icy face to his. He kisses me, I kiss him back, and I hold on to him so as not to fall away in this storm.

- 10 -

San Francisco

I *AM* YODA. NO MORE SELF-PITY. THE STAGES OF GRIEF CAN screw off. Kate and I are *dancers*.

Thanksgiving's passed, finals are nearly done, and high school is close to being a distant memory. We rehearse night and day. I babysit and teach and am polite and matter-of-fact with Simone, who has at last abandoned her campaign of voice mail pleading for me to *Talk to me, darling. Tell me what you are thinking!* She simply smiles, corrects me in class, compliments my turns; she's given in. Surrendered to the fact that The Plan lets no one in the way.

We are racing downhill toward auditions, to our futures. Our lives. Things are the way they're supposed to be.

Especially tonight, like every first Saturday in December since we were five. Kate and I with Mom and Dad, three back from front row, our seats on the aisle at the War Memorial Opera House for the San Francisco Ballet's *Nutcracker.*

Kate's in her traditional sparkly snow-white chiffon sheath, which ends at her knees and makes her legs look about nine feet long, and every guy in the lobby turns to stare. I am wearing eyeliner and one of Mom's skirts, though Kate does not approve of the leotard I've got on in lieu of a blouse.

"I'm a dancer. Get off my back," I say as we make our way to the resplendent lobby—sparkling trees lit and star-topped, spilling light up into the domed ceiling, and voices echoing, volleyed from the marble floor and walls. Perfume and hot apple cider and cookies . . . I'm so hopeful and happy. I squeeze Kate's arm and sigh.

"You know I love you," she whispers. "You know that, right?"

"Yes!" I whisper back. She's been so shmoopy tonight. We pose, smiling, for Mom's and Dad's camera phones before the tallest lobby tree, a million lights and gold ornaments on every branch.

"You girls are gorgeous!" Mom says.

"This may be your last year watching, so enjoy it!" Dad says.

Chimes ring. The show is starting.

We move with the crowd to our seats, worn velvet beneath the ornate blue and carved gold opera house ceiling. The curtain hangs in rich red folds. I turn around to see the people in the risers and the balconies. *Our* audience soon. Not long now.

The lights go down. We applaud the set, the music, the orchestra pit so close to our feet; no music could ever be more beautiful. I turn to Kate.

She takes my hand.

Here we go.

Act one is not my favorite—exposition must play out, so aside from the little kids from the SF Ballet School, there's not much company dancing, although the costumes are amazing; the story is set in pre-1906 earthquake San Francisco, so the party ladies are in Jane Austen–type dresses, empire-waist gowns that flow and swing around their legs. Clara finally goes to sleep, the rats come, the nutcracker's soldiers deal with the situation, and finally, at last—the moment Kate and I wait all year for. The light changes. The music turns. It is winter.

Snow.

Kate holds my hand even tighter.

They glide from the wings, pointe shoes silent, shimmering white tulle and satin, perfect strong arms and legs. The music fills my chest; my heart pounds. Violins, cellos, and flutes come in; the song swells.

The snow falls.

I turn to Kate.

Light reflects in the tears on her face.

I squeeze her hand back, lean close.

"There we are," I whisper.

Her face crumbles and falls into her hands.

Mom leans forward. "What is it?"

I shake my head. Someone nearby shushes us.

"Hey," I whisper, "are you okay?"

She shakes her head and stands. Walks up the aisle.

Dad and Mom crane their necks. "I'll go," I whisper to them, and follow Kate up the aisle, turning back to steal glimpses of the dance we've waited all year to watch.

There's a knot in my stomach, in my throat—Is she ill? Then wildly—Does she know Owen asked me out? How could she? And also who cares, because I said no anyway; I would never do that to her—she knows—but ugh, my hands are sweaty anyway.

The usher at the doors is stern. "Quietly, ladies," he growls, and pushes us into the lobby.

Kate sinks to the top step just outside the door, beside a towering golden nutcracker statue.

"Kitty," I say. "Talk to me. Are you sick?"

She shakes her head, mascara all over her eyes, face back in her hands.

"Should I call your mom?"

"I can't audition for San Francisco."

I sit beside her. "Yes, you can! What's wrong? Come on, breathe. . . ."

I rub her back and she cries.

"I can't. I'm so sorry. Harp, I love you. I'm sorry."

My stomach tightens.

"I don't want to ruin everything. I have to say it now, but I love you. I'm so sorry. Please don't hate me. . . ."

"Hey," I say. "Listen to me. Nothing could ever, ever make

me hate you, not ever. Please just tell me. We'll figure it out. Tell me."

She closes her eyes tight. Breathes in that caught, hiccupy way of really hard crying.

"I won't be here," she says. "In January. I'll be in New York."

My hands go cold.

"New York?"

"I have to go to the finals. For the Grand Prix."

"I don't understand?"

"I went to YAGP. Last weekend."

Through the doors, the muted "Snow" music soars. Act one is nearly over.

I unbuckle the silver sandals I've borrowed from Mom. Tighten them one notch. And then another. Anything to not look at Kate.

"Simone took me. She said it was my last chance to be seen by so many companies. They were all there—Boston. Chicago. New York. Harp, I won. First place."

I hear my voice, "Simone hates YAGP."

"She does. But she says I've been stupid to stay so long. She's been on me about it for a long time. I've put her off, I swear. I told her no way, we've got The Plan, but . . . I'm too old, she says. To pick and choose. It's too hard to fly every-where, audition all over the country. Video auditions don't ever read well, she said—"

"But you want San Francisco."

"They were there."

Applause. The music ends. Beautiful, soaring "Snow" music. The doors open.

"Did you use my dance?"

"Harp."

"Did you?"

She won't look at me. "Your choreography got the highest score."

The crowd streams from the doors, flows around me and Kate sitting on the steps before them, we are rocks in a people river.

You must be willing to eat your dogs.

I stand. Kate stands, her face pink, makeup destroyed.

I let the crowd carry me forward, through the lobby and away from Kate's voice calling me back, out the grand front opera doors to the wet sidewalk. I've left my coat in the coat check. Just my leotard. But I'm not cold. I hail a taxi.

\- \- \-

I let myself cry for exactly thirty-two minutes, the amount of time it took to ride home in the cab from *The Nutcracker* (wasted two nights' worth of babysitting money on that one) and text Mom and Dad: *Got sick, sorry, I'm home, take Kate home pls.*

Once home I combed Bay Area audition listings for every ballet company, professional or amateur, in a thirty-mile radius, anything happening this month, *now,* which turned up four: Berkeley, Concord, Palo Alto, Oakland.

I say nothing to Mom and Dad or Luke or anyone, nothing about anything. I fly unnoticed beneath the radar of Mom's semester finals, Dad's holiday bakery orders, and Luke's moving-out prep. My last day of school comes and goes unceremoniously. Teachers say goodbye; I fill out paperwork and walk home, not turning to look back. I babysit Willa; I teach and go to ballet class religiously on time—never early. I slip in, put my hand on the barre beside Lindsay, and bolt the moment each class ends. I erase every text and voice mail Kate and Simone send, and after a few days, they back off. Give me what I clearly want, which is for both of them to leave me the hell alone, so I can concentrate on:

The New Plan

1. Audition and be offered a contract at one or more companies, which I will have to
2. Turn down when I accept my company position at the San Francisco Ballet, which will
3. Prove Simone and Kate (and the horrible cancerous doubt I've let them plant in my own heart) wrong.

In a studio at SF State, I record an audition tape and send it to forty-three companies in as many cities, all currently accepting applicants. And I wait in hallways crammed with crowds of short-torsoed, long-legged dancers with perfect feet, paper number pinned to my chest. At the first audition, I don't even make the first cut. Barre exercises and I'm out. At the second, I don't even get to touch the barre. I am cut from the lineup.

The final two auditions happen on the same Saturday, which involves intricate public transportation transfer tickets, sprinting from one station to another, and incredibly fortunate timing, but I manage to arrive in plenty of time to be cut in the first round from Dance Theatre of Berkeley and then, two hours later, from a nonprofit dance cooperative in Oakland.

I sleep on the train back to San Francisco, wake up past my stop, and walk three miles home along busy Nineteenth Avenue. Cars and trucks barrel past, exhaust fumes and cigarette smoke, ambulance sirens and police cars and blaring horns and clanging Muni cars, and tweekers and homeless guys, and I cannot wait to tell this story—the failed auditions, Simone and Kate, and how I never let them get me down; how, instead, the whole mess lit a fire in me. *I am a Scott.* How that fire carried me to the San Francisco audition, where the director saw what no one else seemed to. How every dancer's path to their destiny is unique and never easy, but if you truly know yourself, believe in the gift you were born with and meant to spend your life using to make art that helps the world be more beautiful, and if you work hard your entire life for this one, single dream you have and ever will have, then nothing, no one, can stop a person from achieving this dream; it is impossible that it will not come to pass.

Here I am, I will insist. *I am proof.*

Aut moriere percipietis conantur.

- - -

I'm up at five the morning after my walk of shame, after my final failed fire-lighting audition. Only a few days before Christmas, today is my Sunday to work at the bakery. Mom is asleep; Luke and Dad were up and gone before me. I stretch my poor legs, sore from the miles of pavement walking. Yuan Yuan Tan and Robert Falcon Scott stare down at me from the ceiling. *It's up to you,* they say.

Got it.

An hour later, I'm showered, dressed, and pushing glass doors open into the warm, sweet yeasty air of our Fog City Bakery.

The bells above the door ring bright, evergreen and holly berries everywhere, mistletoe and twinkle lights. Dad *loves* Christmas, busy as it is. Every seat is occupied. The counter line snakes around itself and nearly out the door. I toss my bag and tie on my apron, and Luke kisses my cheek as I pass him behind the register.

"Dude, ick! What's up with that?" I say.

"You're here!" He smiles, tossing a bag of sugar cookies to a kid waiting at the door. The closer we get to January, to his new life with LucasArts, the giddier he is.

"Harp!" Dad calls from the kitchen. "How are you?"

"Great!" I answer brightly, The New Plan urging me forward, no room in it for worrying him or Mom. "You're nearly out of croissants."

He gives me a thumbs-up and disappears to the ovens.

I get down to work, taking orders against a backdrop of Johnny Mathis Christmas hits. It is nearly impossible to be in here and not feel wintry happy.

Finally, around nine-thirty, there is a lull. I duck down into the glass pastry case to straighten the rows of sugary dough in all its forms, and the bells ring. I stand.

"Hey!" Owen smiles.

"Hey." I brush flour and red and green sparkle sugar from my hands, tuck stray hair off my face, back into my messy work bun. Why am I either sweaty, distressed, or half naked every single time I run into this guy? "Luke," I call. "Owen's here!"

"Dude!" Luke shouts from the ovens. "Be out in a minute!"

"I will have one bagel," Owen says, stepping to the register.

"We don't make bagels."

"Really?"

"Really."

"Huh. Okay." He examines my neat rows in the case. "Plain croissant?"

I slide the very last one into a paper sleeve. "Three fifty."

He pays with a five, puts his change in the tip jar.

"Thanks."

He smiles and takes the croissant from the bag, pulls off a section, and chews. "Oh, wow . . . ," he mumbles. "That's a lot of butter."

I nod.

He stands there and pulls the whole croissant apart and eats it, one section at a time.

I find a clean rag and go back to the case to wipe the crumbs from beneath the paper liners. Through the glass, I watch Owen brush croissant from his hands, toss the paper sleeve in the recycling bin, pour a glass of lemon water from the pitcher near the door, and down the whole thing.

He even drinks in a casually dashing way. Oh my God, *dashing*? I am not well.

"Okay," he says. "What are you doing today?"

I look up from the case. "Sorry?"

"Today. What are you doing?"

"Uh . . . you're looking at it."

"All day?"

Johnny Mathis is in a marshmallow world, and he's not shy about his love of it. Owen perks up. "You know Johnny Mathis grew up here? Richmond District. Seal Rock."

I did know that. But I'm amazed Owen does, too.

I've been not only sloppily dressed and unshowered, but

also way less than receptive to his attention every time we've talked. So why does he keep trying? And what exactly is he trying at?

Dad steps out from the kitchen.

"Owen!"

"Hi!"

"How are things at Star Wars?"

"Oh, you know . . ." Owen smiles, mostly at me. "Pretty good."

Dad stands there, wiping his hands on his apron.

"Harp."

"What."

"Go home."

"What?"

"Baking's done, and Luke and I can handle the afternoon. Go. What're you up to today, Owen?"

"Not a thing, sir," Owen says.

"Oh, Owen, cripes, call me Dave."

"Not a thing, Dave."

Dad nods. "Owen, want to walk Harp to the bus for me?"

"Absolutely, Dave."

"Uh, *Dave,* I'm on the schedule till three," I say, low.

"Now you're not. You don't sleep anymore. Go take a nap. Or something."

"I'm staying. I need the money."

"Good Lord, Harper," Dad says, pulling some cash from

his wallet. "I am *paying* you to take a day off, okay? Come on." He hugs me, covered in flour and sugar, and now I am, too. "You're bony," he whispers into my hair. "Go eat a burger. Please."

I take off my counter apron and hand it to Luke, who is talking with Owen, and I go in the back to wash my hands and face, run water over my hair, and then give up. I look ridiculous.

"Ready?" Owen says when I come out.

"Sorry?"

"I'll walk you to the bus."

"Oh, that's—no, I'm fine," I say. "Thanks."

He follows me out, calling, "See you, Luke. Bye, Dave!"

The bells ring. Outside, the sun is shining cold. I pull my coat on.

"So. Off to nap?" Owen asks.

"No." I walk away from the park, toward the N-Judah Muni stop.

"Going home?"

"No."

"Mind if I join you?"

"I've got errands."

"What kind?"

I stop walking. Owen does, too.

"Did you ask Kate out and she said no?"

"She asked me."

"Oh."

"I said no."

Thin clouds move swiftly from the ocean, hazy in the bright blue sky. The sea air is clean and cold. Seagulls float above the Jordan almond–colored row houses; blackbirds sit on the telephone wires.

I love this city.

"I have errands," I tell him again. "Really boring ones."

He smiles.

- - -

We get off on Market Street in the Financial District. Owen follows me out of the cold winter sunshine into San Francisco Dancewear, the place nearly every penny I earn ends up.

It's busy. Little girls with their mothers, older girls alone, and chattering groups in the racks and racks of leotards. Tchaikovsky blasts from wall speakers: "Dance of the Sugarplum Fairy."

My chest hurts. I've never been here without Kate. She's not at Saturday breakfast anymore, no more slumber parties.

The staff of willowy, long-haired current and former dancers are up and down ladders and stairs, in and out of the curtained stockroom.

"Harper," my favorite, Mirielle, calls above the chaos. "Where's Kate?"

"Home," I say. "I need shoes."

"Sit and hold on a minute."

Owen tags along to the square of parquet flooring in the center of the room, mirrors on every wall and freestanding barres to stretch and rise with. I sit in a wooden chair. Owen sits beside me, hands on his knees. The music plays, and we watch girls try on slippers and shoes, model leotards, throw tantrums. Owen is the only guy in the store. He smiles. Nervously.

"You okay?"

"Yeah," he says. "It's just . . . do the male dancers have a separate store or something?"

I laugh.

Owen beams.

Mirielle brings a stack of narrow shoe boxes, whips off the lids, and offers them to me one by one, in case I've changed my mind since last month. There are so many brands of pointe shoes—some last longer, some are more flexible, some have stiffer shanks, some are more salmon than pink. But I've found the ones that fit my narrow feet and arch, the kind I can make last nearly a week before they're destroyed and ultimately fail me, and I'll never switch.

"Freed, please," I say. "Three pairs."

Mirielle smiles. "I've got a surprise for you." She pulls from the stack a Freed of Londons box, my Classics, and stamped on the leather sole is a familiar maker's mark.

"Maltese Cross," I whisper. "How many?"

"Just the one," she says, "Let's see."

I move to pull my boots off, but see Owen watching, and I turn to him. "Look away."

"What?"

"Don't look. At my feet."

He frowns. *"Why?"*

"You like this girl?" Mirielle asks him.

That smile. "Yeah," he says. "I do."

"Then trust her," she insists. "Do *not* look."

He rolls his eyes and covers them with his hand. I ease my boot off.

He gasps.

"Owen!"

"I'm sorry!" he yelps. "You can't tell a guy 'Don't look' and then think he's not going to look! A guy is *always* gonna look!"

"Yeah, at, like, boobs or something. This is different! Now you'll never see me the same way. I'm a monster!"

Mirielle laughs. Owen looks completely horrified.

But also impressed.

"Whatever, dude," I sigh. "I was just trying to help you out." I wrap a wad of lamb's wool around my ruined toes and slip my feet in the Maltese Cross shoes. I rise to demi, then full pointe. In the mirror, I catch Owen wincing.

"She doesn't feel a thing," Mirielle assures him. "Nothing but calluses."

He nods, eyes wide.

"Thanks, Mir." I sigh.

"You're welcome. If those are good, I'll grab two more—save the Maltese for San Francisco. Need anything else?"

"Extra ribbon?"

"Yep. Meet me up front."

I pull my socks and boots back on before Owen gets any more time to ogle.

He follows me to the register, where I pay in cash—$328 with tax—for the three pairs, which will last me, if I'm careful, till the beginning of February. Once I'm in the company, maybe San Francisco will be buying all my shoes. I take my bag, and we are on the sidewalk in the chill wind.

"Want to walk?" he says.

He's seen my feet. Might as well.

We walk past the tall buildings of the Financial District, toward the bay, two blocks before he speaks.

"Is there wood in there? In the toe—is that how you balance on it?"

"Flour-and-water plaster," I say. "And satin."

"And why do you like the ones you wear?"

"They fit."

"They all looked the same."

"No. These have a short . . . it's called a vamp, and a wide box, full shank, not too flexible . . ."

"Ohhh, right, the short vamp, I totally missed that. Well, no wonder, then."

Oh my God, this guy is . . . Kate's. Hos before bros. Even if you hate the ho.

I don't hate her, and she's not a ho.

"And what's the Maltese Falcon about?"

"Maltese *Cross*." I almost smile. "There are thirty people in the Freed factory who make the shoes by hand and bake them dry. That's why they're so expensive. They each have their own mark they stamp into the leather when they're done to keep track—my favorite dancer uses these shoes, Freeds, but only the Maltese Cross maker is allowed to build hers. Sometimes you'll find them in the stores. It was lucky I got these. It's a sign. *Feels* like a sign."

He nods. "What are you auditioning for?"

We walk. "Why are you pretending not to be bored by all this?"

"It's not boring. At all."

"Because I will admit, if I had to go to the video game factory, I would never stop complaining."

"The factory probably *would* be boring. But LucasArts is fun."

"Are you aware what you're getting yourself into, living with Luke?"

"Can't be any worse than the other three of us. It's a big house. Lots of space to hide from each other."

"You'll need it." I smile.

We walk. Seagulls cry and we are at the piers, crossing at

the light to the Ferry Building. Students from the Conservatory of Music are playing "In the Bleak Midwinter" on cello, harp, and mandolin, and it is so beautiful that I stop, and Owen stops. The strings echo all around the cavernous marble hall.

Kate won't come over for Christmas Eve. What if her mom is at a party? Will Kate be alone? What about Christmas Day?

I drop my last twenty dollars into the open cello case.

"You okay?" Owen asks.

I wipe my eyes on my sleeve. The sleeve of my ratty old Sunday-at-the-bakery hoodie. My hair, sloppy at the start, is now a total falling-apart mess thanks to the San Francisco wind and two Muni rides.

Owen, on the other hand, I have a feeling came to the bakery for a reason. He is wearing clean jeans. A really nice wool sweater, blue and gray, striking against his warm complexion, his brown-black eyes. Hiking shoes that look like they've never once seen the dirt of a trail.

Kate doesn't even own any ratty clothes. Once they've been worn a few times, she gives them to me or to the West Portal Goodwill.

Kate asked *him*? He said *no* to *Kate*?

"Harper?"

"Yeah."

He offers me his strong, lean arm. I wrap my own around it. He smiles. "Let's walk."

- - -

We sit on a bench on the dock beneath the Bay Bridge. We watch the ferryboats come and go, the sun on our faces. Owen's eating a sandwich from one of the Ferry Building deli counters, and without my asking, he's brought me a huge salad. Dressing on the side.

I wolf it gratefully.

"Who's the Maltese Cross ballerina?"

I chew, swallow. Drink some of the water he's also brought to me. "Yuan Yuan Tan. San Francisco Ballet."

"Sugar Plum Fairy."

"Yes! How do you—"

"Bus ads," he says. "She's on every single Muni shelter near the Presidio. My mom loves her."

"Does *she* dance?"

"My mom? Oh God, no." He laughs. "She just likes that Yuan is Chinese."

"Oh."

We eat.

"She became a ballerina on the flip of a coin," I tell him. "She was a little girl and she loved ballet, but her dad wanted her to be a doctor. Her mom was okay with her dancing. So they flipped a coin."

"Huh. What is *up* with Chinese dads and the doctor pushing?"

I smile. A little.

Ship bells ring. Tourists and bikers get off the Sausalito

Ferry; another group boards. The ferry backs out, chugs toward Alcatraz.

"You and Kate in a fight or something?"

I sigh. "Or something."

"What's the audition for?"

I swing my feet. "San Francisco Ballet. January third."

"Oh, wow, with Yuan! So the shoes really are lucky."

"I hope."

"You auditioning alone?"

I nod.

"Really?"

"Yeah."

"Huh." He tosses our trash into a can, sits back beside me. Moves closer. "I'm sorry," he says. "It sucks. You seem lonely."

I nod.

"You miss her."

"Yes."

"So call her! Say you're sorry and she will, too."

"I'm not sorry."

"Say it anyway."

"I can't."

"Really? So you're fine never seeing your best friend again, ever? I just watched you balance all your weight, which, granted, is not a lot, but still, your entire body held up by one sad, thrashed toe, and it didn't even hurt—but you can't call your best friend and say two words? Just text her, then."

"Okay, Dr. Phil, you don't even . . ." I can't finish my half-assed attempt at pithy. My throat swells, and weeks of missing Kate unleash their misery. So I tell him. Everything. The Plan, Kate, Simone, the failed auditions. The New Plan. All of it. This guy I don't know except that he's best friends with Luke.

And that, in a group of girls all dressed alike, dancing all the same steps around Kate—he saw *me*.

And he listens. Doesn't say anything for a long time. We sit. Knees touching.

"You really wouldn't want to teach?"

"No."

"That Willa kid seems to think you're really good at it."

I nod.

"Free trip to England, at least?"

"No."

He picks my hand up in both of his.

In the midst of this sadness—butterflies.

"You'd never know, with these perfect hands, that your poor feet were so abused." Not exactly holding hands, but he's pressing the warmth of his into the chill of mine.

"You know what?" he says. "Maybe Simone's on glue. And those Oakland people, those auditions—because I know I don't know anything about ballet, but oh my *God*. You are amazing."

I shake my head.

"You know why I wanted to come see you? You understand I came to the show to see *you,* right?"

My heart thumps. *"Why?"*

"My parents are real big on people having a hard-core work ethic. Like, obsessively. Luke would talk about his family, about *you*—everything you do to pay for classes, the teaching and babysitting on top of rehearsing and performing and graduating early with honors—by comparison, my entire family seems super lazy."

"I have a Plan."

"I know. That's what I'm saying. I like that."

A seagull strolls to us, cocks its head, and studies us. Owen smiles at it.

"I have to go home," I say.

"Okay."

He walks beside me to the bus stop. The wind is cold.

"Luke is in love with Kate," I say.

"Is he?"

"Did you ask her before you knew?"

He frowns. "I already told you, she asked me."

"You said no. To Kate."

He stops walking. "Harper. Of course I did." He takes my hand and holds it.

I hold his back, and we walk to the bus shelter. He waits with me.

"No one else knows," I say.

"Knows what?"

"Anything. Any of this. Not my parents, not Luke. They don't know, because I haven't told them, and I've been wanting so badly to tell someone. . . ." My throat's tight again.

He's looking so intently at my eyes, so close. "You told me."

"I've needed . . . Thank you so much. For listening."

"Thank *you*."

The bus is approaching. We step out of the shelter stop to the curb.

The doors open. He lets go of my hand.

"Harper."

"What?"

"Can I call you Harp instead?"

"What?"

"Everyone else does!"

I climb the steps.

"Hey, Harp—call Kate. Text, email, *something*."

"Why?"

"You miss her. And I bet she needs you. I don't blame her; I've spent maybe three cumulative hours with you, and I'm pretty sure I've never known a better person."

I stop on the top step, my hands tingly, and say to the driver, "Hold on just one second. Please."

Owen sees me lean out the door, he moves close to meet

me, and I do not think, I do not tell him the words ricocheting around my head, my thumping heart: *No one has ever said anything so kind to me, ever.*

I hold on to the bus and my pointe shoes with one hand, his shoulder with the other, and kiss him. For one moment he seems stunned, nearly as stunned as me—then his hands move to my hair. He pulls me even closer and kisses me back, takes over, seawater salt on his lips. I'm light-headed, and he keeps kissing me until I pull away, until the *bus* is pulling away.

Dazed and ignoring laughter from the other passengers, I stumble to a window seat. I watch Owen stand on the curb, breathing hard, staring after the retreating bus until I can't see him anymore.

And I do not text Kate. I call her.

- 11 -

Antarctica

I HAVE FEARLESS HAIR, AND IT IS DRAGGING THE REST OF ME, kicking and screaming, into fearlessness. Starting with reading the emails that have been piling up since the day I left home.

I take a breath and begin with Willa's.

>>>Dear Harper,

I am saying this letter and Mom is typing it. I am almost seven, but she says if I type it, you will be home before I get done, so I wish I could type it. Please come home. I'm sorry you were so sad you had to go to Antarctica. Lindsay teaches Saturday and she uses boring music. Also, we are at the barre for almost the whole time! [Note from Hannah: She wanted ten exclamation points. I'm keeping it simple. I love you, Harp.] We never get to turn or jump or anything fun! Mom says if I clean a litter box, we will get a kitten, but I have to show I can do it first, but if I don't have a poop box to clean, then how can I show her? [That's not happening, BTW.] If I do get a kitten,

I want gray stripes and to call it Foggy, or if it is a girl, I will name it Harper. Because for you. I love you. I miss you so much I am typing this part this is me please come home please don't be mad at Madame Simone she loves you too I miss you SO SO SO SO SO much I love you.

Love, Willa Emaline Moore Jr. Esq. MD PhD DDS

[She's been reading the phone book for fun and is fascinated by acronyms lately. Love you and miss you. Call your parents more, okay? XOX Hannah]

I stupidly, wrongly assumed that out of everything in my crowded in-box, Willa's email would have the least chance of breaking me. What was I thinking? When did she become a dentist and a doctor, and what the hell is an esquire? And why is Lindsay not letting them do floor work? They'll lose their center of gravity if she doesn't let them use it—they can stretch on the floor, for Pete's sake—let the kids spin a little!

Gah. This is exactly why I cannot read any more. I close the laptop.

My tenth Sunday on The Ice, and I have become a woman. A banner day, one worth journaling. May 10: *Wore a bra today. Because I had to.*

Cinnamon rolls, butter on my bread, and no ballet have made remarkably rapid changes to my body. There is a softness in my shoulders, my hip bones are not so sharp, and I no longer use a pillow to cushion my knees when I sleep. I'm regretting owning only two bras. I'm in for a lot of hand-washing of delicates in the sink.

I would be losing my mind over the weight were I at home, and not being told by Aiden that these curves are *so beautiful,* spoken low, into the nape of my neck. He sometimes comes over after work to visit—when Vivian's nice enough to be out at the library or the lab.

It took us twenty minutes to move everything Vivian brought to The Ice into my room, where she claimed half the drawer space and sleeps on the second bed, and still we barely speak. Kate and I never had to try; we fell into each other's lives and stayed. I am failing with Vivian. Charlotte's hope of cultivating our lifelong friendship has ended before it began, it seems, though Aiden still holds fast to his own hopes and dreams for the situation; from day one he's asked repeatedly if each night will be "Tickle Fight in Panties Night."

"It's been postponed for hair-braiding and ear-piercing time, but keep asking, perv," Vivian snaps. When she is in the room, she's reading, earbuds firmly in place.

But she's very nice about my vow to keep the Christmas lights lit until the sun returns. So except for when we're together in the dining hall, Aiden and I know each other's faces only in dim, twinkling shadows. I may have cellulite. I can't bear to check, even in the shower. If it's there, good for it. Welcome to my ass, Fat.

Aiden still believes I'm mourning the loss of a horrible boyfriend. "'We would rather be ruined than changed,'" he says, lying beside me (fully clothed, of course) against the threadbare cotton McMurdo pillowcases. "'We would rather die in our dread than climb the cross of the moment and let our illusions die.'"

I smile in the dark against his shoulder. He's sometimes a little Irish-Rover-over-the-top—this from a person who obsesses over poems about San Francisco—but sometimes I wonder if Aiden's Googling poetry specific to my current situation? Does he get points for that, or is it charm in the place of sincerity?

"W. H. Auden," he says.

I nod, as if I knew.

Would I rather be ruined than changed?

I still dream about ballet.

When I swing in the greenhouse hammock, Allison's classical music takes me straight to rehearsal. Shackleton's not been back—maybe I'm getting better? I close my eyes and feel my muscles stretch and lengthen, my feet arch, arms strong, pulling me up and around, pirouette after pirouette, jumps and turns. . . . In the most secret part of my heart, do I think Simone is wrong? Are the directors of every company I auditioned for wrong?

The truth is really, really hard to admit. Hurts still.

I miss San Francisco. I miss the ocean and the bakery and Golden Gate Park. I miss Kate and class and rehearsal. I miss my babies in their leotards and skirts. I miss Simone. I do. I miss Willa. My parents. I miss Luke. I miss my hair sometimes.

I miss Owen.

I open the last of the video audition rejection emails from ballet companies in Oregon, Wyoming, and New Hampshire. The end. I don't delete them. I put them in a folder marked T3.

And there is still the unread actual letter from Owen, hidden at the bottom of my unmentionables drawer. He's unmentionable.

"Aren't you too warm?" Aiden says. "Do you need three T-shirts?"

I'm not giving The Ice *everything*.

Amazingly, Aiden doesn't seem to mind my ironclad limits. Each rebuked attempt to take just one more layer of clothing off me, off himself, let his hands wander the unexplored frozen continent of my new body, only seems to make him like me more.

"Hey. Sunday. Should we go to church?" he asks.

"Should *you*? Are you Catholic?"

"Cafeteria Catholic. My family picks and chooses the parts they like—mainly the celebrating holidays and drinking wine and judging people parts."

"Super."

"Do you have a church?" he asks.

In my mind, beams of foggy sunlight through the windows of Simone's studio make patterns on the wood floor. Every day. Religiously.

"Not anymore" is all I offer.

"You are a mystery, Harper Scott," Aiden says.

"Not really." I kiss him and try hard to forget everything. Everyone. San Francisco. Home—Owen. All of it. For a little while.

- - -

"Winter is for hibernating," Charlotte says, unhooking the top row of her button-fly jeans, "and for storing fat to survive in the cold."

"Not when there's central heat," Vivian says.

We eat rolls and drink hot tea every morning, and most days Charlotte's been adding whole milk to hers. She's getting more intent each day on finding conclusive data to support her thesis about the effects of the pollution on the Adélies. She wants to start writing before midwinter and finish before she's off The Ice in September, so we've been in the lab some weekends and a lot of late nights.

She looks up from her lab table one Friday, leans back, and pulls her head to the side, cracking the vertebrae in her neck.

"That's horrible for you," I scold her.

"How're you feeling?" she asks, reaching for a handful of cheddar Goldfish from the bowl near her notes.

I shrug.

"I haven't said anything about it, because people do things for all kinds of reasons and it's none of my business and it was the least of my worries for you, but I feel like I can tell you now. I *love* your hair."

I fidget with an Erlenmeyer flask. "Honestly?"

"Oh my God, *yes.* Viv, don't you love it?"

Vivian looks up, her own head featuring basically the same cut. "Seems like a lateral move."

"Vivian, good grief," Charlotte says. "We're used to how cute it is on you. This is brand-new for Harper!" She reaches to put her warm hands on my head and looks into my T3 eyes. "Seems better . . . little bit?"

"I think so."

She smiles. "Well, the cut is gorgeous. If I had your eyes, I'd do it in a second."

It *is* a little nuts how big my eyes suddenly became once the hair was gone. But Charlotte is crazy. Her meter is skewed; she herself is objectively gorgeous. She's an Antarctic twenty, mainland ten. Ick, why am I even thinking that? Guys can be such pigs.

"I can't feel your spine or your ribs when I hug you anymore. I like it."

I nod. My phone alarm chimes. Greenhouse.

"That's what's done it!" She smiles. "I told you you'd love it."

"I do," I admit. It's so warm, so clean—I sleep better there than in my bed sometimes. "You should come with. There's always a free hammock. You would love it. Vivian, you too!" Earbuds. Vivian's not going anywhere.

"You go soak it in for all of us." Charlotte hugs me, taking care to squeeze the softness of my arms and put her hands on my less-gaunt cheeks.

"Feels weird," I admit, halfway out the door. "Not sure I like it. The weight."

"Babe, first of all, there's no 'weight'—you could easily use another ten pounds. I swear to God. You're still just this side of bony. Please let it be for a while. See how it feels. Okay? Promise? Look, I'm way ahead of you. I've got my annual Winter Over muffin top, and I'm all, *Welcome, friend!* I'm not saying let's get diabetic fat; I'm saying it's cold out, settle in. Okay? Please?" She massages a soft curve of skin at her waistband. "Well. Maybe not those damn cinnamon rolls every day, but you know. Sometimes."

She takes such good care of us.

I nod and jog to the greenhouse before the tears fall.

The cold is no match for the ache of missing Mom and Dad.

- - -

Allison's got some Celtic pan flute something or other playing for the plants today, and her entire face is shining with a secret.

"Look," she whispers as I lie back in my T3 hammock. "Don't tell anyone." She opens her hand above my open palm and a tiny cherry tomato rolls in a circle.

"Oh my gosh!" It is a testament to my All-in-Antarctica attitude that this wee little fruit gives me a thrill. There's been no salad, no fresh fruit, for weeks. Allison's lettuce is being groomed for the Midwinter Formal, but tomatoes—those are precious. And unexpected.

"Go ahead," she says.

I close my eyes and bite. It's barely ripe but good enough. It floods my entire brain with sweetness. Tastes like the sun. She tucks a blanket around my feet.

"Allison?"

"Yes, sweet pea?"

"Have you been to the pole?"

"A few times, yes."

"A *few times*?"

"For projects, work, sure. Why?"

"What was it like?"

She smiles. "It was beautiful. Life-changing. Freezing cold. Worse than here, if you can believe it."

"Are you going back?"

"Any chance I get. Close your eyes now."

She mists the lettuce with a spray bottle, takes notes on a clipboard, replaces bulbs, fills water containers. Every sound familiar and reassuring and hypnotic.

I give up trying to shut down the dancing my brain launches into the moment I lie back. This music is lending itself to some grand jetés across an endless ice field. No slipperier than coconut snow, probably. Leaps and turns. My legs twitch, and I wish I could think of something—*any*thing—else. My breath is shallow from the stillness of my limbs, it's been so long. . . .

"That was unexpected," Shackleton says. "The hair stunt."

Oh jeez. Back on his dumb pile of snow, feet propped on a jagged block of ice.

"I thought you wouldn't be here anymore," I sigh.

"Why?"

"I feel better. Warmer."

"Oh, really?"

"Yes."

"Do you?"

"I think so."

"Are you dancing?"

I swing the hammock.

He clucks his tongue at me. Just sits there, radiating . . . what? Disappointment? "You most certainly are a Scott."

"What's *that* supposed to mean?"

"Aut moriere percipietis conantur." He crosses his tall fur-lined boots and watches me swing. "Do you know about me?"

I close my eyes and settle in for what promises to be, based on his instructive tone, a great big, long monologue. "Some."

"Okay, look. I'm going to nutshell this for you."

"You're going to . . . Why do you talk like me?"

He shrugs. "I am you. And I think we've established the larger part of your problem is that you lack much of an imagination lately."

"Fine."

"All right. So we brought the ship *Endurance* through the Ross Sea, intending to camp through winter, then make the first transantarctic crossing, but the ice moved in too quickly. We never made it to the continent—the ice crushed her. Our ship."

I nod.

"So we regroup. We live on *Endurance* until she sinks. Then we float on ice floes, hoping to reach solid land. It never happens. When the weather turns, we sail small wooden lifeboats across the open sea to the nearest island."

That sounds horrifying. But saying so might make this go on forever.

"Days being tossed around giant, freezing waves in these tiny wooden boats, but we finally reach Elephant Island, which is just rocks and dirt and penguins. And some seals. First solid land we'd stood on in over a year. Three hundred miles from where *Endurance* went down."

"Did you eat penguins?"

"Yes, ma'am."

"What kind?"

"Chinstrap, mostly."

"Okay." *Thank God.*

"So we rest there a couple of weeks, and then I take five men, my *Endurance* captain and the carpenter, and three of the stronger sailors. And we leave the rest of the crew on the rocks, twenty-two men alone on an island with no shelter beyond two overturned lifeboats. We sail the eight hundred nautical miles to South Georgia Island's whaling station. Fifteen days and storms so bad we have to land on the south end of the island. The whaling station is on the north end, thirty-two miles of mountainous terrain away. I take the captain and the strongest sailors and fifty feet of rope, and we climb icy mountains for thirty-six hours to reach the whaling station."

"Jeez."

He nods. I swing and feel warm, and Shackleton's voice makes me drowsy.

"But this is what I want to tell you; we set off for the whaling station, frozen, seasick, and starving, having not slept for days. I brought these men, I risked their lives, to climb through an entire night and day and night, never stopping."

"That's not possible." I yawn.

"See?" he says. "No imagination. You must will the truth you intend."

"I'm sorry. What?"

He sighs. "Near the summit, the men's heads were dropping forward. They were nearly sleepwalking. So I told them, *Rest now. Sleep.* They lay in the snow, and I told them I would keep watch and wake them in two hours."

"So they *did* sleep."

"Yes."

"And when you woke them, did they plow through to the whaling station?"

"Yes."

"Sleep is everything."

"*Yes.* Except they didn't sleep for two hours. I woke them fifteen minutes after they'd put their heads down. I told them they'd slept for two hours, and they were renewed, determined, and strong."

"You *lied.*"

"You will the truth you need to survive; you make it so."

"Okay . . . wait, what do I . . . so do I lie to myself, convince myself I actually *am* a dancer and then everyone, all the company directors will believe me? Or have I already willed myself into believing I'm a dancer in the first place and I need to wake up from my fifteen-minute nap and face reality?"

"Oh, Harper Scott." He shakes his head.

"Just tell me! Why are you here if you're just going to make me pan for wisdom in the, you know, the river of your parables? I don't get it. I can barely tie my shoes! You have to tell me—please. What am I supposed to do?"

"That was not a parable. That shit really happened!"

"Great."

"If I tell you, you're not learning. You'll just reconcile your confusion to fit the situation you think you're in based on whatever grandiose proclamation I come up with. Like that Irish kid."

"Aiden?"

"I'm getting a little tired of all his poetry recitations. Look out for that one."

"Says the guy running circles around a simple statement that would help me navigate the entire rest of my life! And PS, what are you—Santa Claus? Are you ever not watching?"

"I see what I see."

"Boundaries. That's not right."

"Fine."

"I thought maybe I'd see all three of you."

"Three of who?"

"Scott. Amundsen. *You*. Everyone's unique take on the failure of my life. Past, present, future . . . you know, Dickens?"

He stands and smiles down at me. "You know what, Harper Scott?"

I turn my head to face him. "What?"

"You're close. You're getting near."

"Fantastic."

"And the weight looks great on you. My wife, Emily, was never one to turn down a scone, and her dance card was never in want of a—"

"All right," I groan. "I get it."

"Just sayin'."

I close my eyes. When I open them, there are only the

plants, and the music, and Allison—smiling at all the rest I've gotten.

- - -

Back at the lab, there is a Post-it on my side of the table from Charlotte—she's not feeling great and she'll see us on Monday. Vivian's already gone. I turn out the lights, and in the dining hall, Aiden, smiling, comes through the swinging door to sit beside me while I pry the lid off a little can of mushy fruit cocktail.

"Want to go somewhere?" he says.

"When?"

"Tonight. Outside."

Look out for that one.

I lick syrup from the metal can tab. "You're high. It's forty below."

"Oh, come on!" he laughs. "Aren't you sick of being cooped up?"

The worst part about canned fruit cocktail is the peeled grapes. They'll always be Halloween eyeballs to me. Maybe T3's not our biggest concern—maybe it's scurvy.

"I think I need to sleep," I tell him. "Tomorrow?"

"I will miss you beside me, but I shall forge on tonight."

It's like hanging out with Dylan Thomas.

Oh, really? Shackleton's voice pipes up in my head. *He's mainlining annoying poets again? That's interesting.*

I tap on our door and find Vivian asleep beneath the twinkle lights, earbuds in. Quietly I pull on a sweater and one more pair of long Johns, and open Charlotte's ancient laptop.

I can do this. I am a Scott.

You certainly are. That guy could procrastinate like nobody's business. Look at this mess!

My in-box numbers procreate daily.

Maybe some organizing will minimize the intimidation. I divide and conquer. Folders for everyone.

Mom. Dad. Mom and Dad together. Luke. Kate. Willa. Simone (only two).

Which leaves a long row of Owen. Almost daily, then every other day, then every few, and most recently weekly. But there they are. Most of the subject lines are blank; a few read, *Hello* or *Good Morning.* It is nearly impossible to not open just one, read just a few lines.

Not even close to nearly.

>>>Dear Harper,

Today we spent the afternoon at the Legion of Honor. First Tuesday of the month is free admission day, so cheap date, but that just means more money for food. Which we'll get to in a moment. But first we park near the part of the stone wall that faces the bridge into the courtyard, where the bronze cast of Rodin's *Thinker* sits thinking, and we laugh about why he is thinking naked and he looks like he's on the toilet—but then we stop being jerks and admit it is really amazing and how could a person sculpt something so lifelike from stone?

We go inside, to the paintings. A kid screeches, and that's always nice because someone is taking a little kid to a museum, and that's pretty cool, because some little kids love museums.

I sit back and rub my eyes. What is he talking about? *We* who? And what's with the present tense? Is he rubbing it in that we'd been there together, but it means nothing because he's over me? Not that we were ever "together"—but weren't we? And can I even be mad, because how about the making out I'm doing with the Irish Rover?

Seriously. I really am the worst. I have no idea what I'm doing.

After the Legion, we go for lunch at Park Chow. We sit upstairs under the skylights close to the fireplace and order, not salad, but—wait for it—ricotta lemon curd pancakes with raspberry sauce, which I think I'm only writing about because I'm hungry. But also, it's good date food. Right? We share and we eat the entire thing.

It's okay we eat all that, though, because after we walk through Golden Gate Park, all the way to Ocean Beach, and we sit on the sand and watch kids fly kites and surfers ride the waves and pretend not to see confused naked guys walking around because they think they're on Baker Beach. We stay until the sun sets, and the stars come out.

At the end of our streets is sunset;

At the end of our streets the stars.

It is a perfect day.

"Harper." Vivian's voice in the quiet startles the crap out of me. "What are you doing?"

I rush to close Owen's mail, shut the laptop down, and find I cannot answer her. Because I'm crying too hard.

I sit and cry, for the longest time, before I hear her ask, "Are you sick?"

I shake my head.

"Do you need help?"

"No," I sob. "I'm sorry. I'm sorry to wake you."

She sits up and pulls her earbuds out.

"Vivian," I choke out at last. "Have you always loved science?" I grab a wad of tissue and wipe my nose and eyes. "Was there ever anything else you wanted to do?"

"I don't think so," she says.

"Not *ever*?"

"Well ... I might have thought about being a horse groomer at some point in second grade, but ..."

I laugh for half a second and it turns right into more crying. "I'm sorry," I say. "I didn't mean to wake you up."

"It's okay."

"I'm sorry Charlotte made you move. It's my fault, stupid T3."

She shrugs.

"What do you listen to? In your earbuds?"

"Music."

"What kind?"

She hesitates. "I don't know. All kinds."

"Huh." I get my shower caddy from the closet. "I'll be right back," I say with a sniff.

"Okay."

I brush my teeth, wash my face, and tap on the door again when I return. Vivian's lying back, music in her ears. I climb into the millions-of-kittens bed and stare at the lights.

"Vivian," I whisper.

She sighs. "What?"

"Can I listen to your music?"

She's quiet for a long time. "It's not music."

"It's not?"

"No."

"Can I hear it anyway? Is it that deep-voice guy?"

She sits up. "If I let you listen, will you promise to go to sleep and not ask me anything or talk about it to anyone ever, including and especially me?"

"Yes!"

She sighs again. From her drawer in the dresser, she pulls

out a speaker dock, sets her iPod on it, and crawls far beneath her blankets.

"Vivian?"

"What?"

"Thank you."

She flops back onto her pillow and presses Play.

"Well," the deep voice drones softly into the room, *"it's been a quiet week in Lake Wobegon, Minnesota, my hometown."* And then he launches into a story. About nothing. About some dudes walking down their driveway to the mailbox, and they go have lunch.

What the . . . ?

"Vivian, do you *know* this guy?" I whisper. "Is he sending you . . . what, audio letters? Is this the town you live in?"

She hits Pause and sits up. Even in the dim twinkle light I see the exasperation on her face. "You kept your promise for about ninety seconds."

"Sorry."

"Are you finished?"

"Yes."

"Are you sure?"

"I promise!" She rolls her eyes, but hits Play and lies back down. Sternly.

I wish someone would send me a letter like that. About San Francisco. About people I know doing regular stuff.

Is this what Owen was aiming for?

I close my eyes and think about Dad, up early catching the train to the bakery. Is Mom in class lecturing, running a lab? Is the house lonely and quiet for them? What does Luke do at work? Does he like living with roommates? What is Willa gluing to construction paper these days?

Who is Owen with? Where is Kate?

I wipe tears onto my pillow and concentrate instead on the voice in Minnesota. On these people I do not know and do not miss.

The mailbox guys finish lunch and get on a pontoon boat to go fishing.

I am asleep in half a minute.

- 12 -

San Francisco

THE AUDITION IS A SATURDAY MORNING, THE THIRD DAY OF January, and I leave before Mom wakes up. Dad and Luke are already at the bakery, but in the kitchen there is a jam jar of white sweet peas and a note: *Break a leg! We love you!*

It appears that Owen is an excellent secret keeper. No one, not even Luke, knows anything about anything. I've not seen Owen since before Christmas—since shoe shopping and curb kissing—because I am so tightly wound and focused and trying to concentrate on nothing but this audition, and he is also kindly keeping a promise he made me, not to text or call until it's over. Kate is in New York with Simone, competing in the YAGP Finals, and I am alone.

Owen was also right about calling Kate. It gave us Christmas together and a tearful slumber party, where I stayed silent about my failed auditions—about anything involving Owen— and she filled me in on Simone's urging her, all year, to think beyond San Francisco. What if San Francisco didn't want her?

Why not be seen now, before she's any older, build a career, let a bunch of companies fight over her?

"She got me all panicked," Kate admitted through tears. "She made it seem like if I didn't go, I'd end up in a Grey Gardens situation, living with my mom until I die, and never be a dancer, ever."

"But do you *want* New York? More than San Francisco?"

She fell back, tortured, in the blue chair. "I don't know. But I think I'm curious. Aren't you? Even a little?"

I smiled. Sadly. Shook my head. "San Francisco."

She nodded.

"Did you ask Simone why I couldn't come, too?" I asked her.

Kate looked at her feet. At the wall. "She said your talents lie in teaching. I told her that was crap, that you're a gorgeous dancer, because you *are,* Harp. She said I couldn't see the truth because I love you too much. That it isn't fair to you."

"Do you believe her?" I asked.

"I do love you more than might be healthy for either one of us."

To which I could only say, "Me too."

I wished her luck when she left on New Year's Eve for New York. She wished me luck in San Francisco.

None of it felt real.

This was not The Plan.

Today, *now,* does not feel real. Walking through the

early-morning fog to *our* audition, to the start of our lives together fourteen years in the making—but alone.

The hall outside the audition studio is impassable, legs all over the floor and up the walls, quiet conversations but mostly silence, earbuds in iPods and nervous pliés and relevés beneath framed photographs of soloists from 1933 until today. Yuan Yuan as Juliet, Coppélia. As the Snow Queen.

Through the closed door, we hear the pianist finish barre music, then begin again and again, the same short Shosta-kovich theme over and over, auditors calling combinations, corrections.

I whack my Maltese Cross pointe shoes against a metal doorframe, soften the shanks as much as possible, so they show my arch. I tie them securely. Retie them.

My lucky leotard is clean, black. Thin straps that don't fall off my shoulders, lucky pale pink cotton tights, lucky hair tie, brand-new hairpins. Paper number safety-pinned to my back: *232*. Through the door, the music ends, everyone around me in the hall freezes midstretch, looks up.

Sweaty dancers file out the studio door, spill down the stairs.

"Group eleven. Ladies."

I shake my limbs, rise to demi-pointe.

We take our places at the barre, me and ten other girls, rest our fingers lightly. Why are they all so much taller? Per-fect? *Are* they? I close my eyes. Head up, eyes forward, spine

straight, energy directed into the floor. Don't fight gravity—
use it. . . . Core strong, in, shoulders back, down. First position.
Tendu.

The music swells. My heart swells.

Tchaikovsky.

I couldn't love anything more.

Aut moriere percipietis conantur.

Do or do not. There is no try.

- - -

Up narrow stairs, out the heavy stage door to the sidewalk,
hands on my knees to catch my breath. Audition over. I stand
tall.

Head rush. I sit down hard on the curb.

"Harper."

Owen helps me to my feet.

- - -

"I drove," he says. "Want to go to the park? The beach?"

I nod.

"All right." He opens the passenger door of a car, some
kind of hybrid Subaru-type thing—*Oh, great, he's an environmen-
talist too? Can he be any more wonderful? God!*—and he gets us out
of downtown and into the avenues. I lean my head against the
window.

"Cold?" he asks. I'm only in my lucky tights and lucky leotard, boots, paper number still pinned to my back. It crinkles
against the seat. He cranks up the heater, warm air on my legs.

Through Golden Gate Park to Ocean Beach, along the shore past Seal Rock, and we park on a hilltop beside a low stone wall on the cliff edge, beside the fountain at the sculpted white Legion of Honor museum.

We sit on the wall, with the Golden Gate Bridge view, so near we hear its muted Saturday traffic. Cold ocean wind sweeps fog around our faces, and Owen wordlessly drapes his hoodie over my shoulders. I zip it up, still warm from his body. Smells clean. Like his sweater the day we kissed. Soap, and . . . something sweet?

"Do you wash your clothes in grapefruit extract?" I ask.

"Yes!" he laughs. "I mean, not extract. It's just, like, grapefruit-scented or something? Trader Joe's, Whole Foods, one of those."

I hold the sleeves, way too long on me, over my face and inhale. "I like it. Smells like you."

"I'll buy a fifty-gallon drum of it tonight."

"Good." I lean into him, and he pulls me close with one arm.

Below us, the actual Golden Gate—the narrow, treacherous ocean opening leading into San Francisco's bays—crashes against black rocks.

Ship horns sound from the horizon. The fog thins and rolls so the rocky Farallon Islands are sometimes visible, a tiny black patch where the sea meets the sky, where the great white sharks feed.

"Why anyone wants to live anywhere else in the world is beyond me," Owen says.

Only later will I think how humiliating it would have been had he moved away instead of pulling me nearer when, those words barely out of his mouth, I turn, suddenly thankful for all the stupid make-out scenes in all the dumb ballet movies, because how else would I know how to even attempt this, and I kiss him. Again. I mean *kiss him,* kiss him.

If he is surprised, he gets over it fast. He pulls me closer, both arms firmly around me now.

After a long while, I hold on to his hand and pull away. He steadies me on the wall and won't let me turn my gaze.

"Do you want to talk about it? How it went?"

I nod. But I can't speak.

Seagulls tilt into the sea salt air, through Point Bonita Lighthouse's bright white light flashing through the drifting mist.

"Would you rather I ask yes-or-no questions and you can let me know that way?" he asks.

I nod.

"Okay," he says. "Ready?"

I squeeze his hand.

"Was it . . . I mean, was it hard?"

I nod.

"Are you glad you went?"

I nod.

He takes a deep breath. "Will you be okay?"

I shake my head.

"Oh, Harp . . . ," he says quietly. "I'm so sorry. I don't know what to say."

I breathe deeply, in and out, the salt air. "I think I may start crying in a second, but I don't want every single time I'm with you to be me crying. It's getting ridiculous. I feel stupid."

He pulls me to him again, holds me tight, keeps me warm. "You have no idea," he says, "how *not* stupid you are."

My heart breaks for the years I've spent preparing for this one day, this single moment. For the life I'll never have.

Number 232, you are excused from the barre.

An entire life—my whole existence—for nothing.

At last I am so tired, it subsides. The grief. I am empty.

And still Owen holds me.

"I think," he says, after a long while, "the best parts of San Francisco weren't born till *after* the earthquake. The bridge. West Portal. The entire city was in ashes, and it rose again more beautiful than before. This place is a phoenix. San Francisco is in your blood."

He is trying so hard. Even if such a thing, another life, were possible—how would I live it, still mourning the one I've lost? This is . . . an end. It is panic. I'm drowning.

Lost city of my love and desire.

When the sun is low and the water under the bridge is pink, I ask Owen what time it is.

"Um . . . five. Fifteen."

"Take me home?"

"Of course."

Once more through the park, and we drive beside the beach, past the college, and into West Portal.

The fog is swirling down the street, around our house and Owen's car. I reach behind the seat, grab my bag, and the paper audition number crinkles. I turn my back to Owen. "Can you . . ."

He carefully unhooks each safety pin, his warm hands against the bare skin between my shoulder blades. He drops the pins in the center console thingy and holds the number out to me. "Want to keep it?"

I shake my head. "Thank you," I say. "Thank you."

"Harper. Please call me. Just to let me know you're okay? If you don't, I'll call you."

Even in the near dark I can't help staring at his eyes. "Why?" I ask.

"Because—what do you mean, why?"

"Why do you want me to call you? So I can cry on you some more? I'm a complete disaster."

"You're extraordinary."

"You don't know me."

"I'm trying to."

I smile sadly. "I can't believe I'm meeting you now. This is awful."

"I can't believe I met you at all. This is wonderful. Call me. Please."

"I will."

"Promise me."

I move to get out of the car, but once more, his hand lightly on the back of my neck, he kisses me.

"Okay," I say. "I promise."

- - -

I walk slowly up the drive to the house, all the days and weeks leading to today unraveling again and again.

This shouldn't come as a surprise, Harper.

But it did. It is.

My head hurts. Too much foggy sun. Not enough water.

Number 232, you are excused from barre.

I let myself in quietly through the kitchen door and drop my bag on the table. The familiar, hollow clunk of my pointe shoes turns my stomach. There is television light in the living room; Mom is on the sofa, wrapped in blankets. She turns around to me and pauses her movie.

"Baby!" she says quietly, climbing off the sofa to squeeze me tight. "How was it? Dad told me to leave you alone about it, so I was good all day, not one text. Aren't you proud of me? Tell me now. It's killing me!"

I go to the freezer, move things aside, find the foil package, and unwrap my sand castle cake.

"Harp."

I get a fork, sit at the table, and hack into the chocolate. I put a huge, frozen forkful into my mouth and chew.

Mom stands and watches me wolf the entire thing, and then my stomach swims. I hold on to her and stumble to the door, but too late. The barely swallowed cake is all over the immaculate kitchen floor.

"I'm sorry, I'm sorry, I didn't mean to, I'm so sorry. . . ."

"Breathe," Mom says. She leads me to the sink and I rinse my mouth with cool water, rest my cheek against the faucet.

Yet another benefit of the ballet bun: no one has to hold your hair back when you throw up.

I press my hands against the sink edge and turn to look under my arm. She's anxious. Already mopping.

"Mom, I'll do it. I'm sorry . . ."

"Stop! Just hold on for a minute. Drink some more if you can." She bleaches the floor, done in ten minutes, and I'm on the sofa, head back, my face beneath a cold, damp kitchen towel. She sits beside me and offers ice tinkling in a glass of ginger ale. Too sweet. She frowns and presses her wrist against my forehead.

"You're pink. But not too warm."

I shake my head. "Sunburn."

"How?"

I shrug. Outside all day with no hat. Doesn't matter now.

"Where's your coat?"

I shake my head.

"Harp."

Stage five: acceptance.

"Mommy."

I spill it all, weeks' worth of a mess worse than what wound up on the kitchen floor.

Mom's face is blank. Then baffled. "Simone would never say that."

"She did. She's right."

"She's not. Where is Kate now?"

"New York. With Simone."

"No."

I nod.

Mom tears up. "Why didn't you say anything?"

My throat is tight.

"Dad and I will talk to Simone. This doesn't make sense."

"Please no, don't. There's nothing to say."

"There's everything to say. This is bullshit! She should have spoken to Dad and me before she went to you. What the hell is her problem?"

"There's nothing to say," I tell her again. "Honestly. She didn't want to say it. She had to. It's true."

"Honey, no."

"Mom, I didn't even make it past barre. They don't want me. No one does. It's true."

"It isn't. Stop saying that."

I blink through stinging tears. "I'm scared," I whisper.

"Of what?"

"Everything. What have I done?"

I lay my head in her lap. She pulls the pins from my bun. Carefully, one by one, because they're in so tight. She pulls my ponytail loose, unwinds the elastic, pulls off the hairnet. She massages my head and combs her fingers through the long, straight strands, and I soak her pajamas with my tears. I can't breathe; I can't stop crying. Until finally I do. She rubs my head, and after a long while, I stop choke-breathing and just breathe. I close my swollen eyes.

"I knew practically from birth," Mom says, "that I would be a mermaid when I grew up. I had to face facts, but marine biology is at least in the mermaid ballpark. Grandma could barely yank me out of the tide pools. So when I met Dad at State, I thought, *Oh my God, my soul mate!* Because he knew he was, too. He was obsessed with whale migration."

"Who was?" I ask.

"Dad."

"My dad?"

"Your father."

"He was not."

"He was. He wanted to work at the Monterey Bay Aquarium, and his apartment was wallpapered with posters of sea stars and elephant seals and every known species of whale. I mean, he . . . Oh, I was smitten."

I cannot imagine Dad obsessed with anything not involving dough and an oven.

"Don't make stuff up."

"I'm not. But our sophomore year, of course, I got knocked up with your brother. Grandma and Grandpa let Dad move in with us. We lived in my bedroom . . . and he took extended leave from school to work so I could finish. He had to find a night job so I could be at school during the day once Luke was born. That meant janitorial work, or baking."

"What are you even talking about?"

"I wish you could have known him then. I'm telling you—the ocean was his life. It was. But after, like, two weeks at the bakery, he had forgotten about whales."

"Mom."

"What?"

"You don't need to make stuff up."

"I'm not! This is the absolute God's honest.

"I don't believe you."

"Ask him! Wake him up right now! I'm just saying, you know . . . you never know. You just don't."

"I do."

"We'll figure it out."

"No. It's not the same. I'm not anything anymore. I'm nothing."

She pulls my head to her shoulder, finds the remote, and turns her documentary back on.

A calm, meditative guy is talking about ice worms. In Antarctica. The soundtrack of my toddler and elementary-school years.

The continent is plunged into six months of darkness, silence, and temperatures consistently near a hundred degrees Fahrenheit below zero.

Mom is putting the Antarctic marine life unit she was teaching when I was little back in rotation. The documentaries we watched again and again when I refused to sleep, the stories of our Scott, Shackleton, and Amundsen racing to the South Pole that lulled me finally to dream night after night of their ships moored in ice, studying penguins, eating their dogs.

As I am in Mom's arms, curled on her lap, my heart unclenches. I sit up. She makes room for me beside her, covers me with her blanket, and we watch the rest of this film and then one more. And another.

Aut moriere percipietis conantur.

The answer comes as abruptly as the end of the only life I've ever known. And the answer is a relief.

I need time to stop. I need to take a breath and be still and think, just let me think and figure out what is going on. Let me navigate this sea change. I need to be alone in the dark and quiet. I need to be frozen.

- - -

I don't go to ballet Monday. Monday is the Golden Gate Bridge's eighty-second birthday, my seventeenth. This magical January 5, which, I have learned from the books about Scott I've borrowed from Mom, is also the date in 1922 when Ernest Shackleton died. Who tried, and failed, to reach the South Pole first. Or at all. But while he and his crew waited for the ice to swallow the *Endurance,* he got some major thinking done. And figured some shit out.

Mom has filled Dad in on my "situation." Luke, too, I suspect, because everyone's being extra super nice to me, and to be honest, they're all generally really nice already, so it's pretty obvious and kind of suffocating even though I appreciate that they want to help and that they feel bad—so I plan an escape.

"On your birthday? Let me call her. This is ridiculous!" Mom says.

"No, please," I beg. "I'll be back soon. She just needs me for a couple of hours. Last-minute. I want to help her."

Mom gives in and lets me go to Hannah's, who does not need me to babysit. And who will be surprised to see me, but desperation calls. I promise Mom I'll be back in time for my birthday dinner, and I race to Hannah's and knock. Willa is thrilled.

"Are you staying? Are you going to ballet today? Can I come with you?" she yelps, jumping and yipping around my legs.

- 235 -

We bribe her with television and a Popsicle, and I get Hannah alone to ask, "Who do you know in Antarctica. At McMurdo. Right now?"

She blinks.

"Honey," she says, her hands on my gaunt cheeks. "How are you? You feeling any better?"

The whole world knows. Thanks, Mom.

"No," I sigh. "I'm not. I need help."

"Of course. Anything. What can I do?"

"Antarctica. Who do you know?"

"What do you mean? Like, people? Working there?"

"Yes."

She frowns. "I don't understand."

I heft my backpack to the kitchen counter and pull out Mom's NSF books, the books I've borrowed from the library, and piles of printed Wiki pages. "What do you know about the NSF Senior Winter Over Grant? Do you know anyone who can get me in?"

Hannah sits at the table. "Harp," she says, "you can't go to Antarctica. You don't just hop on a plane—that senior program only offers two spots and they've been filled for months. Plus, it's for students going into college for science and research majors, and the thing is, Winter Over is . . . harsh. It's *intense*. I know you've had a horrible time lately, but I'm pretty sure Antarctica's not your answer. Have your parents talked to Simone?"

I'm about to cry. Again. I feel it in my chest, crawling up to squeeze my throat, and I fight it back, like I've fought the nausea that keeps creeping in when I think about Kate, and Simone, and the studio I miss so much it physically aches, about the kids I'm ditching, who now must have class with impatient, scary Simone.

"There's nothing to talk about," I say for the millionth time, straining not to break, "and it would be incredibly humiliating to have my parents go talk to her about . . . what? Tell her to make my genetics different? Tell her to change my anatomy and toss me in a time machine so I can go back and relearn everything from the past fourteen years except this time do it the correct way with the right body? Hannah, I need help. Please."

She sighs. "Harp, people totally overqualified for the jobs there apply year after year and never get hired. It's a thing; it's on people's stupid bucket lists."

"I know."

She looks me up and down. My hair in a sloppy ponytail, unwashed for days, skanky old hair gel residue still left from my San Francisco audition bun. The deep shadows and creases beneath my tired eyes, matching the never-thinner rest of me. I can't eat. My stomach burns. I can't sleep.

"All right," she says. "There may be someone—I don't know for sure, but—"

"Who?"

"I'm not promising anything. Okay?"

"But you'll talk to him?"

"Her. I'll try. I'll push the 'Scott' thing, see if that works."

I throw my arms around her, nearly knocking her off her chair. "Thank you," I whisper. "Thank you so much."

"I'm *not* promising."

"For trying. Thank you for even trying."

"Your mom will hate me forever."

"She loves you. She's never hated anyone, ever. I'd figure out a way with or without you. This isn't your fault."

She shakes her head. Encircles my wrist with her thumb and pinkie. "I'll tell you one thing right now: Winter Over requirements are unforgiving. No matter who you are or who I know or who *they* know, no one is setting foot on that ice in poor health. Physical *or* mental. Gets *Shining*-esque down there pretty quick. Isolation. Freezing. The *darkness*."

"Sounds like heaven." I hug her hard. "Thank you."

- 13 -

Antarctica

THERE COMES A SPECIAL TIME IN A YOUNG LADY'S LIFE WHEN, constant darkness messing the hell out of her circadian rhythms, she stumbles at five in the morning straight from the shower, wearing jeans, a faded T-shirt, and no makeup, all T3-screwy and blinking in the fluorescent lights of an Antarctic science station dining hall to find an Irish guy in an ill-fitting tuxedo kneeling before the oatmeal pot, offering her a bouquet of dusty silk flowers, and his hand.

The other kitchen guys are crowding around near the ovens to watch.

"Harper Scott." Aiden's voice reverberates around the hall, leaning heavily on his already distinct Irish accent for effect. "Most prized maiden in all the village, would you do me the honor of allowing me to escort you to the festivities this midwinter eve?"

I nearly drop the three paper cups of hot tea I'm juggling.

Scientists and mechanics and every random person getting

breakfast at this ungodly hour stop to watch and whisper. Every single pair of eyes, Aiden's included, is on me and waiting for what I'll say.

Through a frozen smile, I whisper, "What festivities are we talking about?"

"The dance!" Aiden whispers back. "Midwinter Formal. You know this, come on!"

"When?"

"Harper! *Tonight!*"

My entire life spent dancing, and I've never been to a *dance*. No one has ever asked me, but I couldn't have gone if I wanted to, always rehearsal or performance.

I turn to look at everyone watching, smiling expectantly at this ridiculous situation—it's laundry day, and I'm wearing my dumbest work clothes while the good ones are in line for the washer. This sucks *so much*.

But look at him—all dark hair and green eyes and smiling. . . .

"Where did you find a *tuxedo*?" I ask. "Did you bring that with you on the plane?"

"Hey!" a familiar voice calls from the assembled audience. "We've got places to be. Get on with it!"

And then someone else yells, "Shut *up,* Ben!"

Oh, good. Beard.

Aiden smiles hopefully up at me. "The floor is killing my knee, Scott," he says. "Help me out here. . . ."

"Okay, jeez, give me a second. . . ." I can't tell if I'm mortified or flattered. But I set the hot cups on the nearest table and do my best to announce, loud, "Uh, kind sir, I . . . shall . . ."

"You can just say yes," he whispers. "That'll do just as well."

"Oh, okay—*Yes!* Let us prithee . . ."

"Take the flowers!"

I do, and he stands and raises one arm triumphantly, using the other to pull me into a close embrace while the crowd cheers. "You're the loveliest, most awkward girl I've ever met in my life," he says. "I think I need to marry you."

Again, the rush of *Is this humiliating, or am I swooning?* It's a joke—he's tossed it off lightly—but his arm around me, his focused attention on me, he's so . . .

Charming, Shackleton sighs in my mind. *Charm and sincerity— do not confuse the two.*

Okay, but this is the first time a boy has asked me, ever, to go somewhere with him—

Not true. Owen did. He did, and we spent a whole day together. He asked me. Just not like this.

I slip from Aiden's embrace as the crowd rushes in to congratulate him, shake his hand, and I gather the tea cups and cinnamon rolls for Charlotte and Vivian. At the door I catch Aiden's eye and wave. "Eight o'clock," he calls above the din. "Be ready!"

- - -

In the lab, Charlotte is half asleep, forehead on her arms, beside the lab table sink. Vivian's sitting there, watching her.

"Hey," Charlotte says, pulling her head up. "Is it just me, or is your sleep all screwed up?"

"I'm going to the dance," I blurt, still standing in the doorway with tea cups and cinnamon rolls clutched in my arms. "Aiden asked me to go, and I said yes and so we're going. Together. To the dance." I sound like I'm twelve.

Vivian takes the bag and a cup from my hand. "This is lukewarm," she sighs, and fires up a Bunsen burner.

"Harp, really?" Charlotte says, brightening. "Hooray! I've already got a roped-off nonbooze section set up for you three!"

"What three?" Vivian says. "I'll be in bed, asleep."

"Vivian, you're going. Don't be ridiculous." Charlotte sighs. "Harp, when did he ask you?"

"Just now! Right now, in the dining hall!"

"Oh . . ." Charlotte smiles dreamily. "That's so romantic!"

"Is that what you were wearing?" Vivian says.

"I know," I groan, finally surrendering the tea and slumping on a lab stool. "And in front of about a million people. Beard was there. It was . . ."

"Humiliating?" Vivian chirps, and pops her earbuds in for the day.

"*Romantic,*" Charlotte repeats, shooting Vivian a look. "You look beautiful just like every day. He's lucky to have you for his date."

Date. I think of Owen, of sitting beside him at the ocean, and my stomach burns. All the kissing and making out I've been up to with Aiden, but it's *date* that plummets me into guilt—what is *wrong* with me?

"Do we have to be roped off? Can't I just sit near you?" I whine, already freaking out.

"Oh God, I'm not going," Charlotte says, tearing into the center of a roll.

"You have to! You said we have to!"

"Babe, I'm sorry," she says. "I'm exhausted."

"So am I!"

"Yeah, but I'm . . . I can't fit into any of my clothes other than sweatpants, I'm cranky and preoccupied . . . I can't do it. I'm going to wash my hair and crawl into bed."

"Wash your *hair*? Like that's an all-night event?"

"It is!" she cries piteously, and drops into her recliner. "I'm black and so is my hair, it's a whole big production!"

"I cannot believe you," I say. "What am I supposed to do at this thing?"

"You're supposed to hang out with your date!"

"And what the—what am I supposed to *wear*?"

"We'll find something you can wear. Get a hold of yourself. Did you freak out like this before your school dances, too?"

I shake my head.

"Well, it's no different from those, just—fewer teenagers

and no one's spiking the punch, because they'll be drunk already. We'll go to costume storage at lunch and find something that fits you."

"Costume storage?"

"For when people do plays," Charlotte says. "The maintenance crew put on a horrible production of *Pippin* last year, but the costumes were pretty great, so don't worry."

The tuxedo.

"*Pippin*? What am I going to wear, circus pants?"

"What are circus pants?"

"I don't know! But I don't think this is a good idea. At all."

"Harp," she says, "calm down. Go. Have fun. For me?" She glances over at Vivian. "And work on her, will you? See if you can get her to at least go to the dinner part?"

"There's a *dinner*, too?" My head drops to the lab table.

- - -

"Maidin mhaith, Antarctica! Aiden Pot-o-Gold-Riverdance-Soda-Bread Kelly with you on June twentieth, this glorious midwinter eve! From this day forward, we're nearer every moment to seeing our dear old sun rise above the Transantarctic Mountains, but until then, here's hoping you're all preemptively hydrating and got your fancy pants pressed for an evening of drunken abandon, fine cuisine, disco dancing, and the treasured Midwinter Plunge. I'm off to pick up my own lovely lady for the festivities, so I'll see you all. Welcome to midwinter!"

Aiden's coming to get me at eight. Which gives me two hours to persuade Vivian to put on a dress and join us—or to nap.

Or I can just sit in front of this computer while *Vivian* naps and dare myself not to open any more Owen mail.

I've gotten off my ass and read and answered all of Mom's, and Dad's, and Mom and Dad's. Which were nearly all variations on the theme of: How much they love me. And miss me. And hope I am okay. They do not bring up ballet. Or Simone. They do not ask if I am dancing, and it makes me love them more. And so every week I try to be an adult about it, and I write them to tell them, truthfully, how much I love them back. And miss them, too. And that I hope they are okay, and then untruthfully I say I am okay, and then I talk about working with Charlotte and how super fun my co–grant student Vivian is.

I resist Owen by opening the most recent of Luke's.

>>>Harp,

Mom says you're getting all this mail but that if you don't answer it's not a thing. You're just there to do stuff like not answer mail. And I've got a whole long list of things I'm not supposed to write about. Which I'm sure is obvious. But maybe not.

You seriously can't call? Because this feels like when a person's in a coma and you have to sit there and talk to them like they're awake so they know they're alive. Makes me kind of worry you're not okay. But maybe you are. I hope you are.

Also they say telling you about my stuff is good, so here's

some stuff: LucasArts is AMAZING. I'm in a cube with three other guys, I'm finding a crap ton of bugs in every level of this game I'm testing. Last week I surpassed the previous record for number of legit bugs found. They got me a cake with a Stormtrooper on it. From Dad, haha! For a second, I was like, "Noooo . . . worlds colliding!" But it was good, so I ate some and just went back to work, like a BALLER.

The cafeteria—I shouldn't call it that. It's like a restaurant with the best view of the Golden Gate and this huge salad bar and a fajita thing, and everyone says George always comes for burrito Friday. I haven't seen him yet. But you should come. I can bring guests in for lunch.

Okay. This may be the worst thing or maybe you won't care, but Kate says she's written you, and of course we all told her you don't write us back, either, but did you see her email? You should maybe Google her because I can't keep the shit straight, like positions and principal and soloist or whatever. But anyway. Are you sure we can't talk on the phone? Because she's back. It's been maybe a month? She said she loved New York, but someone from San Francisco Ballet went to a performance she was in in New York, and I guess they lured her back home with a better contract. Or something. For real, Google her and it's all this stuff about how she broke her NYC contract to come to the SF Ballet, and how awful and irresponsible she is. Which I think is stupid. But anyway, she's over at our Presidio place a lot. Which, in case you were wondering, is still also AWESOME. We call it the Cockpit. (Because of some Shakespeare theater, Owen says. Don't be gross. But yeah, it's all just dudes, so . . . pretty hilaire.) But anyway, she and Owen talk all the time and go out to lunch sometimes, so I'm sure he's getting filled in on the whole sitch.

Anyway, I didn't know if you knew, and if you did, that's good because that means you're reading her letters, and if not, then I'm really sorry. I don't know what to say except that. Sorry. It's so messed up. But I know the main reason she said she's back was to be near you. When you come home. Which I hope you do, soon.

Luke. (I am your brother.)

I am colder than I've been since I got here. My hands are ice, my scalp is tingling, my stomach is frozen.

The San Francisco Ballet. Without me. Hanging out at the Star Wars house, Cockpit, whatever. *Going out to lunch with Owen?* She's a professional ballerina; is she even allowed to *have* lunch?

That was *their* date. The Legion of Honor and pancakes at Park Chow and the beach. But *why?* He said *no* to her. He stayed with *me* all day. . . .

Says the girl about to go on a date herself. With Aiden.

Hanging on the door are two dresses that Charlotte and I scavenged from the costume closet. One is blue satin; the other is sparkly and slinky and strappy, slip-like and practically nonexistent. Like something Kate probably wears on her San Francisco lunch dates. Her museum-and-pancakes dates. With Owen.

I take a shower, a long one. Fifteen minutes, most of which is spent standing, still staring at the drain while water runs into my open mouth. I knock on Charlotte's door and push it open. It is sleepy warm in there, and dark.

"Sorry!" I whisper. "Got any makeup?"

"Yay, midwinter fanciness!" she cheers hoarsely, directing me to a small bag on her dresser top. "You *are* going to have fun! Good for you!" She yawns.

My short hair is finally starting to grow in just a little, enough for a barrette to hold on to some swept across my forehead. Back in our room I let Vivian sleep and use some charcoal pencil from Charlotte's bag to give myself a stage-worthy smoky eye. My lips are glossed, legs shaved; this dress fits perfectly.

I have no shoes for a dress. Rather than bother Charlotte again, I just pull on my snow boots.

Aiden knocks to fetch me, and I open the door to his smiling face and a sweater the color of his eyes, which widen as he takes me in.

"What?"

His green eyes move from the sparkly Kate-and-Owen-date slip dress, to my new body in it, to my feet. "You gonna wear those boots?"

"Yes."

"You still want to go to the party?"

I laugh. *"Yes."*

"Because we could just stay here. In your room."

"Um, no, you cannot," Vivian's sleepy voice comes from her bed.

"Sorry, Viv!" I whisper, grab my key, and follow Aiden out the door.

- - -

Antarctica is a free-for-all. The dining hall is draped with flags of every nation claiming some part of this continent, reminiscent of the photograph in our dining room at home of Scott's last midwinter dinner, Union Jacks and silk sled flags sewn by the crew's wives and mothers hanging above the beautifully laid table. The last celebration of their lives. It is all very elegant and formal. Except Charlotte's carefully taped UNDERAGE ONLY table has been trampled already. I feel like a grown-up because (long story long) not only am I wearing a bra with regularity, I also have now tasted alcohol. Vodka, I think—or whatever is in a cosmo, a drink I have chosen simply because (depending on whom you talk to) it was invented in San Francisco. It is a deceptively delicate shade of translucent pink, but it's a legit drink that provides legit results, especially in a small person who has never had even a sip before.

Being a ballerina is sort of like being a monk.

I wish I could enjoy this. My first dance, first actual date.

A planet away but foremost in my thoughts, Kate is in San

Francisco. Kate is a member of the San Francisco Ballet. Kate is with Owen.

I ask Aiden to bring me another drink. He's more than happy to.

He maneuvers through the crowd and finds us a place to sit, never taking his hand off the small of my bare back. Were Charlotte in her right mind, not so exhausted and overworked, I'm pretty sure she would not have chosen this dress for me.

Dinner is an amazing, fancy buffet, and I eat some rice and start feeling a little better—at least not as tense and very warm and sort of buzzy—especially when I am three drinks in, and people start leaving in small groups. There is laughter and straight-up shouting, and the formal crowd is half gone.

"What's this?" I slur, "Where are they going?"

"How're you doin' there, teetotaler?" he yells above the Diana Ross album the Midwinter party-planning committee decided to favor us with.

I am very fine so far, and I tell him so and ask again why everyone's leaving.

"You want to see?" he asks.

We run to get into our parkas. But not before he catches me in the dark doorway of the dorm room, pushes me against the wall, and kisses me. Hard. Which makes me want to ditch the parkas and stay here, but thank God Vivian's sleeping because I am not in a state to make decisions like this. Drunk and reeling. *Kate is home, she's a company member of the San Francisco Ballet, and she is with Owen.* So instead I pull him along to go outside in thirty-degrees-below-zero air down the main road and out just a bit into the vast darkness, until we see floodlights set up on the dark ice around a group of clearly insane people.

They've taken a chain saw to a thin patch of ice near a crevasse, exposing a large rectangle of the ice-cold Ross Sea.

People are jumping into it. In their underwear.

There's some kind of warming pool nearby, and the moment they submerge themselves in the freezing ocean, they practically fly back out and straight into this makeshift black plastic hot pool, where they yowl from the instant temperature change, then lean back and revel in the experience.

"The water's warm," Aiden tells me, low beneath the screaming of jumpers. "It's what, thirty-five below out now? The water's around one or two degrees. So it's a huge temperature swing once you've disrobed and you're in and out. Hot tub's supposed to be nice, though."

"Uh-huh."

If I wait one more second, it won't happen.

My parka is off, boots and sweaters, and finally I hand Aiden the sparkly dress. He accepts it without comment, and I'm running on the ice in a black bra and underwear. Years of existing in various states of undress for quick changes in front of stage crew have rendered me unfazed about being half naked around fully clothed people, but even if I were— fazed—I might not be in this moment.

The soles of my feet are on fire, bare on the ice.

People are cheering for me. A guy hooks a wide belt around my waist, attached to a rope on a pulley. I am the only woman out here. Probably because the others have the common sense not to be, and they aren't underage drunk and missing ballet, and *Kate joining the San Francisco Ballet without me and having lunch with Owen—seriously,* is *that a euphemism?*

I drop in. The water is a meter deep, I slide beneath the surface—*Oh God oh God burning burning burning cold*—and I am out and running to the hot tub and in it. Aiden's still standing on the ice where I left him in the dark, clutching my huge parka and all my clothes.

"Come in!" I shout to him.

He smiles. "Divers only!"

I climb out, accept a towel some nice stranger hands me, and race again across the painful frozen snow to the door of our building, followed closely by Aiden who drops my clothes and wraps my parka around my icy, basically bikini-clad form.

Beard stares. Huh. I had not noticed him when we ran past.

"Let's get you warmed up, Drunky." Aiden smiles, then picks me and my clothes up, a fireman rescuing a frozen hammered lady, and carries me up the stairs toward my room.

"Oh, wait, stop, first I have to pee so badly," I whisper, *loud,* above the Bee Gees blasting from the party downstairs as we pass the restroom door. He sets me on my feet and wraps the cold towel around me. His hand lingers at my waist, I turn my face to his, and we stand in the hallway, kissing.

"Hey," he says, and pulls me back to whisper, "want to let Vivian have some time and stay with me tonight? You know, in case you get hypothermia. Or something."

Kate will be a soloist. She will be Gisele. She will dance with Yuan Yuan Tan.

I can never go home.

"Yes," I whisper back. "Please."

I duck in the bathroom, dive into the first stall, and it's like I've never peed in my life; every glass of water and tea I've consumed since birth has been waiting for this moment. My head is so floaty. Did I really just tell Aiden I would spend the night with him? What the hell is happening?

The tiled walls echo someone being sick in the stall two over from mine. There're only a handful of women in this building, I've met them all but only in passing, so I'm not sure what to say besides, "Um. Hello? Are you okay?"

More being sick. Booze. Stupid party. So far I feel fine, but what if my body hates vodka and I get sick, too, and have a hangover? I never should have done this—

"Harp?"

I'm out of my stall, standing outside the one Charlotte's in. "What is it? Do you need the doctor? I thought you weren't going to the party. Are you drunk? Oooh, what did you wear? I think I got your dress wet. . . ."

"Harper."

Her voice—the tone—is sobering me up pretty quickly.

"Charlotte. Unlock the door." But she doesn't even have to. I push it open with my shoulder.

She's sitting, exhausted, on the gross tile floor beside the toilet. In her pajamas.

She leans her head against the toilet tank.

"Oh, Char, are you drunk? Don't get drunk in your room alone! Call me next time because do not tell my parents, but I'm drunk, too!"

"Not drunk," she says, closing her eyes. "Pregnant."

I close my eyes against a wave of dizziness, and all I see are the McMurdo condoms. Piles, and baskets, and Halloween-candy-sized bowls of condoms.

"Charlotte," I say. "That's not possible."

She is sick again. I hold her hair back.

"Antarctica," she pants. "It's all possible."

- 14 -

San Francisco

THE THIRD SATURDAY IN JANUARY, I AM UP BEFORE THE SUN, eager for my secret day of errands, and early enough to cross paths with Dad and Luke in the kitchen before they're off to the bakery.

"Baby." Dad frowns. "What are you doing up?"

I shrug. "Can't sleep. Thought I might as well get up."

"You're coming tomorrow, right?" Luke asks carefully.

"Yes," I say. "Definitely. What's tomorrow?"

"Harp!" Luke says.

"Moving day!" Dad says. "You better be kidding."

I'm not. I have completely forgotten Luke is leaving, which just shows (a) what a horrible sister I can be, and (b) just how down in it I am.

"Yes," I say. "I'm there. Yes."

They leave me to wait around until the sun rises, and it's time to go.

My legs hurt. Not dancing, not stretching for hours each day for the first time in years, is wreaking havoc on my body. Lindsay has reportedly taken over teaching my babies, which is definitely better than Simone unleashing her nuttiness on them. Unless they pick up Lindsay's barre-clutching habits. Then it's a wash.

Kate came back from New York with second- and third-place wins for both her solos in the Grand Prix, and went right back to attending class with Simone while she waits for an offer from a company. Which could be any day. When she first came home, I begged Kate to tell me everything—how class was, who was doing what—but then I couldn't bear to hear any more. Her sleepovers became visits, which became phone calls, which have now been reduced to texts.

My heart aches for her the way my legs do for turns.

I think of Owen in the spaces that ballet and Kate aren't filling. He is there in the mess of longing, and he calls and texts, and I return them all and we've spoken a little, and he is being incredibly respectful in regard to my pleading for being left alone just now.

But I miss him.

Mom and Dad have kept their promise to not chase after Simone for a "talk," but *she* tracked *them* down instead.

"'A hundred messages I have left Harper,'" Mom reported Simone said. So they went to the studio, and she explained about my hips. And my feet. My arms and neck, all the reasons why, no matter how much of my life and heart and everything I give to it, it will never change the truth.

"But you love it so much," Mom says night and day. "You can't just stop. Please don't let it go."

She doesn't understand. And honestly I don't, either. I just know going to the studio seems more impossible than not going. So I don't. And I think about Antarctica instead. Better than dwelling on the eighteen rejection emails I've gotten from the video auditions.

At 7:31 a.m., I leave the house, stop by our mailbox, and peer inside. My high school diploma. Perfect. I walk to West Portal Avenue, and in front of the bookshop, Hannah is idling in a car. I climb in and kiss Willa's sleeping face in the booster seat behind me.

Hannah cranks up the heater.

"I can't thank you enough," I tell her.

"Better save the gratitude till we see how the day goes. You never can tell."

"Got it."

And we're off, on a marathon tour of the Bay Area, one government building and doctor's office at a time.

First up, our family dentist, who, like our doctor, thinks my parents know all about the National Science Foundation forms I'm filling out for them regarding the state of my teeth (X-rays, thorough cleaning) and my general physical well-being (blood work, internal exam).

Wintering Over means living on The Ice for months with no way to leave. No way for anyone to come in. Too cold for planes to land, too stormy. Medical emergencies must be avoided at all costs. Only healthy people are allowed to Winter Over. I've been eating. I can fake my way through this. And all those years of fastidious personal hygiene are about to pay off.

While Hannah and Willa wait, I go into a nondescript office park in Oakland to take an hour-long multiple-choice true/false quiz about my mental health, answering a couple hundred questions such as, *Yes or No: I hate my mother.* And *Yes or No: My close friends have often told me I have a drinking problem.*

I am increasingly, maybe foolishly hopeful. One of Mom's past teaching assistants is on The Ice and staying through winter. Hannah says this woman absolutely loves Mom. She may be my way in. I'll clean the Antarctic toilets—I don't care— just so I get there.

Hannah's miserable about keeping secrets from Mom. I'm guilt-ridden asking her to—but we're both still doing it, which is a testament to how worried Hannah is about me. And how worried I am about myself. The intense purposefulness that went into preparing for my life with Kate in the San Francisco Ballet has now found itself poured into getting me on a plane in March to Antarctica. To the frozen dark. To the resting place of explorers, even those I'm not related to by blood, whom I have begun to feel a true kinship with: their years of preparation, laser-beam focus, the all-consuming joy felt in the attempt—and then in a moment, it is gone. Nothing matters. Without ballet, without Kate and our Plan, I am nothing, and when I think about it, I can barely stand up straight. I need the frozen dark in a way I cannot describe but that Hannah seems to understand. And so she is helping me.

At last, we are done. Nothing more to do now but wait for NSF approval, and for some scientist at the bottom of Earth to take pity on me. It is an agonizing wait. An audition for The Ice.

- - -

It is a gorgeous day in the Presidio. Rolling green hills and perfect white stucco officers' homes, renovated into beautiful single-family and rental houses, rise in the blue winter sky. The house Luke is moving into has peekaboo views of the Golden Gate Bridge from the second story. It takes dividing the rent four ways to make it possible, but anyone could see it is worth it.

I'm scared and impatient to see Owen, hoping he's not here one minute, praying he is the next. I've had to be single-minded of purpose to get this chance for Antarctica figured out, but not one day has gone by I haven't missed him, haven't wanted to see him. He texts and leaves messages, and I answer them— but maybe he's done trying to get me to act like a normal person, with common sense and manners. He doesn't know about Antarctica. No one does. Just Hannah. Well, and Willa.

My hair is down. I'm in my best jeans, a cute sweater.

I'm terrified.

Dad climbs into the back of the U-Haul pickup he's rented for this auspicious occasion: Luke's first foray into independent adulthood. His stuff is covered with a blue tarp—a small pile of recent Craigslist finds. Preassembled, barely used Ikea bed; an estate sale dresser; rugs and lamps from various garage sales. Boxes of game junk are labeled and carefully taped. I put my *Antarctica: Terrible Beauty* book aside to heft one of the smaller boxes up flagstone steps and through the front door of the house.

Wood floors, tall windows.

Owen.

"Hey," he says. *Smiles.*

"Hey."

Two weeks, but I have not forgotten how very dark his eyes are. And those arms. His voice.

"Come take a tour." He holds out his hand. The safety pin hand.

I give him mine.

Dad and Luke unload the truck, and Owen takes my box under one arm, up a narrow staircase to the sunny second floor.

"Bathroom, bedroom, other bedroom, other bathroom, Luke's room . . ." Here he sets the box onto the bare floor.

And then we step inside the last room. He closes the door quietly. We are alone.

"I missed you," I say, barely audible.

"I missed *you*."

"You did?"

He just stands there, looking at me. My heart races.

"You have no idea," he says. And then my back is against the wall, his hands in my hair, blood thundering in my ears, and we're kissing like he's been away in battle, like it's been years—

"Harper!" Dad's voice calls up the stairwell. "Come bring up some of this stuff! Let's go!"

"Oh my God," I pant, pulling reluctantly from Owen's arms. "Luke can live in the car. I don't care. . . ."

"Me neither," Owen breathes. We move to sit on his neatly made bed.

"Harper!" Mom's voice comes through the open window facing the ocean.

"Ignore them," I whisper. "They'll go away eventually." And then he stops kissing me because he's laughing.

I sit up. "This isn't funny," I say. "I *missed* you."

"Yeah, well, whose fault is that?"

"I'm in the midst of a crisis!"

He hugs me, one of comfort, and pushes my hair off my face to kiss me again and ask, "What have you been doing?"

"Wallowing," I admit. "Trying not to."

"That's fair."

"But I may have figured out what to do about it."

"That's great!"

"Yeah. Maybe." Suddenly, his hand in mine, Antarctica seems like a horrible idea. But maybe it won't happen, so it won't matter anyway.

Owen smiles. "Listen, I'm not going to keep promising to not come around anymore. This is stupid."

"Okay, stalker."

"Whatever. Get a restraining order."

"Harper!" Dad practically yodels. Owen stands and pulls me up.

"Let's go," he says.

"But"—I pull him back—"I *missed* you."

"Yeah," he says. "I can see that, and the feeling's mutual, but your dad will kill me if he thinks we're up here doing what we're doing, so let's make an appearance."

He opens the door and reaches a switch above his head. Two lightsabers, crossed and mounted above the door, glow red and blue.

"Oh, brother," I sigh. "How old are you again?"

"I am nineteen years old. But Jedis live forever."

"Do they?

"I don't know." He kisses me once more and raises a bamboo shade off the window, and the room is bright. Blue bedspread. Probably hiding Star Wars sheets. Dresser. Lamp. Rug. Books.

"Should I have ignored your request and just come over? What do you think?"

I smile. "I think you are the kindest person I've ever met. Thank you for not."

"Okay."

"How are *you*? Work good and all that?"

"Sure."

"Good."

"Was showing up at the audition a total creeper move? Because, I swear to God, I didn't mean it to be. Honestly."

"Owen. You saved me. That was a bad day. There've been a bunch of bad ones since, but *that* day . . . Thank you. If I forgot to say it then, which I'm sure I did, thank you. So much."

We stand in the doorway, breathing quietly. He closes the door with his foot.

"Just two more minutes," he says in my ear.

"Two or five," I whisper, and he backs me toward the bed again until, through the open window, we hear Luke call, "Hey, Kate!"

I get up, despite Owen's pulling my hand back, and go to the window. Kate's crossing the front lawn.

Owen comes to the window to see for himself, hugs me, and says, "Want to hang out here? Hide in the closet or something?"

"Yes."

But I follow him reluctantly down the stairs.

"Hey, Kate!" he calls. I drop his hand. Kate walks up the steps toward us, lugging a laundry basket of books.

"Hi!" She smiles brightly at Owen and hopefully at me. He takes the basket from her and jogs it upstairs to Luke's room. I move forward and hug her.

She squeezes back, so hard I think my lungs will collapse, and, oh, I've missed her skinny, strong arms. "Hi," she says again, beaming.

"I'm not carrying any more of Luke's tighty-whities. Come on." We sneak around the house to hide in the back and sit on the grass beneath Owen's window.

"I miss you," she says, "in class."

"Me too."

She pulls at the grass, plucks tiny white daisies from the lawn. "I heard from New York."

"Oh." My voice is suddenly high, constricted. "Who?"

"New York City."

"Oh God. Wow."

"And ABT."

New York City Ballet. American Ballet Theatre.

My head is spinning.

"That's—Kitty. That's amazing." I hate myself that the words are nearly impossible to say with genuine enthusiasm. "As a student?"

"Positions," she says quietly. "Apprentice. In the company."

"Wow," I whisper again.

"I mean, just corps, but it's . . . I don't know what to do. I have to decide by next week because I'll start the following at either one. They want to know."

"You'll start the following week—so in two weeks you'll be in New York."

"Yeah."

"Professional ballerina."

She draws circles on the dirt with a stick. "Yes."

We sit in silence.

"Hey, ladies," Owen calls, materializing at the side lawn. "Hiding from the heavy lifting?"

Kate stands. Smiles. "Maybe."

Owen reaches down and pulls me to my feet.

Kate's smile falters.

We get everything up the stairs and into Luke's room, and then Dad tries to be cool by offering an Igloo chest of beer, which Luke can't drink physically *or* legally, and Owen also underage, politely refuses. I take one, and Mom snatches it from my hand, whacks Dad on his arm for plying children with booze, and gets on her phone to order pizza.

Luke gives Mom and Dad and Kate the official tour. Owen hangs back with me in the sun on the front steps.

"Where are the other two Jedis?" I ask.

"Surfing. You'll meet them later."

I nod. "Break Luke in easy."

"He'll be fine. Excited to have your own bathroom?"

"Hell yes. Tossed his Axe spray and foot-fungus cream already. It's all potpourri and fancy soap up in there now."

He smiles. "You're gonna be okay, Harp."

"Did I say you could call me Harp?"

"Dude. It's one less syllable. Everyone else does it!"

"Everyone else knows me."

"Not the way I do."

"Oh my God," I sigh, smiling.

"How's that?" Kate says. She steps around us to stand on the path at our feet.

"How's what?" Owen asks.

"What *way* do you know her?"

"He doesn't," I say. "He's joking."

"I'm not," Owen says. I give him a small shove and a *look*.

Kate's smile is strained. She looks from me to Owen. "What's up, Harp?"

"With what?"

"Come on."

"Nothing! Nothing's up!"

Owen frowns. *"Nothing?"*

Kate's smile flattens.

"He's just kidding," I say again weakly.

"I'm not," he says, looking directly at me. "Why would you say that?"

"I only mean, there's nothing *bad* going on, there's not . . ."

"Wait, hold on," Owen says, "Is there a *thing,* like some conflict of interest happening that I don't know about?"

Holy crap, guys can be dumb.

"I don't know," Kate says, kind of . . . mad? At me? "Is there? *Harp?*"

What the—*what?*

My gloom and anxiety are turning to anger as my addled brain assesses this screwed-up situation. "Wait," I say. "Everyone just . . . Kate—did Owen ask you out?"

She stands there for a while. "No."

"I told you," Owen says. "*She* asked me."

Kate's eyebrows and vocal pitch are up. "You *told* her that?"

"I didn't know it was a secret!"

Kate stands. "Harp, can we take a walk?"

For some stupid reason, my heart starts thumping in my chest. This is *Kate*—why am I scared? She is my *sister.*

"I don't think Harper needs to go anywhere with you right now, Kate," Owen says.

Kate's perfectly pink cheeks flush bright.

"Please don't speak for me," I say, low.

"People!" Dad calls from the door, "We ready for pizza?"

"In a minute!" the three of us yell in tandem, which is kind of hilarious. I wish I could laugh.

"Harper," Kate says, my full first name and in a voice I've never, ever heard her use. "I'm sorry. Honestly. I'm sorry I'm a better dancer than you." Her voice breaks. "I'm sorry I can't stay in San Francisco with you and live in a crappy apartment, waving a flower around in the chorus forever. I'm too good for that. It's a waste of my talent. I can't give up my entire life for you."

"Jesus, Kate!" Luke says, standing behind us in the doorway.

"Jesus *what*? It's true! I'm sorry, Harp, I love you. Enough to tell you the truth."

"Okay," I say. I push myself up off the step.

"Okay what?"

She's . . . God, she's so *mad*. How did this turn so fast—how am I the villain? She wants a fight. I'm too tired to give her one.

"I'm sorry, too," I sigh. "I'm sorry I held you back. I'm sorry I don't have the money you do. I wish I didn't have to work so much, because maybe if I'd had the money for private lessons and more time to take luxurious naps, maybe I could have been better—but let's be honest, never as good as you. I'm sorry a boy you like doesn't like you back. I'm sorry he's slumming it with your sidekick instead. I'm sorry for everything."

I cannot believe these words are coming from me. Neither, clearly, can Kate.

Kate, my mind clamors, *I don't mean it. Forgive me.* But those words don't get spoken. Just the mean ones. I turn and walk toward the ocean. My MO as of late.

"Where are you going?" Mom calls. "Harper, what's happening?"

"I don't know," I call back. "Home. Antarctica." A bus passes me. I wave and run ahead to the stop, and catch it just in time.

- - -

Thank God for babysitting money and refunded, un-danced-in pointe shoes. (Except for the Maltese Crosses, still in their box in my closet.) Because REI does not hawk subzero winter gear for cheap. I pull an enormous parka over my bony arms, and my phone buzzes.

Owen.

"Hey," I say.

"Hello. Where are you?" he asks.

"Hiking."

"Meet me tomorrow. Union Square at two. Can you?"

"Owen."

"Just be there. Where are you? You're not hiking."

"Maybe I am! You don't know!"

"Tomorrow. Five o'clock in front of Tiffany."

"Tiffany? Barf. And I can't."

"Why not."

"I'm packing. I'm leaving."

"Not for five days!"

"It takes a long time."

"Look, I'm not going to beg. I'll see you there. At two."

He hangs up.

This parka is ridiculous.

- - -

The Muni is so crowded I nearly have a panic attack, get off three stops early, and walk fifteen blocks in cute but uncomfortable shoes to Union Square, which is also packed, and Market Street is blocked off.

Chinese New Year. I'm so dumb.

I fight through the crowds to stupid Tiffany. He's not here. I should've stayed home and watched Mom cry some more. She and Dad have forgiven Hannah, but Mom is heartbroken I would do this—go to The Ice without telling her, not ask her for help—mostly just sad I'm leaving.

"Six months," I tell her over and over. "I'll be right back."

It doesn't help.

A hand is on my arm.

"You're here!" Owen says.

"Tiffany?"

"It's an easy landmark. Now let's go in and pick out a ring and get it over with."

My hands go cold.

"I'm *kidding*!" he says. "You really *are* depressed. Come on." He takes my hand. I hold on tight in this crush of people. He navigates through the crowds. "So explain to me," he calls over the noise. "How exactly does this work? Where do you get the money to fly to . . . where do you go?"

"New Zealand first. I don't. I'm an employee and also it's a grant. For students. They send me."

"Okay."

"And they've got the hard-core cold gear. I get paid practically nothing, but there are no living expenses, so I can save a little stash. And then, when it's over, I get a one-way ticket around the world in either direction. That's it."

"Huh."

We make our way into Chinatown, which I cannot believe we're going into. Belly of the beast.

"Is this the best idea right now?" I shout.

"Only option," he shouts back. "Hang on!" We maneuver through the sea of people and music, vendor carts and craft tables. The festival is in full swing. He pulls me out of the crowd, down a small side street, into a dark hall, and up an even darker stairwell.

"Listen, if you're going to murder me . . ."

"I would have done it already. Here." He rings an apartment doorbell. "Take off your shoes."

"Why?"

The door swings open. "Owen!"

"Dad!"

A smaller, older version of Owen grabs his younger self and kisses his head, then frowns at me.

"Oh, this is my friend, Harper," Owen tells him. His dad smiles, gesturing for us to enter.

We take off our shoes.

"Sorry to shanghai you," he whispers.

"That's racist," I whisper back.

"Well," he says, "you can't change a nation."

"Dude."

A roomful of people greets us. Afternoon winter sunlight streams into a huge room from picture windows that look down on the street. The party is going on directly below us.

"Gung hay fat choy!" everyone calls, and hugs and kisses.

"Mom," Owen says, "this is Harper."

His mom, taller than his dad and with a head of salon-styled curls, glares openly at me. Owen rolls his eyes.

"Harp, these are my cousins. This is my aunt, my uncle, Grandpa. This is Harper." His grandpa looks like he's around a hundred and three years old. He gives me his cool, papery hand. He smiles and nods. I do, too.

"It's so nice to meet you all," I say. Everyone else smiles and nods, too.

There is a long table in the dining room piled with food. Owen's mom tries to get him to eat. He speaks Mandarin to her. Or Cantonese. One of the two, and I think he's telling her we came by to say hello but that we are going to the parade now.

"Is Josie already gone?" he asks a girl cousin.

"Hours ago," the cousin says, dipping some food thing into a bowl of some sauce thing.

"Okay," Owen says. "See you after!" There's more shouting and hugging and then we're back in the dark hall.

"Thanks," he says. "That was fun!"

I follow him down the stairs back into the alley.

"Who's Josie?"

"Jealous?"

I stop walking. "Who is Josie?"

He sees my face, walks back, and whispers close, "I *like* you jealous."

"I'm *not*—" I begin, but he kisses me.

"Josie's my sister," he says casually. "She left the party early."

"Jackass."

"I'm not the one with a jealousy complex!"

"Okay. So one sister? That's it?"

"And a ton of cousins." We're back out on the street. "I grew up in that apartment."

"Your mom looked mad."

"Oh, she was."

"Why?"

"Because you're white. Cross here." He runs, against the light, across the street and back toward Union Square.

"You can't have white friends?"

"Not white girlfriends."

"So she needs to chill. There's no problem."

"Oh, there's a problem," he says. "You like egg rolls?"

"No. Sorry."

"You've deeply offended my culture. How about dim sum?"

I shrug.

"Is Luke right? Do you really not eat?"

"No, it's . . . complicated."

"Not really; it's just food. Hold on. Don't move. At all." He leaves me on the sidewalk and runs to a food cart, takes a paper bag from the guy, ducks into a bakery, comes out with a pink box, and takes my hand again. We go up some narrow backstreet. He pulls down a fire escape ladder, we climb up, and we're on a roof patio. Grass. Flowers. Adirondack chairs.

"My dad's friend's house," he explains. "They're out of the country and said we should use the roof. Have a seat."

From the chairs we can see the avenues below us, lights and talking and a bright hum of music.

"The parade goes right past here," he says. From the bags he pulls cartons of stir-fried vegetables, plain white rice. Pink box of almond cookies. "So, now, what's your deal with Chinese food? Which, this isn't even—this is American Chinese food."

"It's not the Chinese part; it's the fried part."

"Thought so."

"Not sure how to navigate food. Lately. Or ever."

"Okay. Well. It's here if you want it."

"Thank you." He tosses me a bottle of water and breaks apart disposable wooden chopsticks.

"Talk to Kate lately?"

"She's gone."

"New York?"

I nod.

"Oh, wow," he says. "I'm sorry."

"Not your fault."

"No, I mean sympathy. I'm sorry. For the loss."

"I'm not like that," I say. "What I said to her."

"You were sticking up for yourself. She wasn't being the nicest."

"She's not like that, either," I say. "Not at all. Something's wrong."

"What is?"

"I don't know. Her parents are kind of awful, but I'm too wrapped up in my own stupid tragedy to pay attention to anyone else's and offer help. So."

"Why do you do that?"

"What?"

"Take all the blame. Belittle your sadness."

"Because . . . other people have real problems. People are sick. And starving. And they have terrible families. I'm in perfect health with a family who loves me, and I'm moping about *ballet*. And not just moping—I'm fully *agonizing*. I'm destroyed.

I don't know what to do without it, and that's . . ." I'm getting worked up to cry. Again.

"Okay," he says. "Yes, you're lucky you're middle-class and white, and you've got a great family, and they paid for classes when you were little—fine. But it's not *luck* that you've worked your ass off for the past fourteen years. If you were Chinese, my mom would be in love with you. She'd be planning the wedding."

Drums and bells crash in the street below.

"That's the second marriage reference you've made in the space of an hour."

"Harp, it's a huge, catastrophic fuck-up you're getting through. It's okay to be sad about it."

"Can we ever talk about you?"

"There's nothing to talk about."

"You were premed. Now you make games. Your mom seems kind of racist. That it?"

He puts a bunch of rice into the vegetable container.

"I love science. I thought I wanted to be a doctor. My parents *really* wanted me to be a doctor. But it turns out? I also really love sitting around in my boxer shorts playing *Halo*."

"I thought I made that up. Is that a thing?"

"Hell yes. It's just reality."

"Okay."

"And there's *my* guilt—I could be dedicating my life to helping people, healing them. And I choose *video games*?"

"So go back to med school."

"Yeah," he says. "You'd think. I was going to take just a semester off when Lucas first offered. Then it turns out that nearly every single minute of every day, I am so happy at work. Even when it's really hard—especially when it's hard."

"Wow."

"I know! And they do this thing, with Make-A-Wish— you know, where kids are really sick and they can have a wish granted, like the thing they love most in life to happen just once?"

"Yeah?"

"So, some of the kids choose to come see us making games. That's their whole wish in the entire world—to watch us drawing, or see how we build the levels or whatever. A kid came in a few months ago, and she's bald and super little, and you just think—if you could trade places. But the whole time she was there, she was *so happy*. And I thought, that's a worthwhile thing; making something that makes people happy—that matters, too. That's a life."

The parade is starting. It is crawling along the wide streets below us, music and lights, convertible cars with political candidates waving from jump seats. Firecrackers.

"This is the Year of the Sheep," he says.

"Oh yeah?"

"It's a really good year. Fortune-full."

"It's going great so far."

He smiles kindly, puts his hand on my knee. "And you were born in the Year of the Tiger."

"I know. I've seen the paper placemats in restaurants."

"So you know you're spazzy and can't settle down in relationships, but you're an incredibly hard worker?"

"You're making that up."

"I'm a Rat. Cheerful. Impatient. Supremely talented in a million ways."

"Of course."

"Harper."

"Owen."

"Tell me this is none of my business and to shut the hell up and I will, but—running away to Antarctica . . . doesn't seem like it's going to solve anything. I mean, isn't the whole issue that you love to dance? Isn't that the point? Why can't you just . . . *always* dance?"

An enormous flatbed goes past, covered in little kids and poster-paint signs reading, WAH MEI SCHOOL.

"My mom," Owen says, pointing. "She jumps on midroute. That's her school. Mom! *Mom!*" She waves, smiles, looks up, and see us. Sees me and frowns.

"Don't worry about it," he says. "She'll love our kids—the Chinese half at least."

"Not even a ring on my finger and you've got me popping out kids. Plural."

"I sent you to Tiffany. There could have been a ring, but nooo—oh, look, there's Josie! There she is! *Josie!*"

"Where?"

"There, right there below us!"

"I can't see past the Miss Chinatown float. I don't see where you're pointing."

Miss Chinatown looks up, sees Owen, and waves.

"Oh . . . ," I say. "Right. Okay."

"And she's still premed."

"Of course."

"Plus her boyfriend is totally Chinese."

"Well, sure. And you brought me to your childhood home to meet your family because you like to stir the pot."

"What pot?"

"It means I think my being white is a thing with you."

"A *thing*?"

"A novelty. A way to stay the black sheep."

"'Black sheep'? Now *that's* racist."

"No, it isn't! That's a saying!"

"Oh my God. Okay."

"It *is*."

"Harper," he says. "Do you *have* to do this?"

"I need to."

"*Why?*"

"I'm a Scott."

"Are you scared?"

The dragon music is starting. The gorgeous silk-and-paper dragon puppet is snaking its way around the street, undulating and dancing.

An empty stomach makes a fierce dog, Scott said. My *life* is empty.

"No," I say. "I'm not scared. At all."

He leans close to me. "It's obvious the biggest competition I have for your affection is San Francisco, and believe me, San Francisco doesn't want you to go."

"Don't," I beg. "Please. This isn't easy."

"I'm sorry. I can't not say this. Please don't leave. I don't want you to go. You can figure it out here. Your family will help you—*I'll* help you."

"I'm trying to save myself. I'm so lost. Please don't—"

"I am completely selfish. Stay with me."

My head is light. Tingly. I'm barely breathing. Firecrackers explode in the street below us. I tilt my head up to the sky. No stars; too many lights.

"I wish I could," I admit.

"You can! I just found you. Please don't go."

"I have to," I say. "Already gone."

"Stay. Please."

Nothing to say to that. So I don't.

I only kiss him back.

- - -

In the San Francisco airport there is a yoga room, and also there are therapy dogs walking around with trainers, and the dogs wear vests that read, PET ME. These things are supposed to calm anxious travelers. But I am not anxious. I am eager. Mom, on the other hand, has been in the yoga room for forty-five minutes, and the last time we saw her, she was practically French-kissing an Australian shepherd and holding on to his coat for dear life, and then the trainer awkwardly eased him away from Mom's grip, while Dad backed Mom slowly toward the Cinnabon.

Luke is here. And Hannah, and Willa. Who has not forgiven me. She keeps asking if she can "help" by "holding" my boarding pass and ticket while eyeing the garbage can.

An unread letter from Owen, delivered by Luke, is in my backpack, but Owen is not here.

Because I asked him not to be. Because being near him would make it impossible for me to leave.

Kate is in New York.

I am alone.

"So, when does the last mail flight get to The Ice?" Mom asks for the bazillionth time.

"End of March. Don't send anything later than next week. I won't get it till August."

"And you'll be there when?"

"Three days. I'll call from the hotel. And then I'll email. Okay?"

Hannah and Dad and Luke hug me, Mom clutches me once more, and then I have to get in line. I take off my shoes and pull out my phone and passport. Willa makes a last dash to put her arms around my legs.

I pry her arms apart. "I have to go," I whisper. "I'll bring you a penguin, okay? Willster?" She's crying. "I'm sorry," I tell her. "I'm sorry. I'll come back. I promise. Okay? I *promise*."

"Bring me a polar bear."

I get on my knees and hold her tight. "No polar bears," I whisper. "That's the *North* Pole."

North in the *Arctic*—a word derived from the Greek *Arktos,* meaning "bear." So *Antarctica* means "no bears."

An entire continent named for what it lacks.

I am nothing now. I am only what I lack.

No bears. No ballet.

Willa runs back to Hannah, who picks her up, and they wave and walk away.

I am going. To be in the dark and quiet. To be frozen. To Winter Over.

- 15 -

Antarctica

THERE ARE SOME HARD-CORE VETERAN WINTER OVERERS WHO would love it if the Internet had never been invented. "Antarctica has lost its sense of isolation," they complain, isolation being the reason so many people come here year after year. Solitude. Escape from the rest of humanity. From life.

I'm starting to sympathize with them.

Ballerina Comes Home

It took moving 3,000 miles away to New York City for Katherine Grey to realize, "San Francisco is my home. It's where I'm meant to be. This city is in my blood!" She laughs, as some of this San Francisco blood spills from an open blister on her foot and onto the studio floor of Grey's lifelong ballet teacher, Simone Beaulieu.

"Kate could never be anything else," Beaulieu

says, intently watching Grey's lightning-fast turns across the floor of her West Portal dance studio. "She was born to this."

Which makes it no surprise the seventeen-year-old was chosen earlier this year by New York's world-famous American Ballet Theatre to be an apprentice company member, a coveted position most dancers only dream of.

"But as soon as I got there, though the training was wonderful, my homesickness turned to something deeper," Grey says.

Oh, really. Perhaps it's the *deep* realization you've betrayed your best friend and lied to her for ten years. Or it could be you got a bad street-vendor pretzel. Who knows.

"I can dance anywhere. But I couldn't belong everywhere," a feeling Grey says she was willing to ignore, and she threw herself fully into participating with daily rehearsals at ABT.

"The managing director of the San Francisco Ballet was in town. He'd seen me at a competition earlier in the season and liked what he saw." Then came San Francisco's unique move of facilitating negotiations to get Grey out of her nine-month contract with ABT and offering her a two-year corps position contract with the San Francisco Ballet instead. Which Grey was "thrilled to gratefully accept!"

"Everything I've ever loved has always been here in San Francisco, in West Portal. Now I can say that for certain."

"Harp?"

Charlotte is awake but still in my bed, beneath every blanket I could find. I close her laptop and reprimand myself yet again for being weak—I have got to stay the hell off Google and stop dumping entire containers of rock salt onto these wounds.

I go to the chair I've set up beside her. "Hey," I say. "What do you need?"

She closes her eyes, her arm over her face. "It's a million degrees in here. Can I get some of these covers off?" She shoves them aside and I fold them at the foot of the bed. "Thank you for staying. You don't need to. I'm used to it—I'm so sorry I ruined your night."

"You saved my night," I sigh. I'm nursing a huge headache, my eyeballs are parched, I'm wrecked recalling alternately first how impossibly close I came to spending the night with Aiden and then plunging my thoughts right back into how much

I love Owen's laugh, his beautiful eyes, his intelligence, his kindness, his voice, sitting together by the bridge above the ocean and the lights and sounds of the New Year parade—

Poor Charlotte moans pitifully from the covers, sick and miserable.

"I'd almost rather have anything—strep throat, bladder infection—than nausea. I hate it so much!" she whines.

There's a tap at the door, and I step into the hall, where Aiden hands me saltine crackers, a liter bottle of flat ginger ale, and a cup of ice.

"She okay?"

"Just the flu. She'll make it. But I'm staying with her, okay? Sorry."

He pulls me to him, hugs me in my far-less-sexy sweat-pants and T-shirt ensemble. "Me too. I'm really sad our slumber party got hijacked."

I nod into his chest, thinking miserably of Owen, awash in guilt, deserving of how awful my head feels, and so grateful I found Charlotte when I did—but then look what Aiden does. Brings her soda and crackers, kindness and care for us both.

"Thank you," I say. "This will really help."

"Here, I've got these," Vivian says, suddenly standing beside Aiden, her face hidden behind an armful of folded blankets she's found in Charlotte's room.

"Oh my gosh, Vivian, thank you."

Aiden's eyes are wide. "Is *this* Tickle-Fight-in-Panties Night?!"

"Perv," Vivian says, and shuts the door.

"Sorry!" I whisper to Aiden. "Thank you, thank you, call me later!" I slip into the room and lock the door behind me.

Charlotte sits up.

"I found these," Vivian says, and piles them on top of the stack at the foot of the bed.

Charlotte falls back against the pillows. "I am the worst mentor ever. Holy crap, I'm going to get sued. I'll be thrown in jail for contributing to the delinquency of minors, and I'll deserve it. This is *so* bad. . . ."

"Oh, relax," Vivian says, dropping onto her bed. "You're a science teacher, not a den mother. No one's going to find out."

Charlotte and I stare at her.

"*What?* Harper, you're not going to tell anyone here. You're not telling your parents, right?"

"Of course not, no!"

"Me neither," she says to Charlotte. "It was nearly impossible to persuade them to let me come here. I'm not about to prove them right about how McMurdo pretends to be a science station but in reality is nothing more than a sex den of debauchery. So there you go. No one will find out Charlotte's a South Pole dancer, and no one's going to know Harper got drunk and made out with some dude in the hallway. All is well, and the world will go on turning."

"Vivian," I say, "I *like* you in a crisis."

"This is not a crisis!" Charlotte wails. "Wait—oh God! Harper, did you tell me in the bathroom that you're drunk? Are you *drunk*?"

"Not anymore."

"Oh, sweetheart, please," she begs. "You can't, you cannot do that. Promise me you won't—"

"Trust me," I say. "I feel terrible. I hated it. And my parents will never find out about that, either."

"Please just let your brain develop some more before you screw with it, okay? It *is* my fault; I'm your supervisor. Your mom would never forgive me. But also, Harper, my God! You know better! You've got to use the common sense I know you have. Was Aiden, too?"

I shake my head. "I don't think that guy can *get* drunk."

She rolls her eyes. "I'll talk to his supervisor. This is why no one wanted to offer these grants. You can't have teenagers in this kind of situation. Where the hell did he get the drinks?"

"From the bar, I'm guessing."

"Was that him out there just now?"

I nod, pour the ginger ale over the ice, and it foams up a little.

"You tell him it's the flu?"

"Of course!"

She closes her eyes again. "This is so dumb."

"None of his business. No one's but yours. Drink this."

"Well, mine and the medical staff who aren't equipped for childbirth.

"How many . . . like, how far along . . . ?"

"Five, maybe six months."

"How long have you known?"

She counts in her head. "Eight . . . teen weeks? My period is never regular in the winter. Sometimes it never comes at all. Core temperature can get so low it messes with it. But apparently not enough." She pulls the covers back up around her.

"Girls at my school got knocked up all the time," Vivian says, reaching for some saltines. "At least you're an adult."

I frown. "They *did*?"

"Sure. I mean, two or three a year, but there were only, like, five hundred kids in the whole school, so that's a lot. Statistically."

"In *Minnesota*?"

She rolls her eyes. "Yes, in *St. Paul*. People have sex there. Haven't you seen *Purple Rain*?"

"I thought that was Minneapolis," Charlotte says.

"So," Vivian says, "aside from the barfing, are you . . . okay? I mean, what are you going to . . . Does the father know?"

She shakes her head. "No."

"You gonna tell him? Is he here?"

"It was *one* time, the stupid New Year's Eve party. He left on the Last Plane Out. Flight-scheduling guy. I need to figure out how to not let this ruin my entire life before I bring a guy who couldn't care less into it."

"How do you know?" Vivian says. "Maybe he would care . . . more."

"I don't even know his last name. He may not have known my *first* name."

"Oh."

"In my defense—once you've taken a million hikes and watched all the movies and gone to the library and played air hockey, there's only so many recreational activities a person can fill their time with here. Also, we were completely drunk, so all I can say is, heed this life lesson—drunken sex with a guy you barely know? Not the best idea. Also? McMurdo serves perishable food from boxes with expiration dates in the previous decade. Condoms have a shelf life, too."

"Gross," Vivian mutters.

"Yeah. Well. And now I'm awake night and day freaked out about unsavory diseases . . . Oh God, I can't think about it!"

"So get tested!" I say. "You're having regular visits anyway, for the baby, right?"

"Harp, *no* . . . they can't know."

"Who can't?"

"I've got to stay and finish. I'm being dramatic. I'm sure it's fine disease-wise. The battery of tests they put us through to get here . . . but I can't see the doctor for *any*thing, because if they find out, they'll make me go back at Winfly."

"Which of course you will be doing . . . ," Vivian says. "Going home at Winfly. Right? Because you aren't stupid?"

"What's Winfly?" I ask.

"Viv," Charlotte says, "haven't you ever seen that *Oops, I'm Pregnant!* show? Or whatever it's called? People carry babies to term all the time, and they don't have any idea they're doing it till they're peeing or taking a bath one day, and *Whoa!*"

"Charlotte," Vivian sighs.

"I'm not kidding! People smoke and drink and climb really high stepladders, and here come these perfectly healthy babies. I'm not doing any of that. I can't handle booze, I hate smoke, I feel perfectly well except for all the throwing up—which is a *good* sign, by the way—and obviously I'm gaining enough weight. I'll see the doctor the second the Winfly plane takes off, I swear. I'm a biologist—that's practically a doctor anyway."

"It is not!" Vivian shrills.

"Okay, well, it's science at least! I have to stay and finish. If I can keep it quiet till after Winfly, they'll have to let me stay."

"What is Winfly?" I ask again.

"Seriously?" Vivian says. "I thought you were an 'Antarctica-ist.' Did you read anything in the manual at all?"

"Winter Fly In," Charlotte says. "NSF's got to get McMurdo set for October Main Body—resupply, get the labs and rooms ready. At the end of August, there's this predictable tiny window when the weather clears up just enough while the ice is still firm and they can land a plane with a crew of, like, two hundred people to prep the station, and they bring all kinds of stuff with them. We'll have lettuce again, and eggs and milk. Oh, and mail! Then the next day, the plane takes off, before the weather traps it here. It's Santa Claus for Winter Over."

"And when Santa goes home, you'll be with him," Vivian presses.

Charlotte frowns. "Winter's not over till the end of September, your contracts and mine."

"Who cares! You've got a really good reason to get off The Ice. They'd *want* you off, right?"

"*Yes,* but I can't yet."

"Charlotte!" Vivian cries. "Do not stay for the penguins. You can finish later! You can't have a baby on The Ice. It won't even have a country of origin."

"Yes, it will! It'll be Antarctic American. Also, the penguins *are* worth staying for—I've got to finish this research."

"I know," I say. "But, Char . . ."

"*And* I've also got to turn it in on time to matriculate, or I won't have a degree in my possession, and therefore I won't be able to accept job openings *now.* If I leave it undone, I'll never come back—not for years, and how will I support this baby then? I can't dump a kid with someone while I go live on The Ice for a year. I need to be done, degree in hand, so I can have a real job at home and pay for rent and diapers and toys and candy."

"You can't give a baby candy," I say.

"*I'm* gonna."

"Oh jeez."

"Listen to me. I can't start over. Years have gone into getting here; a woman in science has to be three times smarter just to prove she deserves to be here, and then I'm black, so of course I've had to work *ten* times harder to prove . . . who the hell knows what. . . . But I've done it. And I'm here, I'm nearly graduated, and I'm fucking exhausted." She throws the covers back off, boiling again. "I can't start over. Not with a baby to take care of. She'll stay put till winter is over, I promise. Please help me."

I barely remember the surgery performed on my feet. But I recall vividly begging Mom and Dad to let me do it. Promising to pay for it. Which I partly did, with babysitting money. *It's just shaving the bone,* I'd sobbed. *It's completely routine. Dancers do it all the time. If I don't, I'll never be on pointe, please. Please help me.*

"She?" Vivian says.

"Who?"

"You said 'She.'"

"Oh. I can tell. This kid's a giant pain in my ass already. She's not going to take crap from anyone, ever. Including me."

Vivian looks at me. "Fine," she says. "No one's going to know. But if you drop this kid on the ice and we get busted for knowing, it's on you."

"Got it."

"Can I admit something dumb?" Charlotte whispers.

"Oooh yeah!" I squeal quietly. Vivian shakes her head.

"When I first found out and recovered from the stroke, I was . . . *happy*. I love kids. I *love* them. I want one. And I worried sometimes. About how, with my life this way, was I ever going to find time to meet a decent guy, get married, and have a baby before I turned forty?"

I think of every kid I babysit. Sneaking them ice cream and tucking them in. I see Willa's face. My Saturday class, grabbing my legs, trying their best for me onstage, dancing their hearts out. Loving me.

"She was meant to be!" I sigh happily.

"Yay for faulty condoms!" Charlotte cheers weakly.

"Nice," Vivian says.

"It would be kind of amazing if she *were* born here. You could name her . . . Nacreous."

"Because no one makes fun of kids named Nacreous," Vivian adds.

"Ugh, I'm so sick of being sick," Charlotte moans, and rolls over to her side. "Hey," she says, "was I hallucinating or were you in the bathroom sitting on a towel, wearing a black bra and underwear?"

I help her sit up and put the ginger ale to her pale lips. "Yes."

"Yes what?"

"You were hallucinating. But that's going around, so no big whoop. Eat a cracker."

She tells us she'll be fine, she can go back to her room, but Vivian and I agree we'd feel better knowing Charlotte's getting some sleep in case she needs us in the night. So we tuck her in, Vivian lies down in her bed and turns away from the glow of the laptop, and I stalk Kate and read the rest of Mom and Dad's emails. At eleven-thirty I find Ice 104.5 on the radio dial.

"Top o' the midwinter to us all. Let the rosy sky warm and brighten a little more each day! Except for the predicted record cold snap on its way preceding Winfly. No matter. We'll bundle up together, won't we, our Antarctica family? Tonight I've got love in my heart for you all, and here's a song to send you off to sleep, whoever you are. All of us. Together beneath the moon on this most beautiful ice. Samhradh sásta, family."

"That guy," Vivian sighs in half-sleep.

And then from the tinny radio speakers comes a single note. A fiddle. A long, sweet draw across the strings and into an Irish lullaby.

I close the T3 folder, cover myself in blankets on a chair, and drowse in the warmth while Aiden plays us all to sleep.

- 16 -

Antarctica

JUST AS AIDEN SAID, EVERY DAY THERE IS A LITTLE LESS PITCH to the black of the sky. Not that we see much of it, Charlotte and Vivian and I. Aiden goes out for night hikes with the kitchen crew and his radio friends, disappointed I'm less amenable to the cold as the months go on. And I couldn't say for positive, but maybe he's still disappointed our sleepover never happened. Charlotte and Vivian and I are working twelve-hour days, struggling to get every sample cataloged, indexed, and aggregated to make a cohesive, compelling narrative that will save the Adélies from more human-caused illness, let their babies live and thrive—and let Charlotte's life and baby thrive as well. Staying busy working and keeping huge secrets help keep me from mourning the loss of San Francisco to Kate.

Fourth of July brings another excuse for the scientists and support staff to drink and get sick and use all the *probably expired* condoms they want. Charlotte makes a beeline for her room the minute our work is done for the day, hiding her ever-expanding midsection beneath the shapeless sweaters she's borrowed from Vivian and the LEAVE ONE TAKE ONE box in the hallway. I worry about her being inside all night and day, breathing circulated air, but she's worried the cold would be worse. I beg her to go to the greenhouse with me, and she points out, rightly so, that lying on her back in a rope hammock would be a dead giveaway; Charlotte is very thin—this baby is appearing slowly as a volleyball-shaped addition to her narrow frame. Allison's not dumb; her whole life is spent encouraging living things to procreate.

The Fourth party is raging beneath the disco ball when I go in to get Charlotte some dinner to take back to her room. Aiden's working in the kitchen, and I've had enough partying with drunk scientists for one lifetime. Also, Vivian and I are pretty occupied with procuring food at odd hours for hungry pregnant people who want a soft pretzel with mustard *right now.*

Aiden waves from the kitchen, and I sneak in to him, inhaling the aroma of simmering sauce made from canned tomatoes, and the warmth of baking bread.

For a moment I am lost in missing Fog City. That we have a bakery, our family has a bakery, that feeds so many San Franciscans has always made me proud. To have people grow up on our bread. Every day after work, Dad or Luke take the end-of-the-day stuff to food pantries all over the city, and a percentage of every year's quarterly profits goes to the food banks.

I've known all this forever but can't remember if I've ever said, "Hey, Dad. Nicely done."

He is a good man. They are good parents.

I miss home so badly. I can never go home and live every day being Salieri to Kate's Mozart. It's a big world. There's got to be someplace I'll love as much as San Francisco.

More lost than when I began. I need a sign.

"Hello there." Aiden smiles and pulls me to him by my waist. "Going to the party? I made a flag cake—Martha Stewart showed me how! Did you know she made peach cobbler in *prison*?" There's a torn-out page from a *Martha Stewart Living* magazine taped to the cupboard.

Indeed, there is a sheet cake on the counter. But the strawberries and blueberries making the stars and stripes are thawed from freezer bags and leaking juice all over the white frosting.

"Might be a little soggy," he considers.

"Looks beautiful to me," I lie. "It's a valiant effort, especially from an Irishman. Martha would be proud."

He turns my face to his and kisses me, in front of all the rest of the kitchen staff, who whack wooden spoons against hanging pots. They hoot and cheer, alerting the cranky kitchen manager, who probably has T3 also and who hollers, "Hey, staff only! Get the hell out!" I slink sheepishly away.

"I'm off at two!" Aiden calls.

"I'll be asleep!" I call back. "Charlotte's starting at six tomorrow, but come over after?"

He smiles and nods, and stands looking sadly down at his well-intended but truthfully ugly cake.

I load a plate with steamed frozen vegetables and canned fruit, bagels and cream cheese. I want some lettuce more than I can express. Oh, a bell pepper would be so good. . . . Allison's leaves are growing well, but nowhere near the rate needed for everyone to have a salad every day. I'm looking forward to Winfly like it's Christmas.

I knock on Charlotte's door, and she lets me in, then flops back on her bed. "I'm so tired," she sighs.

"Could be the twelve-hours-every-single-day working situation."

"Yeah, or the giant baby messing around in here."

"So not giant. You look like you had a big lunch."

"Well, I did," she says, and tears into a bagel.

I move some fruit around in a bowl. "You know what?" I stand and stretch. "You need fresh air. Just for a minute. Come on."

She's totally ensconced in a nest of blankets. Shakes her head.

"Yes! It's . . . hold on. . . ." I go to her desktop and see the current temperature. "Twenty-three below, perfect! Hasn't been this warm in forever. Who knows when it'll happen again. Get dressed. I'll be back in ten and we're going."

"I need to eat first . . . ," she whines pitifully.

"Fine, shove the rest of that bagel in your face and we're

going. Boots on. That parka's not going to fit forever." And I'm out her door to go get Vivian.

- - -

"What are you going out for this late?" Beard crabs, practically hucking radios at us. "You know it's snowing, right? Can't go past the church, and no Ob Hill. *Scott.*"

"Lady time," Charlotte demurs. "Don't worry about it." She is all about the honey-attracts-more-bees-than-vinegar way of dealing with this guy, but I'm not sure why anyone would want to attract bees on purpose. At least not on The Ice, where there's nothing to pollinate.

Except ladies. Heh.

I've taken my newly invented Antarctic Wind Advil Cocktail, which is three Advil tossed back with a big cup of hot tea, slammed back fast, no chaser.

Outside, snow is swirling and the wind does feel good, what seeps through our layers to chill us. Its sharp, frozen cleanliness wakes us. We fill our lungs and clear out the warm, stale, recirculated McMurdo air. We cannot talk over the wind, so we walk past the buildings, our attention on the black and red flags, away from the streetlamps, to the edge of the frozen white. The storm is covering the Transantarctic range tonight. No moon. But here we are.

Charlotte holds her arms over her belly. Vivian's are deep inside her parka, and I hold mine out, *Titanic*-style. I jump around, move. My poor body. Doesn't feel like me anymore.

Charlotte looks over at me and does some knee bends, whacks Vivian on her shoulder to get her moving, too. We are doing ridiculous calisthenics on Antarctic ice. But our blood moves. The icy snow stops pelting us; the wind seems to rage a little less. We close our eyes in our ski masks and inhale deeply. There is a sliver of a low moon in patches of the starry black sky.

And then I gasp from the coldness in my throat.

The sky.

Paintbrush strokes of color, flung from a palette of violet and crimson, of green and blue. Vivid, pure color, and it seems to move and shimmer, not like the pearly nacreous clouds; these are ribbons of pigment.

Aurora australis.

This is a really crazy time of year for the southern lights to show.

It's a sign.

Of something.

- - -

We say good night to Charlotte. I take a hot shower and lie down on the kitten bed in the twinkle light, not sleeping. Vivian's at the library. I get up and pull open my unmentionable drawer, search around in my underwear, and find Owen's letter.

Nothing could get any worse. If he's "lunching" with Kate, probably bringing her roses to opening night . . . and what am I doing with Aiden?

What am I *doing?*

I open the letter. Handwritten. LucasArts letterhead.

Dear Harper,

I'm going to try to just write this and give it to Luke to give to you, not agonize and edit and try to sound smart and casual, which would take hours, so forgive me if this is terribly written. But the thing is, I worry you left San Francisco because you think you owed it something and that you failed. I worry you think maybe you don't deserve to live here anymore. If this is how you're feeling, you could not be more wrong. You are more worthy of San Francisco than anyone I've ever known. Including Tony Bennett—that guy can go straight to hell. San Francisco needs to shape up and be more worthy of you.

You may be in Antarctica by the time you read this. If you read it. What is life like there? How is your job, and what is it, and have you seen penguins?

On a purely selfish note, I barely got to know you and tomorrow you'll be gone. And I already miss you. A lot. You are in the middle of some really difficult—I was going to say crap, but it's not crap, it's your life. And I didn't mean to intrude, and I'm sorry I flat-out begged you to stay and pretty much accused you of running away, because that's not true. I know that, and it's none of my business. I'm sorry. And I wish I could have helped more. If I'd known how, maybe you wouldn't be going.

But then on a trying-not-to-be-selfish note, you know better than anyone what you need to do. Which is, sadly for me and your family and San Francisco, leaving.

So. Here's a thing. I feel like we never got to go on a date. Like a "Hey, I'll pick you up at eight!" date. Not to assume you would have agreed to one with me, but I never even got the chance to ask you to. There are so many things in the city I want to do with you. I want to ask you to show me the places you love best, and I want to show you my favorites, and wouldn't it be great if some of them overlapped?

So here's what I'm going to do. I am going to ask if you will go on dates with me while you're gone. I am prepared for this to be one-sided. I have no idea how Antarctica works, if you'll be able to respond. But it's six months. (Six months, you are so brave!) If I don't hear from you by September, when you're supposed to come back, I'll end this nonsense and leave you alone. But until then, I will get to know you by dating your family. Shut up. It's not like that.

Here's what I know about you so far: You are a person full of love and hard work. Graduating early with a 4.0, working and dancing, like, thirty hours a week—who does that? You love that Willa kid. She adores you, and those little girls you teach were crowding around you after THE NUTCRACKER like they worship you. Which I think they do. I like little kids a lot, and the way people interact with them tells me a ton about who that person is. Kids and dogs.

Your family seems to know you really well. I'm going to see what I can find out. In exchange, I'll send you reciprocal fun-filled information via email about me and tell you all about the dates we would have gone on. *All the WHEN HARRY MET SALLY stuff. This will get you more information about me than if you spoke to my family, as my dad's English kind of sucks and my mom still hates you, so I feel like it's pretty even. Good times. The Ice hasn't turned you Chinese by chance? Calm down. I'm mostly kidding.*

I plan on bragging to anyone who'll listen that I know a person who lives there. (Temporarily. I hope.) Seriously, how did you manage that? What seventeen-year-old does that? And I wasn't going to mention dancing, because—obviously—but I'll say this one last time and never again if you don't want to hear it and PS, destroy this letter once you read it. BUT. You dancing in that falling snow was maybe the most beautiful thing I've seen in my life. Ever.

Be safe. Have an adventure. Come home.

Owen

The museum pancake date was *ours.*

I never wrote him back. And now he's having "lunch" with Kate.

I open my email.

So many from Owen. Still coming in on a semiregular basis.

I choose a random email from Kate and hold my breath.

》》》I love you. Forgive me.

I open another.

>>>I'm sorry. Please forgive me.

The most recent one.

>>>Come home.

I open Willa's second and only other email. Her new baby-sitter is nice but is allergic to tree nuts, so now they can't have peanut butter in their kitchen, ever. Lindsay, it seems, is such a bad teacher that Willa has stopped taking class. So have many of the other kids. Then a PS from Hannah:

>>>Don't listen to Willa. Lindsay's not that bad. It's just without you teaching, I feel really uncomfortable taking free lessons from Simone, but I'm saving up and I'll send her back next fall, so please don't worry. We love you! Come home safe—and soon!

I've left Willa without classes. It's my fault. I hate money, I hate that ballet is so goddamned expensive. Willa loves it; she—and *every* kid who wants to—should be able to have a damn ballet class. It's just dancing; it isn't a pony or sleepaway rocket-launching camp. An empty room and record player are all that's needed and they love it *so much*—

My stomach is burning. It is on fire. I'm getting an ulcer! There's a hole in my stomach!

My face flushes and my heart races.

I compose an email to Simone.

>>>You need to call Hannah and get Willa back in class. She loves it, and she needs it. I'm sending the tuition. Please don't ever tell Hannah. Just get Willa back there. And please get someone to help Lindsay teach.

Dad reports:

>>>I've seen more of this Owen kid than I have of your brother. They both come to Saturday breakfast. He asks a lot of weird stuff about you—what you were like as a little kid, what's your favorite subject in school, do you and Luke really get along or secretly hate each other—is he vetting you for something? Please answer the guy's letters and get him off my back!

And Mom says:

>>>Owen invited us to lunch at LucasArts last Friday, and guess who was in line behind me for burritos? GEORGE LUCAS! I asked if he knew your brother, and I told him about Luke being named for LUKE, you know, and George said that was "wonderful" and then we both ordered chicken burritos, and he went to get a yogurt from the cold case, and he turned

around and said to me, "May the Force be with you . . . and Luke"! You could have knocked me over with a feather. Your brother was humiliated. Mike. Drop.

Oh God. Poor Luke.

I compose a new message.

>>>My Sweet Willster,

Please, please go back to class. It is so fun, and so good for you, and I asked Madame Simone to please get a helper for Lindsay. I will see you again. I promise.

Hurts my heart to write it. She may miss me, but I know for a fact I miss her more.

If the aurora *was* a sign, I still have no idea what it meant.

But I can't worry about that right now, because I have to go call Western Union and wire money to the woman who ruined my life so she doesn't ruin Willa's life.

- 17 -

Antarctica

WINFLY IS COMING. THE MONTHS OF DARK COLD ARE STARTING to wear on even the most senior Winter Overers. Every day people are getting more anxious and the hammocks in the greenhouse are all full of T3 zombies. I haven't seen Shackleton in weeks. Allison's pumping as much lettuce into the kitchen as she can, but it is never enough. Charlotte is in overdrive and dragging Vivian and me with her—and oddly, I think it is helping. I'm feeling more focused, no less confused about the shambles of my directionless life, but I'm not freaking out and panicked so much every second of the day anymore. We are working for a very specific goal. And Vivian and I have made it our mission to monitor Charlotte's wellbeing and counteract the stress of finishing her thesis, to keep that baby where she's supposed to be as long as she's supposed to be there.

Of course, I've also decided to make myself insane by

alternating spending time with Aiden and then having a date with Owen. One afternoon or evening, an icy snow walk beneath the star-filled and gradually but ever-brightening sky, watching the aurora and feeling small in the universe. The next night, me with the laptop in bed, reading in order the twenty-five (and counting) emails detailing my and Owen's "dates." And exchanging information about himself for stories he has gotten about me from Luke, or Mom or Dad.

⟫Today I helped your dad and Luke take the day-olds to the shelter in the Castro, and I got to hear all about how on your birthday and Christmas you always get a million handmade cards in your mailbox from the kids you take care of and your students. I love that you love little kids. Here's my deal with them:

I think I told you my mom teaches preschool at the Wah Mei School in the Sunset? It's in a church basement, and it's the oldest Chinese/English bilingual school in San Francisco. When my parents came here from China, I was three, and they both worked full time, so they put me in Wah Mei. Every day from seven a.m. until six-thirty at night. Those are long hours for an adult; they're even longer for a kid. Josie was already in first grade and she came after school, so we were both there till dinnertime. Then on Saturdays we had to go to Chinese school for three hours.

Okay, I'm going to nutshell this for you.

Where have I heard that before?

I'm at this little basement school all day, just a tiny concrete side yard to play in, and they were always putting on VHS tapes of Mister Rogers for us. And during naptime the teachers would watch Oprah when they thought we were asleep. So here's what I was getting all day at preschool (day care—who are we kidding?):

- I am special because I am me, and there's no one else like me.
- A fulfilling life means being independent, helpful, and kind.
- Always clean up after yourself.
- Crash diets don't work. (Oprah)
- Chase fulfillment, not money. A right-sized life is the best life a person can have.

And then at home, I'm getting a slightly opposing viewpoint:

- Money is security.
- Charity begins and ends at home.
- Happiness is security, which is money.
- Family is the world and tradition is family.
- Don't be lazy.

So I often found my worldview in quite a pickle. When I ditched school to work at Lucas, my parents were furious. I understand why. I was choosing a path that to them meant I would not have the best life I could, because to them, being a doctor meant secure money and prestige and oh, there's the helping-people part. But hours and hours of those great American philosophers, Rogers and Winfrey, had gotten to me. I love my job. I make games that make people happy, which is a way to help, I think. Fun is important. I'm financially independent, I'm starting school again, part time this fall, to finish a degree in programming and design. I couldn't have asked for a better life.

I like little kids, I think, because I remember so well what it was like to be one. I sympathize. Even in the best of circumstances it is often harder than a lot of people remember. I help my mom with the Wah Mei kids on field trips sometimes when I've got a day off. They're fun, those little suckers.

I'm a complete mystery to my parents. But they love me. I love them. We just don't talk about my day at work or the fact that I haven't been to church in five years or that I might be in love with a white girl or that I drive a hybrid car because the emissions are lower, and then we're able to have a great time together.

Good date. Sorry I talked so much. Fred Rogers says it's good to share. And it's thanks to Oprah I'm not intimidated by, instead ridiculously attracted to, smart women. Because I'm learning that you are, even more than I already knew.

Owen

PS: Please explain to your mom that George Lucas doesn't know any of the employees at his company. It is a small city unto itself, and he couldn't care less. Thanks a ton!

I am at a loss for any words that could even attempt to reciprocate the honesty, the smart, funny, impossible perfection of Owen's letters. I start, again and again, wanting so badly to respond and then, embarrassed by the words I've written, delete them all. Not good enough. But silence is worse. What must he think of me?

And also, does this guy ever work? These emails, it's like a novel every time! And also: *He might be in love with a white girl.*

In love.

"Might be. Interesting."

Shackleton's sitting on my bed. On top of my unfolded laundry.

Vivian is asleep in her bed—I watch her breathe. Even, slow.

"Hey," I hiss. "What gives? This is my *room*! It's completely inappropriate and *not* okay. You're freaking me out."

"That greenhouse is entirely too crowded lately."

"Not cool, man."

"That Owen's a nice kid."

I close the laptop.

"Probably wouldn't ply you with liquor and encourage you to risk hypothermia for fun."

"Aiden didn't *encourage* . . ."

"I found a stowaway on *Endurance* after we'd sailed too far to turn back. Want to know what I said to him?"

"No."

"You'll be the first one we eat."

I do not return his smile.

"Listen," he says, "I forgot to tell a really good one."

"Good one what?" I sigh.

"This one's quick. I promise."

"I'll bet."

"When *Endurance* was sinking, we knew we'd be traveling—whether it was ice floe or sled. We had to pack light, take as little from the ship as we could if we were to have any hope of finding land. Food and fuel were the utmost priority, followed closely by clothing."

I close my eyes and settle in. He's not going anywhere.

"But one of the purposes of the journey was to photograph the landscape. My photographer, Frank Hurley, was under contract with Kodak, and they'd given him all the plate glass negatives he wanted."

"Glass?"

"Yes. The negatives were exposed on glass, and each

photograph weighed several ounces. Frank had hundreds of them. Maybe thousands."

"Thousands of pieces of glass."

"*Yes.*"

"Okay."

"I told him we couldn't possibly take them all—the sleds couldn't bear the weight, and it would slow us down. He had to decide. I was his expedition leader and I forced him to choose which to take."

"You give him a number, and he whittled it down?"

"He tried. He wanted to keep them all, and yes, they were all worthy. Every one magnificent. You've seen them, yes?"

I have. Mom's got all the Frank Hurley coffee table books because our Scott is in a lot of the photographs. They are honestly magnificent. Shattered *Endurance* tilted precariously in the pack ice, sinking into the black water. The men playing football on the ice, the dogs. The *James Caird* out to sea, leaving the men behind on tiny Elephant Island.

"We piled every single negative on the ice one afternoon. I held one in each hand and told him he had three seconds to choose. Left or right. The one he pointed to went into a pile on a sled, the other I smashed on the ice."

"*No.*"

"We completed three rounds of this and were left with the collection the world is familiar with today—culled by pure instinct, every one a masterpiece, a treasure."

"You smashed works of art on the ice?"

"The poor man was paralyzed by indecision. But by the last round he completely trusted himself. He was fearless. He knew exactly which to keep; he saved the very best images. And his own life. *All* our lives, by not forcing us to wait for days while he agonized over an impossible choice. Trust your gut. It will save your life."

"How will I know?"

"Do you trust Simone?"

"I don't know."

He stands.

"You'll know when you stop asking."

"Look, Rumpelstiltskin, can you please just say what you mean? In regular words?"

He shrugs. "My mind is yours, so the words are, too. You are my captain."

"Harper?" Vivian mumbles, and rolls over to face me. "You okay?"

I rub my temples, close my eyes, and breathe.

"Sorry," I say. "I talk in my sleep sometimes."

"Okay."

"Hey. Can we listen to your friend some more?"

"What friend?"

"The guy. About your town?"

"He's not my . . . It's two-thirty in the morning!"

"I know." I pile the laundry into a basket, climb into

bed, and pull the covers up under my chin. "Just for a little while?"

She puts her iPod in the dock, hits Play, and falls back on her pillow.

"Well," the guy says, *"it's been another quiet week in Lake Wobegon, Minnesota, my hometown."*

- 18 -

Antarctica

WINFLY IS TOMORROW. BEAUTIFUL, BEAUTIFUL WINFLY. LATE August and the sun is creeping every day higher behind the mountaintops.

We've made it, Charlotte and Vivian and I and *Her*. Nearly. Practically. Maybe.

Charlotte's anxious all morning at work. Two hundred Main Body staff will arrive on this flight, along with the mail and fresh food.

We're busily working quietly, getting so close to finishing the analysis part of her thesis, and Charlotte says, "It's going to be so crowded in the dining hall now. I'll miss winter."

"Oh, come on. You don't even go in there anymore."

"I like it when it's just us. Winter people are a special breed. And this may be my last one."

"Well. Now you'll have your own little Winter."

"Oooh, name her Winter," Vivian says. "That's way better than Nacreous."

Aiden and I take our last Ob Hill winter climb before the crowds descend. All the way to the cross, so near the stars we could reach and touch them.

"I will never understand," I say, my face to the sky, "How Shackleton navigated those tiny wooden boats across the ocean. Twice. In *storms*! How do you use celestial navigation with cloud cover?"

The stars are burning so bright tonight.

"He didn't."

"Yes, he did. What else would he use?"

"First of all, Shackleton wasn't the one navigating. He was the expedition leader, smart enough to choose Frank Worsley as the captain; Worsley navigated. And I've no idea how he did, storms or not. Southern skies are impossible."

"Why?" Stars so densely piled in the black they make a person swoon—how could they not lead the way?

"I'm telling you, in the Northern Hemisphere, Polaris, the North Star, marks the position of the north celestial pole—which just means it's easy to orient yourself in the night sky, find True North. But the Southern Hemisphere has no Polaris."

I feel a disorienting shift. "It *doesn't*?"

"The south celestial pole—the imaginary point in the sky directly above the South Pole—there's no especially bright, outshine-the-others star there. Or anywhere in the southern sky. So to celestially navigate, Worsley had to use constellations—Southern Cross, Centaurus—and measure them against one another's distance, account for rotation . . ."

No path in The Ice. No guidance in the stars.

Why did I come here?

"The southern sky is beautiful," Aiden says quietly. "But it will keep you lost if you don't know your way around the stars."

The ice and ocean and the night sky go on forever. I am lost. Still.

"Five weeks left," Aiden says.

I nod.

"If you decide to go back to San Francisco, I'll miss you," he says.

"I don't know where I'm going."

"No?"

"No idea."

"Well," he says, "I was thinking. If you don't go home . . . would you want to go home with me?"

"Home . . . to Ireland?"

"No! Home. Just . . . the world. Wherever we want."

My breath slows.

"Three months. See how it feels. Then I'm off to Ireland for winter semester at university and you'll . . . know more."

This sky—these deceptive, aimless stars—will never be more beautiful than in this moment.

"Yes," I say without thinking.

I move closer to Aiden, standing beside Scott's cross.

I have taken a step.

- - -

"Good morning, ladies!" I sing as I sail into the lab the next morning bearing toast and tea.

"Is it?" Vivian asks, deep in concentration with a sheet of data apparently confounding her.

"You look rested!" Charlotte says.

I smile. "I feel better. I feel good. There is lettuce in my future."

"Oh, that's right—finally!"

The whole station is eager to watch the arrival of the cargo plane, but the clouds have moved in and it is snowing. Not enough to cancel the flight, but with the windchill where it is, none of us are going out.

At last, they arrive. The Winfly people. Cold blows in and reunions and laughter, and Charlotte is right—long lines for food. Aiden's swamped in the kitchen. He waves and smiles. For dinner they've unpacked the freshies, and Charlotte and Vivian and I feast on huge bowls of lettuce, tomatoes, peppers, and mushrooms.

"I've never been happier in my life." Charlotte smiles.

"I'll be happy when you're home and in a hospital," I tell her. But secretly I'm already happy. Traveling the world, exploring with brave, adventurous Aiden, getting a time-out on San Francisco and Kate, and ballet and Owen and—Oh, see, I can't even think about it without getting nervous and confused, and so I stop and concentrate on my lettuce.

Vivian is working late on the confounding data, so I go to our room alone, turn on the laptop, and tell myself this is the last. One last date with Owen, then I'll write him and tell him . . . what? That I think of him night and day and miss him so much, but this cute Irish guy is offering me an easy way for me to be lazy and put off living my life for a few more months?

>>>Dear Harper,

It is Past Romances Revealed date time. This, I assumed, would be the one that got me super jealous and made me hulk out.

Instead it made me feel like I'm a total creep.

Kate's been nice enough to meet me for lunch a lot. As it turns out, she knows more about you than almost anyone. She spends most of the time crying, but I come prepared with tissues and bullet points to keep her on track as I barrage her with questions about you.

Please tell me you're responding to her emails.

And there's where my involvement with that ends.

Back to our date.

Kate says, and I think I believe her, that you've never had a boyfriend. Not that every single person needs to date—it's no requirement and you're kind of busy every second of every day, but . . . Kate says you two agreed. For ballet. Again, I totally get it. But did you ever want to go out with someone and purposely not do it? Did you ever wish you could?

That's the part that makes me sad. It's just the Rogers/ Winfrey in me that thinks you maybe would have had some fun at movies and beach parties and such. But I could be wrong, and if you never wanted to and didn't miss it, then I am definitely wrong.

So here's my deal. I dated in high school/college:

1. Mia Li

2. Midori Tong

Mia and I dated all of our junior and senior years. We went to prom twice. Then she went to school back east and never wrote once she got there. Harsh.

Midori and I dated on and off during my first year at college. She majored in acting and was smart and funny, but there was this whole "free love" thing going on in the drama department.

I'm making all this sound like it was them not me, but that's because I'm telling the story.

I dated the daughter of one of my dad's work friends. Her name was Vivian Tam. She was really kind and very pretty. Smart. You can see I have a type. She went to do Peace Corps work and never came back from rural China. My mom still thinks we're getting married.

And that brings us up to date.

You will notice all the surnames of past girlfriends are Chinese.

I wondered for a while if I was a soulless robot incapable of true passion, because while the end of each relationship left me sad, there was never crying or Ryan Gosling–level devastation.

I knew you for what, three months? Spent a total of maybe ten hours with you? I will go ahead and tell you what your jerk brother probably already has. There have been some Gosling moments—none involving standing in the middle of a street in the rain—but it hasn't been fun.

One piece of decent advice my mom did give me, and is maybe why I persist one-sided dating you, is this:

Find someone smarter than you. Also, braver and stronger and better looking.

Have I mentioned that I miss you?

Vivian's key in the door startles me.

"Hey," I say, and shut down the laptop. "What's up?"

"You tell me," she says, surveying my red-rimmed eyes and pile of wadded-up Ryan Gosling tissues on the desk.

"Get the numbers figured out?"

She nods. "I am a genius." She climbs into her flannels, gets in her bed, puts her earbuds in. Then she takes them out. "The grants look really good."

"Oh—they do?"

"You're a good writer. You use the stats really well. They're not overwhelming, and they make effective points. You should think about it."

"What?"

"Grant writing."

"For . . . ?"

"Like a job. It's a skill. You can write grants for anything. Like funding teenagers to come to Antarctica."

"Anything?"

She shrugs. "Corporations, people with money are just dying to fund things and write off the deduction. You're good at it."

Anything.

"Thanks. Thank you."

She puts her earbuds back in and lies down.

Anything?

"Vivian."

"What?"

"Do you miss home? Is that why you listen to him?"

Long silence.

"It helps me sleep."

"Vivian."

"Harper."

"I miss home, too."

She pulls her headphone jack out, puts the iPod in the dock, and we listen to the stories and miss home, together.

- - -

Charlotte sleeps late, taking a rare day off work. Vivian and I, both worn out and ahead of schedule anyway, nonetheless work in the lab on our own. Also it's a nice place to hide, as we're not in the mood to deal with the two hundred new people just yet.

"Being pregnant makes you really tired, I guess?" I muse.

"The girls at my school seemed pretty drowsy," Vivian says. "But most them were also always smoking weed, too, so maybe they were just high. Or bored."

"Jeez!" I laugh. "Teen pregnancy and drug use—Garrison doesn't talk a lot about that happening in Lake Wobegon."

"That's because he made Lake Wobegon up." She sighs. "Don't talk about him in the daylight or I won't let you listen anymore."

I smile.

Only hours till we're home free, the second the plane leaves, we can unburden our secret to the doctor, and Charlotte will be in the clear.

"Hey," I say. "I'll go grab lunch. What do you want?"

"Really? Because I'd love more salad. Maybe mashed potatoes?"

"That is a brilliant combination. Be right back!" I rush down the hall until I reach the gridlock at the kitchen.

So many people. Too crowded.

I make my way to the stairs, and Beard sidles up behind me. "What's up, Scott?"

"Not a whole bunch. How are you?" I take Charlotte's lead in suffusing my words with cheer.

"Claustrophobic. But they're here to stay. Winfly left this morning."

I turn to face him.

"Really? I thought it stays a day or two."

"Too cold. Unloaded, refueled, took off right after."

I'm smiling so hard my face hurts. Charlotte and Vivian will be thrilled; I already am. My toes wiggle inside my shoes. No more baby secret. She can see the doctor. I get in the horrendously long food line.

"What're you so giddy about?" Beard frowns.

"Just excited for salad!" I'm tempted to annoy the chef, go back into the kitchen, and grab Aiden for sheer happiness. I crane my neck to glimpse him, but still he's nowhere to be seen.

"Who're you looking for?"

Oh my gosh, Beard. You are so annoying. "No one."

"Not your boyfriend, I hope."

"He's not my boyfriend."

"Oh. Well. That's good. Considering."

"Considering what?"

"Long distance never works."

I turn to him, take the bait. "What?"

His face changes.

"What *is* it, Ben?"

"This is the Irish kid we're talking about, yes?"

"Yes," I sigh.

Ben looks, for a moment, truly reluctant. But he says it anyway. "Do you know he left?"

"Left where?"

"On the Winfly plane. He's gone."

"No, he's not."

"He is. I watched him get on the bus for the runway. Tagged his bags and everything."

"You are an ass."

"Kid, I'm just telling you what I saw. . . ."

"I'm not a kid."

"Harp." Vivian, out of nowhere. "Forgot to ask for orange juice." She looks from me to Beard. "What's up?"

"Scott's upset because her boyfriend's gone."

I can't move. The salmon stream of people crowding around the dining hall entrance is pushing, moving in closer. Everything is suddenly very quiet. Someone, Vivian, takes my arm and guides me firmly away from the crowd, from Beard, up the stairs, to a door and knocks.

- - -

"Are you sure Ben's not just messing around?" Vivian muses.

I hadn't thought of that. "How would we check?"

"Go ask the kitchen staff! Look at the flight record!"

"I'll go," Vivian offers. She's back in three minutes. Shakes her head.

"Jesus Christ," Charlotte whispers. "Do *all* men suck today? What the hell?"

"He wanted me to go with him," I whisper. "When winter's over. We were going together."

"He *said* that?" Vivian asks.

I nod, mopping my face with a wad of tissues.

"When?"

"Last night."

"That's a dick move," she says.

"For sure." Charlotte nods.

Vivian's sitting beside me on my bed, and all at once, as if I've completely lost control of my mind and limbs, I put my head in her lap and cry until I can't breathe.

And she *lets* me.

She pets my short hair. "I'm sorry," she says. "Harper, I'm sorry."

"I don't . . . I don't even . . ." I choke. "Why would he leave without me? And early. Can he even do that? Doesn't he need a compelling reason? I'm so stupid!"

"Harper," Charlotte says from Vivian's bed. *"Harper."*

"What?"

"You are not stupid. His reason is . . . he's a little boy."

I pull myself together enough to sit up. "Oh, Vivian," I choke-breathe. "Your sweater's all cried on."

She shrugs. "It's not one of my favorites."

"Harp, I didn't realize you liked him *that* much," Charlotte says.

"I don't think I do!" I wail. "Do I? It's not even—Now what do I do?"

"About what?"

"I was going with him! I didn't know where, but it was a direction to go, and not alone, with a person who knew me as *just* me, not . . ." I stop short of *ballerina*. "I knew where I was going. I'm lost again."

They both sit and look at me, bewildered.

"Why not go home?"

More tears.

"Hey," Vivian says over my sobs. "Off topic, but can we tell the doctor now?"

Charlotte shakes her head.

"Will you tell them soon?"

"Sure."

"It's making me really nervous."

"Ugh, me too!" I shout, flopping back onto the bed. "That goddamned plane left hours ago. Say something! Go see the doctor."

"I'm waiting for just one small storm, make sure they don't send a plane right back."

Vivian and I exchange a look. "You've got two days," I say. "And it'd better storm. Otherwise we're going there and telling them ourselves. I can't take it anymore!"

"Fine," Charlotte crabs. "But I'm hungry. Can someone . . ."

Vivian stands. "I'll go," she offers. "What would you like?"

"I'll go with," I sniffle. "Might as well keep eating."

We take Charlotte's grilled cheese order and fight through the crowds together.

- - -

I am searching for solitude in the wrong place. So many people, all excited to be on The Ice. The afternoon after Aiden leaves, I practically run to the top of Ob Hill, alone at last but breaking the rules. I've memorized the climb, and each time I'm faster.

At the cross I watch the sky glow mostly gray-pink. That's all it's doing and it's enough. Still beautiful. But freezing.

"You okay?"

I nod.

"Don't seem like it," Shackleton says.

"I'm such an idiot."

"Eh. I wouldn't say that."

"He was so . . . honest."

Shackleton smiles. "Don't know about that, either."

"Okay, well, no, not in retrospect."

"Listen. You've only got to trust one person to know where you belong. And clinging to the coattails of some dumb kid who stands by and angles for a *sleepover* while you drink yourself sick? And give me a break with the 'Home is where you hang your hat' nonsense. That will get you nowhere. Thank goodness he left."

I turn to him.

"Seriously!" he says. "Listen. It takes patience and love and bravery to have a home. To not just run off to the next place when things are hard. Or frightening. Or lonely. I'm not saying you stay stuck in a place you don't want to be if you can get out. And obviously I'm a huge fan of exploring this glorious planet. I'm speaking to the fact that nothing good can ever come from leaving something you love, simply for an asinine notion you're not good enough for it. Or him. Or anyone. *Make* yourself good enough and don't start with me. I get the body structure stuff. I'm saying, you know who you are. You do. The path is in front of you; be brave and take it. *Now.*"

"I can't see it."

"Don't have to."

"How did Worsley navigate the boat to South Georgia?"

"If I knew how, I would have done it myself and not risked his life—I'm the leader, not the captain. I was smart enough to hire the very best crew, each man the best at his job, and *that* is why they lived. They saved themselves."

We look up at the diamond dust of stars in the darkening sky.

"Feels impossible."

"Harper Scott! There is an important distinction between *difficult* and *impossible*—one requires a huge amount of effort," he says. "And the other requires more."

"I had a place to start," I say. "Someone to go with. Maybe I'll go anyway. Alone."

"No more relying on others for the good. Or God forbid blaming others for the bad. Forgive. Trust yourself."

I nod.

He smiles.

"Harper."

I nearly fall off the mountain.

Vivian.

"Talking to yourself is a clear sign of T3."

I nod.

"Except here. Which is so cold you have to persuade yourself out loud not to freeze to death," says Vivian.

I nod.

"Are you okay?"

"Yeah. No."

Wind is picking up.

"Some Indian tribes, when they're in mourning, the women cut off their long hair. Sometimes they bury it with a person who died."

Tiny shards of ice swirl around us. I am hypnotized by the stars.

"*Harper.* Are you in mourning?"

I nod.

"I'm homesick," she says, and jumps lightly, trying to warm up. "I hate going to bed alone. I'm used to sharing with three of my sisters. I can't sleep. So I listen to Garrison. I was glad to move into your room. I sleep a lot better."

I smile. "Me too."

"Where *are* you going? When it's done?"

I shrug.

"You're not going back to San Francisco?"

"Can't."

"What if Charlotte does have the baby on The Ice? Will it be Antarctican?"

"It should be."

"Want to take a walk?"

I nod.

- - -

We huddle together and make our way back down Ob Hill, past the power wires bending beneath the soft weight of snow, past work sheds and buildings to the front steps of the Chapel of the Snows.

The sturdy white chapel is squat and symmetrical, featuring a tall steeple. We fall, pushed by the wind, into the unlocked door and climb out of our frozen parkas and mittens.

The church is lit and warm. The vaulted, beamed ceiling is dark wood, the altar backlit (or would be, on a sunny day, probably) by a window with a stained glass image of the continent of Antarctica embedded with symbols of various religions. And a penguin. The seats are basic wooden, padded office chairs arranged in rows, big American and Antarctic flags on poles. I'm surprised it gets any business, what with all the scientists. I think a lot of the people who come here worship mostly at the Altar of Keeping Warm.

Vivian is in a seat halfway back from the altar. I hug myself warm and walk down the aisle to sit beside her.

"This thing burned down," she says. "Twice."

"In all this ice and snow. Perfect."

"What do you miss most?" she asks me. "Like, when you lie in bed awake, thinking about your life before you came here, what comes up first and most often?"

It is so hard to parse this excellent but dangerous question. Because as I mentally Rolodex through what makes me cry into my McMurdo pillow, it seems to all be wrapped in one all-encompassing ache.

"What do *you* miss?"

"My sisters. Brothers."

"How many?"

"Well. I'm sixth."

"Wow."

"Of eleven."

"*Wow.*"

- 334 -

She nods. "My favorite thing about being here has been that no one knows me as number six. Or anyone's sister."

"Do you all love science?"

"No. They're in the Future Farmers and Girls Scouts, and they like math, some of them. My older sisters have a pottery shed and a kiln out back."

"They must be *so* proud of you. Two students in the entire world, and they chose you!"

She smiles.

"I miss San Francisco," I say.

"*That's* what you're breaking your heart over? Get on a plane, problem solved!"

"No, not *just* that! Partly, though."

"Sure."

"Have you even been?"

"*This* is the first place I've ever been outside Minnesota. Traveling with eleven kids is no picnic. And not cheap."

"You've never left home in your entire life, and the first time you do, it's to New Zealand and Antarctica?"

"St. Paul folks don't half-ass anything."

"Clearly."

"Where have you been?"

"Oh," I say. "I've been . . ." And it occurs to me—I haven't. Been anywhere. One trip to New York to meet Dad's parents when Luke and I weren't even potty trained. Mom and Dad and Luke have been lots of places. I've always begged to stay home with babysitters, happily giving up travel opportunities to never miss class, rehearsal, performances. "I haven't been anywhere, either!" I say. "I never cared. I love home—is that weird?"

"Not to me."

"You know what I miss? *Knowing.* Knowing exactly what I'm doing every day, working as hard as I can and harder, toward a very well-defined goal. Not this nebulous, lost . . ."

"Grant writing. I'm telling you, *that's* your calling." She smiles.

She gets up and goes to the rows of white candles below the window, beside the altar. "I have always been embarrassed that I'm not jonesing to get out of Minnesota—not even St. Paul—the second I graduate. Am I lazy? Or boring?"

She strikes a match and lights a candle. "Or maybe it's as simple as I love where I live, and who gives a crap what anyone thinks of me? They can live where they want and leave me the hell out of it."

And *that* is the news from Lake Wobegon: She *is* a badass.

- 19 -

Antarctica

WORK IN THE LAB THE FOLLOWING DAYS IS MUCH LESS LIKE work. Vivian and I chitchat like old ladies, and Charlotte has taken to wearing giant headphones to drown out our gabbing. A raging storm blew through the ice shelf, and Charlotte let the medical center know what's up—that she's *knocked* up, as she fondly refers to the situation, and no one's panicking. No one's in trouble. And we're nearly done with the grants, the research; Charlotte's thesis is basically complete. So we're free to openly ferry deliveries back and forth from the kitchen to the lab when Charlotte *must* have three slices of American cheese *or I will cut someone.*

Which I'm on my way out the door to get when a mail guy puts his head in the room.

"Harper Scott?"

"Yeah?"

"Package. Last of the pile, took a while to sort."

A box. Wrapped in brown paper, addressed to me in black

Sharpie. Inside there is another wrapped box, and a folded letter.

Harper Scott,

I've been reading up on Robert (Millennium) Falcon Scott. And I came up with some interesting observations:

He was a scientist. The last letter he wrote from inside his tent before he and his men died, he wrote to his wife about their son, "Make the boy interested in natural history if you can; it is better than games." I'll try not to take offense at that last part, but the thing about wanting the kid to like science? Dude loved science.

So why kill himself and his entire crew trying to get to the pole first? What's that got to do with science? He was broke. His family was broke, and getting there first would have meant a regular income. Had he just gone there to do the research, no one would have died, people! Apparently he was a great researcher. The writings they found with the bodies are apparently still really useful.

That whole story seems unrelated, but stay with me. I think my point is this: You love ballet. You are a dancer. A really amazing dancer. Find a way to make it your life. Don't give it up. But also? Please don't die for it. There has to be another way to keep it. Isn't there?

Yours,

Owen

There is a DVD. Our *Nutcracker.*

I unwrap the smaller box.

My audition shoes. My Maltese Cross Yuan Yuan pointe shoes. There is a note tucked in them.

Please don't throw this out before you read it. I begged Simone to ask San Francisco to come see me. They weren't scouting. I wanted to come home. I need to be with you. You're the only family I have, the one I want. I need you. I love you. I think Owen does, too. I'll do anything. Please forgive me. Please come home.

Kate

Vivian reaches for the shoes. "What *are* these?"

"They are mine."

"Are you a *dancer*?"

I reread Kate's note. Owen's letter. I hold the shoes to my heart.

\- \- \-

In the movie room, where people usually watch horror movies about isolation in the snow, I put the DVD in the player, settle Vivian and Charlotte in chairs before the screen, and ask them, for the hundredth time, to "Please just tell me what you see."

They nod. I leave the room, but listen at the door to the music, still more familiar to me than anything else in life.

"Where is she?" I hear Charlotte say. "It's a crowd of skinny white girls all dressed the same, doing the same steps—how can you even tell which one is her?"

"Concentrate. *Right there*—see? The left? And then ...
there, turning, see?"

"Okay, okay, yes. I'm moving closer. I'll lose her in that—
what the hell is that, snow? Is this *The Nutcracker*?"

I hear Vivian heave a huge sigh. "I am deeply concerned
for your child. Pay attention!"

I love them both. So much.

It ends at last, the parts I'm in, and I go in and pull up a
chair beside them.

"Tell me." I ask.

Scientists. Neutral. People who observe, ask questions,
gather information, come to conclusions. Objectively. People
kind enough to tell me the truth.

"You're amazing," Charlotte says. "So beautiful!" She is
crying. Hormones.

Okay. Maybe *one* of them is objective.

Vivian takes a breath.

"There's a difference that I see," she says carefully,
"between you and the other girls. I have no idea if it's good
or bad—better or worse. But definitely you're not like them."

My stomach and my heart unclench.

"Okay."

She nods. "Even if I wasn't watching just for you, I would
have seen it."

I eject the disk.

"What does that even mean?" Charlotte cries. "She's

stunning. Did you see her doing all those turns? What is wrong with you?"

"I'm not saying she's not really great," Vivian yelps. "Harper, that was really and truly amazing. I think you're a beautiful dancer—I'm saying there's something different. That's all. It's an observation. *Science*," she says to Charlotte. "What she asked us for."

Charlotte sits, pulling at the raggedy edge of her sweater sleeve. "I saw it, too," she says. Quietly.

"Really?"

"Just . . . different—but isn't that good? Unique!"

"Depends," I admit. "Not always."

"Are you all right?" Vivian asks.

"I think so."

"Have I said the most horrible, mean thing ever?"

Were my throat not tight for crying, I would be able to tell her the truth. Which is that, in a little over twelve minutes, here in Antarctica just in the nick of time, she and Charlotte have set me free.

"Want to be alone?"

I do.

I close the door and sit. I put the disc back in.

I see it.

What Mom and Dad could never see through a mucked-up lens of way too much love and no dance experience of their own. What Simone was seeing and didn't want to. Wished she wasn't.

What I should have seen and didn't. Or maybe, like Mom and Dad, so much love made it unclear, made it not matter.

And there is Kate. Still, always the way I've seen her all my life, even more. Perfection. She could not be more beautiful, and more than that, *her love is evident*. She is born to it.

I rewind to watch us both, just once more, and accidentally rewind past the start of "Snow."

Here are my angels. Here is Willa.

Their faces turn toward the wings where I know I am smiling, demonstrating the steps, whispering at them to "Look at the audience! Have fun, turn, turn!"

They are concentrating so hard. Heads high, feet turned out, arms strong. Listening carefully to their music, loving every second of every movement.

I walk alone to the basketball court. People are milling around, walking past. Some poke their heads in the open doorway to take a look.

I tie my Maltese Cross shoes securely on unstockinged feet.

I turn carefully across the floor, my head light with no hair, familiar stretch and pull in my legs and arms, in my abdomen. People stand and watch me. I keep dancing. They walk away; they walk on and don't stop. I'm alone—now I've got an audience—now alone. Alive, at last, in every second of every movement. I am home.

"Okay," I say quietly to Shackleton. To myself. "Okay. Understood, Captain."

- - -

I dance every day, and the last winter weeks fly by. My legs are stronger, arms tighter every moment. I eat vegetables, and cheese, and anything I want. Except white bread and butter. My body is lean and strong, no longer bony. And my boobs stick around. Bonus. The sky is lighter every day until at last, all four hundred of us rush outside, and it happens; the fiery light edges over the mountains. It is a new year. Winter is over. The light is glorious and beautiful and hopeful. We laugh and cry and jump around, strangers and friends. We yell at Charlotte not to jump too much, for crying out loud, the poor baby, *jeez!*

In the crowd, a familiar face is near in her red hood. Allison hugs me.

"You look good in natural light," she says. "How do you feel?"

Months of people—of myself—asking me that, but I like it from her.

"Better," I say. "Not so . . ." I gesture around my head. She looks into my eyes.

"Definitely better. I need to ask you something."

Oh, ick . . . I hate it when people preface things with that phrase, makes me feel like I'm in trouble—just ask!

"Do you think about the pole still? Would you want to go?"

I am mute.

"Because I'm on a flight that's going in the next couple of

days. If there's an extra spot, I've been told I can fill it. You'd need to be ready within minutes when I tell you it's time. What do you think?"

I hug her so hard she seems concerned about fractured ribs.

"Hey," Vivian says. "Will you help me with something?"

"Anything," I promise. "Anything in the world."

- - -

"I am *not* doing this!" I yelp. "This is horrible. Do it yourself!"

"Oh my gosh, you big baby," Vivian huffs. "You said you'd do it!"

"Because I didn't know you meant *this*!"

She's sitting on a stool we've borrowed from the kitchen, facing the mirror in our room, urging me to grow a spine and stab her earlobe with a needle.

"No one in my entire family has pierced ears," she says. "No one. I want them. I'm scared to death, and if I don't do it now, I never will . . . please!"

"But shouldn't you be numb?"

"How?"

"I don't know! Ice or some shit!"

"So go get some!"

I run to the dining hall to find even the drink machine line snaking around the room.

Ice.

I stomp back into the room wielding a fistful of Antarctic

ice, chipped off the side of our home, Building 155. I mark perfectly even ballpoint dots on her ears, and I take a huge breath.

Vivian is now the only member of her entire extended family to have holes in her ears.

"Oh, oh my God, oh oh . . ." She moans. "That's awful! Let me see!"

I wipe the blood away with some hydrogen peroxide, and the tiny silver studs Charlotte gave her for this venture sparkle in Vivian's ears.

"I love them." She breathes through the pain. "Hurts like a mother, but aren't they so pretty?"

"Absolutely," I agree.

"Want me to do yours?"

"That's all right." I smile. Simone never, ever allowed any kind of "nonsense" with our bodies—no tattoos, no hair color, no painted nails.

"My hair will grow back," I say. "But absolutely no piercings. I am a dancer."

"Thank you," she says. And she turns to hug me.

"That was horrifying. But you're welcome," I whisper. "Thank *you*."

- - -

In the gym room, I push Charlotte's head slowly toward her knees. "This is going to help, I swear," I tell her, and she holds the position as long as she can.

"My back is killing me," she whines. "How much longer is this kid going to torture me so?"

"Seriously," Vivian says from her own stretch, deep into the floor. "Mother of the year."

"Scott," someone yells into the open door.

Beard.

"Allison's on the phone from the fire station. I'm not your personal errand boy."

Lovely.

But my heart is smashing around—this is it. My chance. I run to Beard's desk, and nearly screech into the receiver, "Allison?"

Fifteen minutes to gear up—half an hour to get there, twenty minutes at the pole, half hour back. "And it's gorgeous weather!" Allison reports. I sprint, breathless, to the stairs.

"Harp!"

Charlotte's face is pale, she and Vivian are stumbling from the dance room together. Charlotte has sadly peed her pants.

Or not.

"Harp, I can't have a baby on The Ice!" she cries.

"You can too!" Vivian snaps. "Harp, hold her other arm, would you? She weighs about a million pounds."

"That is *not* me!" Charlotte sobs. "It's the giant person trying to crawl out of me. Oh my *God . . .*"

It is suddenly very dramatic in the lobby. I hold Charlotte's arm.

"Hey!" Beard yells to us. "Quit screaming. This is a science station!"

I stand, holding Charlotte up, frozen.

"Harper," Charlotte says. "I'm so glad you're here."

Frozen no more.

I beam. "I wouldn't want to be anywhere else in the world. Vivian, prop her up against the wall for just a second!" I run to Beard's desk. He's reading a paperback book with the cover torn off. Gross.

Forgive, Shackleton's voice urges me. *Be kind. Be brave.*

"Bear—*Ben,*" I say, low. "Do you want my seat for the pole?"

His face is blank.

"What?"

"Go to the pole. With Allison. She'll be here in ten minutes. Be ready. If you miss it, it's out of my hands." And I'm back with Vivian at Charlotte's side.

- - -

I've never seen more hair on a baby in my life.

"Was it like birthing a squirrel?" Vivian asks, her fingertips stroking Adelie's tiny head.

"I really couldn't say, Viv," Charlotte says. "Next time I give birth to a woodland creature I'll be sure to take notes."

Adelie Siku. *Siku* is the Inuit name for "Ice." She is perfect and beautiful, a citizen of Antarctica, the United States, and McMurdo Station's first native daughter.

"Are you really coming home?" I whisper to Charlotte. "To San Francisco?"

She nods, worn out but blissed.

"Then you'll never need a babysitter," I tell Adelie. "Auntie Harper's got you covered. I'll wear you in a BabyBjörn to ballet rehearsal."

"No way."

"Just until she can take a class—come on. We're never doing *The Nutcracker,* so calm yourself right down."

"No *Nutcracker?*" Vivian says. "Isn't that ballet sacrilege?"

"Not at my studio," I tell this tiny creature. "Auntie's superior grant-writing skills will mean anyone can take classes, even if they can't pay tuition, and our mommies will sew pretty costumes for our winter performance, called *Aurora.* And you and your friends will be all the colors of the southern sky in winter, and you will be strong and have poise and grace and lots of snow and glitter."

"No . . . ," Charlotte says.

"Oh, yes!" I whisper in Adelie's tiny ear, beneath her perfect dark curls. "Glitter! Lots and lots of glittery snow and ice. Your mom loves *lots* of glitter."

And Charlotte can deny it all she wants, but Vivian and I know; we saw our girl smile.

- - -

The rookery is bathed in ice-cold sunshine, and Vivian's smile is, too.

"Why am I crying?" she says, sniffling in the wind.

"Because you're not dead inside!" I sniffle back.

Allison and a spare flight coordinator are exploring Shackleton's Hut, but Vivian and I cannot leave the Adélies for a single moment. The babies are nuts, running all over, slipping on the ice, hopping bravely into the ocean to climb right back out and find their parents.

"We helped them," Vivian says. "Maybe Charlotte has saved them."

Their tiny faces, black-blue eyes in their white rings, sleek bodies—open, trusting hearts. They walk near us, curious.

"Hey," we murmur. "We love you! Hello!"

They look up at us. Right into our eyes.

"Think they understand?" Vivian asks.

They stand so close, hold their steady gazes in the icy wind. They don't move.

"They do," I say. "They understand perfectly."

- - -

We climb down the cargo plane's steps to the Christchurch tarmac, and the unfamiliar September warmth is delicious. The air here is not nearly so clean, but the grass and flowers and this sun . . . We inhale as deeply as we can.

We are going home.

But first, we will celebrate Vivian's eighteenth birthday tonight, conveniently providing me with an adult chaperone, because tomorrow—we are traveling. Four weeks of exploration. We've got our tickets, a list of hostels, the money we've saved, and only one deadline—the lease on an apartment in San Francisco Kate and I will share starts November 1, as does my three-days-per-week sublease at Madame Simone's studio for my twelve ballet students, Willa included, already registered. We are the Starlight Ballet Studio. Also, I've got a ton of Adelie babysitting to do.

Maybe London next summer. Maybe. Maybe I will apply for San Francisco State's spring semester. Maybe I will double major in dance and choreography. Maybe minor in business so I'll understand how to keep my studio alive.

Vivian's not starting school till January, either—and with her ears pierced, who knows what kind of mischief she'll get up to. She puts her sunglasses on. She's visiting San Francisco in February. I'm visiting St. Paul in June. When there's less snow.

In the airport, I mail a plush Adélie penguin and a letter to Willa. And Kate. And to Owen. A few letters. Letters asking forgiveness. Letters of bravery and love. Outside on the curb, I soak in the sunshine. Close my eyes. The traffic noise, after months of quiet, is delicious.

"What do you think?" Vivian says.

I nod. "You ready?"

"Lead the way."

And she does.

To one more airport, just one building where Cessnas travel to remote places.

Back to the Ross Sea. South Georgia Island, where I sit in the impossibly green grass on Shackleton's grave.

"He died on your birthday," Vivian notes.

I nod, happy we know each other's birthdays because we are friends. "His wife spent half their marriage waiting for him to come home from the ice. Then he dies shipboard on the water, and she realized he'd been home all that time. So she let him stay."

I give him the wildflowers I picked in the field outside the cemetery.

We follow the path over the green hills of the island, ice and ocean around us.

True south.

- 20 -

San Francisco

32 Days Later

OCEAN BEACH SMELLS LIKE MY CHILDHOOD. SOUNDS LIKE MY future. I breathe the salt and cold and then, nearer the park, the evergreens and cypress and juniper berry and the lawn, new soil. I'm in a tank top. No coat. The fog moves in my hair. I want to hug it.

"I missed you, Fog!" I whisper.

The heavy glass doors close behind me, and my heart races at the sight of the words on the walls. *All* of the poem's words come to me:

> Stars that sink to our ocean,
> Winds that visit our strand,
> The heavens are your pathway,
> Where is a gladder land!
> At the end of our streets is sunrise;
> At the end of our streets are spars;

At the end of our streets is sunset;

At the end of our streets the stars.

"Harper Scott," Owen says.

Those eyes. Still so dark, so beautiful, and kind, intent on mine. On me.

"Your hair." He smiles.

I nod.

"Do you love it?" he asks.

"I do."

"Me too. Can I?" He slowly moves his fingers through my hair, standing so near to me that I close my eyes and inhale the scent of him, the grapefruit soap he still uses.

"You got my postcards?" I ask.

"You've been *every*where," he says. "They're taped to the refrigerator; it's a total pain in the ass just trying to get in there for some milk."

"Did you get my letter?"

"Uh, yeah . . . the ten pages asking forgiveness for I'm still not sure what? Yeah. I got that."

"Forgiveness for falling apart. For doing stupid, selfish things in Antarctica, not writing you back right away, all those beautiful letters, every date we went on, I read them over and over—"

"Harper, nothing you've done there or anywhere is

stupid. I was a dick for trying to guilt you into staying for my own selfishness. Which, in my defense, was fueled by the fact that I was, and am, amazed by and in awe of you. So there's that."

"Okay."

"And I wrote you because I wanted to write you. I missed you. If you'd wanted me to stop, I knew you'd tell me."

"Okay."

"And your hair is so freakishly sexy, I'd like to . . ."

I silence him with a kiss, familiar and thrilling and *I have missed him so much.*

"You read them?" he says. "The date letters."

"Yes."

"More than once?"

"Maybe."

"Wow." He smiles at the floor.

"And oh, my *shoes*," I say. "You saved me. My life."

"Kate got them to me."

"Thank you. I'll never be able to say that enough. How can I . . ."

"Harp," he says, and pulls me to him because, despite how hard I'm trying not to, tears are spilling.

"Every single time!" I yelp. "Can I ever spend three minutes with you and *not* cry?"

"I'm prepared now. It's okay!" he says, and he puts a white lace-edged handkerchief in my hand. "That's your welcome-home present. Now you can be proper and fancy with your depression!"

"I'm not depressed! I'm so . . ." He kisses me again. People are milling around the chalet, but who cares? We kiss and kiss, and he pulls me even closer until I have to pause to catch my breath.

"So to be clear, you *liked* the dates?"

"They're perfect blueprints. Can we go in order? Can we start again?"

"Really?"

"Yes, please."

"Does that mean we have to work back up to kissing?"

"Obviously. Let's go." I sigh happily.

"Where's your coat?"

"Not cold. Not anymore."

"You must have been frozen."

"I was."

I take his warm hand in mine. My heart is buzzing. Dancing.

"Where to now?" he asks.

"Anywhere. Everywhere. And then home."

Author's Note

The *truth:* from the ages of eight to eighteen, I loved ballet more than anything in life, and I knew I was going to be a ballerina. The *fact:* there was never any way in hell that was going to happen. Not just because I took just three classes a week at our small town's only ballet studio, in the basement of a former Sacramento Ballet soloist. She loved us and yelled a lot and was glad we came to class, but I think she knew she wasn't grooming any prima ballerinas. The *fact:* I was not born with the ballerina essentials— the body, the turnout, the strength, the extension, the stamina. None of it.

Besides being a former ballerina, I am a playwright who writes novels. I think in scenes, not chapters, and when imagining a story I always begin with Russian actor and director Konstantin Stanislavski's "magic if." The "magic if" is the truth that occurs on stage, which is different from the truth of real life but is absolutely necessary for an audience to believe in a performance. It is a truth informed by facts, but not made up entirely of them. And it often begins with the question "What would I do if this were happening to me?" A question I come back to time and again when writing fiction.

Which is all to say, *Up to This Pointe* is a work of fiction informed by a ton of research about ballet and the lives of Scott, Amundsen, Shackleton, and the Winter Overers at McMurdo Station. Antarctica has always been a brutal ballet to me—a painful, terrible beauty. Both demand a nearly impossible, super-human capability and instinct to survive. And both hold inexplicable sway over the people who fall in love with them.

Rose Wilder Lane said of writing novels, "Facts are infinite in number. Truth is the meaning underlying them." In reality, a teenager would never be allowed to Winter Over in Antarctica. But in the reality of *Up to This Pointe,* in Wilder's words, "It is not a fact, but it is perfectly true."

Below I've shared some of my favorite research sources with you, because trust me—the "magic if" cannot compare to the real-world magic of ballet and Antarctica. The real world we are so very lucky to live in.

- *The Worst Journey in the World* by Apsley Cherry-Garrard

- *Encounters at the End of the World,* documentary film by Werner Herzog

- *Big Dead Place: Inside the Strange & Menacing World of Antarctica* by Nicholas Johnson (companion book to the archived blog of the same name)

- *An Empire of Ice: Scott, Shackleton, and the Heroic Age of Antarctic Science* by Edward J. Larson

- *Antarctica: A Year on Ice,* documentary film by Anthony Powell

- *South: The Endurance Expedition* by Ernest Shackleton

- *Dancing on Water: A Life in Ballet, from the Kirov to the ABT* by Elena Tchernichova, with Joel Lobenthal

Acknowledgments

First and always, to Melissa Sarver White. O Captain, my Captain.

Chelsea Eberly: editor, author, my unbelievable good fortune. Thank you.

Mallory Loehr, Jenna Lettice, Alison Kolani, Christine Ma, Elizabeth Tardiff, Noelle Stevenson, Deanna Meyerhoff, Anna Gjesteby, and everyone else at Random House Children's Books and Folio Literary Management. Thank you.

My Seattle homes: the Elliott Bay Book Company, Eagle Harbor Book Co., University Books, Mockingbird Books, Queen Anne Books, Third Place Books, Parkplace Books, and my very own Island Books.

My Seattle writing family: Mary Jane Beaufrand, Lish McBride, Michelle Goodman, Sierra Golden, Karen Finney-frock, Kirby Larson, Kim Baker, Mel Barnes, Jennifer K. Mann, Tori Centanni, Stephanie Kuehnert Lewis, Anna Eklund, Tara Conklin, Dawn Simon, and Suzanne Selfors. SCBWI-WW and the staff and teachers at Hugo House, Seattle. Linda Johns: author, Seattle librarian, hero. You are all the best, most beautiful part of living here.

Caitlin White of Bustle.com, Sanovia of Creatyvebooks.com, Allie Williams (director of the Parnell Memorial Library), the San Francisco Porchlight Storytelling Series, Joseph Murchison, Sheila Hale, Vivian Bernstein, and Marlaine Figueroa Gray for reading, kindness, and inspiration.

Jenni Holm, Sarah McCarry, Beth Lisick, Arline Klatte, Jessie Scholl, Lisa Brown, Amber J. Keyser, Suzy Vitello, Dao Strom. Fearless writers, all.

Thank you, Bernadette Cheyne, Ivan Hess, Margaret Kelso, and Charlie Meyers of Humboldt State University.

My family: Tim and Vickie Longo, Henri, June, and James Taylor Longo, Joe Hart, Patrick Clark, Daniel Slauson, Deanne Calvin. My sister, Christine Inez. Christine and Dominic Falletti and Kelsey Todd. My Lucas Arts family. Bradley Comito, for every perfect, frozen detail. Ellen, Mike, and Katrina Harding, love and thank you to the stars and moon and back. Sarah, Alex, and Malachi Neuse, in these pages and my every day. The Wallach-Neal family and Julia J. K. Rizzle: rock, river, esteemed colleague. It has been an honor. Analise Langford-Clark, my light in the fog. Robert Irvin, my celestial navigation.

Martha Brockenbrough and Jet Harrington. It is not often that people come along who are true friends and *sublime* writers. You are both. How impossibly lucky to find you.

And to my own little constellation, Tim and Cordelia Longo. My true south.

About the Author

JENNIFER LONGO was a ballerina from ages eight to eighteen, until she eventually (reluctantly) admitted her talent for writing exceeded her talent for dance. The author of *Six Feet Over It*, she holds an MFA in Writing for Theater from Humboldt State University, where her obsessive love of Antarctica produced her thesis play about Antarctica's Age of Exploration. Jennifer lives in Seattle with her husband and daughter and writes about writing at jenlongo.com.